ELISABETH GIFFORD

THE

LOST LIGHTS

OF

ST KILDA

CORVUS

Published in hardback in Great Britain in 2020 by Corvus, an imprint of Atlantic Books Ltd. This paperback edition published in 2020.

10 9 8 7 6 5 4 3 2 1

A CIP catalogue record for this book is available from the British Library.

Paperback ISBN: 978 1 78649 905 9
E-book ISBN: 978 1 78649 906 6

Printed and bound by CPI Group (UK) Ltd, Croydon, CR0 4YY

Corvus
An imprint of Atlantic Books Ltd
Ormond House
26–27 Boswell Street
London
WC1N 3JZ

www.corvus-books.co.uk

For Douglas Gifford

CHAPTER 1

Fred

Five days in darkness deep as a pit and my mind begins to play tricks. I hear the silence as singing, a faint choir in a distant room. Gaelic? English? Not Jerry, that's for sure. Sometimes, it's the darkness itself, blooming into images that swell and fade on the air, fuelled, no doubt, by the throbbing in my hand. Two nails gone, pulled out by the Gestapo. Worst of all is when the air becomes solid and I gasp, heart hammering, sweat on my palms. Then the only escape is to hold my mind steady and stand on my island again, looking out at the Atlantic and the curve of white sand around the bay. Slowly, very slowly, I turn in a half circle to see the crofts and the rise of the hills beyond like a comforting arm sheltering the village. A thin veil of cloud rises over the summit of Conachair, evaporating away as it starts to pour down the hillside, and high above, a sky that's pure blue and endless. I breathe in deeply, the air clean and sea-blessed. Concentrating now so that the scene before me does not flicker or fade, I take a step, and another. Blades of grass, oiled and bright with sun, pass beneath my feet, the turf sprinkled with white daisies and tormentil as I move towards the line of bothies along the curve of the shore. A dog barks a greeting. Mary Gillies sits in front of a cottage spinning, the squeak of the turning wood as she lets the thread in and out, singing something in Gaelic as she works, but she does not raise her head as I pass by. Halfway along the row of cottages, I take the narrow path between a bothy and a byre, moving up past the burn race with the familiar irises and their spear-shaped leaves, yellow flower heads fluttering. One step at a time, I rise beyond the village towards Conachair, the fine webbed clouds over its summit. And now, standing on its heights, dizzy with the wind on my face, the air hazed with a moist brightness, all around is the ocean, a vast disc of rippled glass beneath an infinity of sky. I drink in the purity of so much blue. Some eight miles away, the islet of Boreray and her sea stacs like the hump of a whale guarding her two calves. I stand there, rocked by the wind, and a deep peacefulness comes to me. Nowhere in the world that's as true or as home. Then my eyes scan back down to the village, my vision magnifying the dear houses below.

And there we are, sitting outside the bothy, Archie smoking, both of us reading in the evening light. But where is she? If I could see her one more time. That way she had of teasing and putting us in our place, two students from Cambridge who thought we knew it all.

I hear the rattle of bolts being shot back. The island fades. The iron door of a Tournai prison cell opens, squealing its pain. Just enough light creeps in to outline the barrel-shaped tunnel, ten feet long to the end wall. Damp brick scratched with graffiti, names from the boys of the 51st. No window. I wait for the guard to put a bowl of barley swimming in water on the floor, but instead a man is pushed in. He staggers and falls. Behind him, the guards drag in a body, the head slumped between shoulders pulled up in their sockets like a chicken on a butcher's hook. A boy. They leave him on the cold concrete, face against the filth. I have just enough time to register the first man's grey hair, gaunt, a civilian shirt and grey trousers, before the door slams shut. The darkness floods back. The bolts rattle back in place. I can hear the older man shuffling about. His voice.

'Kenneth, Kenneth, will ye wake now,' patting him on the cheek, urgently. 'Come on now, man.' There's a groan of pain in reply. 'That's it now. I'll bide with ye, Kenneth. That's it, man. Breathe now. You're all right. We'll see the light again.'

'Donal?'

'Aye, I'm here, Kenneth.'

'Are we dead now, Donal?'

'No. We're back in the fort, in the cellars.'

'Dead would be better.'

'We'll come through. One day you'll be home, standing in the lane before your own wee house.'

I flinched at this. What were the odds, really?

'You sleep a while now, Kenneth.'

A shuddering sigh.

'Caught escaping?' I ask in a whisper.

'Aye.'

'Fred Lawson. Cameron Highlanders. I'd shake hands but they've left them a bit of a mess.'

'Donal MacIver, Seaforths. Three of us. The other man shot. And Kenneth here's taken a very bad beating.'

'Is he going to pull through?'

'He's still strong in spite of the past months, but it's the will he needs now. The boys came into this war with such determination and now. . .'

'And now here we are, left behind to rot in a German prison, the Queen's own Highlanders. Not what we planned.'

'But we'll come through yet. We'll come through.' I heard the man shift and exhale with pain. His voice came again in the dark, fainter now. 'But will you excuse me now, son. I may just shut my eyes for a while.'

Both of them out cold. The only clue that they were still there was the intermittent sound of breathing. I found myself straining to make out the particular sound of Kenneth's breath, faint and wetly ragged – ready to crawl over there if it stopped. And do what in this blackness? Give him a talk on wanting to live?

So many like Kenneth in the German prison camps. When the call went out in '39 the boys came in droves from the Highlands and Islands to join the Camerons, the Black Watch, the Seaforths, and the Gordon Highlanders, the Argylls, and the Sutherlands; descended from the men who had once fought alongside Wallace and Bruce, or battled to the death on the fields of Culloden. Along with the regiments from Aberdeen and Dundee, they become the 51st Highland Division – famous in the Great War as the men who never gave up. The fighting 51st.

So how bitter it was when the order came to put down arms and surrender alongside the French army, finally overrun by Hitler's panzer divisions. The Gordons, fighting a rearguard action in the woods of Normandy, had to be issued the order twice. They couldn't believe a command to surrender. Nearly all of them little more than boys.

I was older than most when my call-up papers came, a good few years past thirty. I'd been working as a drilling engineer for mining companies overseas. I was straight in as sergeant, assigned to the radio signals division. And since I was born in Uist, I was attached to the Cameron Highlanders. It was good to hear the Gaelic spoken again after so long. There'd not been much call for it during my years out in South America and Malaya.

Maybe it was hearing the old language again, but you came back to me so clearly then. I'd catch sight of you standing in the doorway as I sat alone on my bunk polishing my boots. Waking in the morning, as the barrack room came into focus, I'd see you, standing near my bed, the breeze from the hills come with you, and each time it would pierce me through with such a longing for days that were gone.

I'd refused you from my mind for so long, stubborn in my anger, but now I was a man wakened from a dream and I saw how I'd let the years slip by. All I longed for was to see you again, just one more time.

I asked a boy from Harris if they'd heard any news there from the folk on St Kilda. He looked at me with surprise.

'And where is it you have been hiding yourself to not know that there is no one on the island of St Kilda now. Not one living soul.'

The blood drained from my legs. I sat down on a chair. 'What are you saying? You're not saying they starved one winter?'

'No. But they came close enough. They were taken off the island after a very bad winter. Did you no see it on the newsreel in the cinemas? Ten years back. Nineteen thirty, it must have been. They live on the mainland now. I dinna' ken where.'

I hadn't followed the news from Europe. I couldn't remember what I'd been doing ten years ago in the sticky heat of Malaya's dusty towns and scrubland jungle of tepid beer and brief evenings with Malay girls. Nothing I wanted to recall with any pride. And now it came to me, a dawning realization of the chasm between us. All those chances to turn back and find you long gone. I had no way of contacting you now. No idea where you were living. Too many years sacrificed to my pride and my anger.

It was your face that had stayed with me as we fought in France. It was you who'd sustained me when we were hungry and without sleep for nights as we fought the retreating action back towards the Normandy coast. We had to smash equipment as we fled, the radios and the boxes of transmitter valves thrown out of the truck and shattering on the asphalt like summer fireworks. But we still hoped we'd make it home. We'd heard the army north of us had been taken off the beaches at Dunkirk by boats and by a miracle were back home to England.

At St Valery we were told to make our way down to the beach where boats would evacuate us too. But as soon as we got there, I saw we were lost. We stood on the top of cliffs three hundred feet high; at the foot, a narrow strip of beach strewn with bodies. The Germans had set up gun emplacements on the cliffs across the bay and were picking off the men as they went down the steep paths single file. A rolling fog had come in. There was no way a ship could navigate its way in. A boat that had come in earlier had already sunk under fire.

No one was coming to take us home.

We turned back to the town, now blazing and exploding like a giant bonfire, the shelling constant. By morning, the French general had ordered a white flag to be hoisted from the church spire. We had surrendered. In the town square there was a huge pile of rifles.

You could hear men's guts creaking from emptiness as the Germans marched us east. They wouldn't let us break ranks to fetch water. In front of me, a man fell, faint from exhaustion. The guard ran down and cracked his head with a rifle butt, shot him when he failed to wake up. At night we were herded into fields surrounded by rolls of razor wire that the Jerry had gone on ahead and got ready for us. 'You can't fault them for how organised the buggers are,' said Tom from Dundee. He let the potatoes he'd grubbed up roll out of his pocket onto the floor and we all shared what we had from our quick foraging in the wide flat fields that ran along each side of the road. A marvel how good a raw potato tastes when you're starving hungry. The next night we collected wood to make a fire as soon as the guard was further up the line, managed to cook them, but by the third night the French farmers had got wise to the threat of ten thousand men raiding their field and stood with sticks to defend their crop, and we didn't blame them.

We passed into Belgium. They shipped us onto empty coal barges, crammed us down in the sooty hold so you could hardly breathe. Then back to walking again.

The first real food we saw was spread out on trestle tables as they marched us into a station. We had our photo taken in front of it with the Red Cross nurses in uniform standing behind the tables ready to serve it out. As soon as they had their picture they packed all the food away without it crossing our lips.

We were herded towards cattle trucks. They started loading us in forty at a time. I knew there'd be little chance of coming back once we were on the trains. A prison camp in the east, labouring for the Reich. I was standing in a group next to the great black engine breathing out its clouds of steam and soot. I sidled to the back of the column. When a fight broke out, I saw my chance, stepped back into the steam cloud and away along the tracks in the fading light of evening.

I made it as far as the coast, living on the handouts that the farmers gave me, risking their lives to invite me in for a meal. One night, a couple insisted that I have their bed while they slept in the kitchen. I'd found civilian clothes by then, buried my uniform, keeping nothing but my compass. So when I was picked up on the heavily guarded Belgian coast, trying to find a boat to get home, I was interrogated as a spy. They gave me the full treatment, plus a month in the Tournai punishment cells.

In the darkness, I listened to the breathing on the other side of the cell. One slow with a wheeze, the other more uneven, a pause as if the next breath might not come. Perhaps I slept. When the door opened next, a faint grey light trickled in as the guard put the bowls down. I could make out the two forms against the distempered brick. The older man, Donal, slumped against the wall. The boy was tipped over, a jacket under his head against the cold of the concrete, a patch where he had dribbled a dark spool of blood. Then the black loneliness that filled our cave came down once more.

The boy began to cry. 'I can't do it. I can't do it any more.'

I could hear the sound of a head banging and banging against the concrete. The scrape of Donal reaching across to muffle Kenneth's sobbing into his chest.

'We have to hope, Kenneth. Think of all the things you want to see again. They are still waiting for you, and you will see them again. Don't you have a girl, Kenneth?'

This made the sobbing more intense. 'Jeanie. Her name's Jeanie. I told her we'd be married when I came home.'

'Can you see her now, Kenneth, in the garden, waiting for you?'

'It's too dark in here.'

'You'll see her. You must hope on it. Just as I turn in my mind's eye now to see my Barra, with the little church waiting for me there on the hillside looking out towards the fishing boats. That's where I'll be again one day. And you, Fred Lawson, don't you have something you hope for as you sit here in the dark, something you believe in?'

'I'm not a man who goes to church.' And then I stopped. That wasn't what he was asking me. 'There is an island,' I began. I paused, searching to find the words.

The boy shifted, perhaps turned his head, both of them listening.

'It's a small island, far out in the Atlantic, a hundred miles away from the rest of the mainland, the most remote place in the British Isles, a place almost from another time. When I first set eyes on St Kilda, I'm guessing I was the same age that you are now, Kenneth. I was barely more than twenty.'

He grunted, a small sound of pain, but it was there, his wanting to hope on something.

CHAPTER 2

Fred
ST KILDA, JULY 1927

Dear Lachlan,

I doubt that I can find the words to adequately describe this place to you, but I will try. You warned me I might find it tedious here, the isolation, so far away from civilization, and it is true that this is considered such a harsh posting for the nurse or the missionary that they are generally only assigned for twelve months. But hardship to be here in the middle of such beauty! A lonely and very windswept beauty, yes, but I am already grieving that I shall have to leave at the end of summer and go back to Cambridge.

So what is this island of St Kilda, or islands to be more exact, as I know you will want me to be? I can see you now, wiping your hands on an oily rag as we stare into the greasy parts of some engine that has ceased to run, me knowing full well that your mind has already taken the structure to pieces and found the problem. Pin it down, man, you'd tell me when making a diagnosis of what ails the motor. Go to it logically. In fact, I have been helping the minister's wife repair her wireless this afternoon, which she relies on for news from the mainland. A radio's not so different a proposition in principle to an engine, though the parts are finer and its paths run through the air. I've been able to blag my way through and pick up how it works pretty quickly, following your method of stripping back a problem to the underlying logic. The look on her face at being back in contact with the world was thanks enough.

But back to the island itself. I will stay away from my more misty-eyed descriptions of St Kilda, even though it does encourage just that, and try to concentrate on what I am here to understand – the underlying rock formations – and so return to Cambridge with enough information in the bag for my final paper.

St Kilda is in fact a group of four islands and various sea stacs, the largest of which, at some four square miles, is Hirta. If you were to walk up from the tiny village on the bay to Hirta's highest point, what you'd see is an ancient volcanic crater, a bowl of green that lies half dipped in the water as if some giant is scooping out a drink with a pan, one side lost under the water and the other rising high to make a semi-circle of steep hills, leaving a green amphitheatre around the village with its half-moon of white sand and its line of low cottages in a curving line a short walk up from the beach. Standing in the village on a fine day in such a sheltered and benign spot one is tempted to believe in a god of blessings behind such loving creation, but climb up to the top of the encircling hills and the shock is deadly. The land ends, falls away into cliffs with a drop of one thousand and three hundred feet, where men fall to certain death. Where, coming to the edge, you must drop to the earth and cling on with fear at the way the wind comes at you with such force, knocking the breath out of your lungs, a fortress of the highest sea cliffs in Europe.

Within that, the hills slope in towards the Village Bay. To one side, the hills continue in a circle of blasted skerries, jagged points sticking out of the sea like a broken jawbone or the rusted-away edge of the giant's bowl dipped into the sea. They were once part of the island but are now cut off by a channel forced through by the pounding sea.

After that there is nothing but open water, all the way to America. Your eye then finishes the broken circle and travels back to the land at the other side of the bay.

Into this natural harbour the deep-sea trawlers run for shelter in storms, unless the wind is from the west, in which case the Village Bay is useless against the gales that blow straight in, any boat thrown up against the rocks. The only hope in such weather is to shelter in the glen over the brow of Mullach Mòr that forms a mirror to Village Bay, though it is a place devoid of any human features other than some basic stone beehive huts, still used by the girls who go to milk the cows in summer and which may date back to antiquity, if Archie is to be believed. I have not gone so far as to see the glen myself yet, but I am told it is there.

I have read this letter back and see that the above does nothing to describe the place adequately. I should have first mentioned the light. For we float on it in the sea's reflection, the damp air luminous. The light encircles us, the far horizon all around us nothing but a deepening blue line of shadow where the water has ended and the sky begun. How the light shivers and shakes over the barley heads, or glistens off the swathes of silver-blue plantain leaves on the slopes by the sea. How the light brightens and darkens in racing patches across the land as the wind shifts the clouds across the sky. And the hundred shades of glassy light in the sea, dark petrol blue to faint jade, or the china blue over the white sand of the bay.

By now you are probably thinking that being cast so far out into the Atlantic, I've begun to lose my marbles – and perhaps you're right. This place never lets your senses be still, always waiting for the next trick of the weather, your head always filled with the din of birds and the wind.

Did I mention that the sky is alive with bird wings? The black-tipped bent spikes of the great gannets' wings, the flutter of scissor-beaked kittiwakes, fulmars, skewars, puffins, petrels – the same birds that supply most of the islander's primitive diet.

Even more birds reside on the two daughter islands, Soay and Boreray, and more still tumble and skirl in the skies around the black rock stacs that rise up out of the water like ancient relics – the head of a massive prehistoric shark, nose to the sky, another in the shape of a Neolithic hand-held axe – ancient and violent eruptions of lava plugs from before time. I will long remember our first sight of them from the tossing boat as we arrived, how they seemed to come to us, pitching and moving with the horizon across the sea like animate beings, and all the while the outlines of first Boreray, and then Hirta beyond, solidified and became green hills and slopes shattered all around with massive cliffs. Arriving here is almost the entry to a legend.

And now back to where we are lodged here in the village. We are snug enough in the minister's house for the time being, though as you can imagine it's hardly Archie's ideal set-up to be under the eye of the minister's wife. He is even now planning for us to move out into one of the abandoned cottages in the village. There are two or three homes standing empty since the population here is not what it was some twenty years ago, and I sometimes feel a poignant sadness to think that I may well be witnessing the end of a unique and rare community that still lives as people must all have lived long ago. Cars or towns with their shops are unknown to them – even a bicycle is a foreign item here.

Archie is away arranging for one of the village women to sweep out an abandoned bothy and hopefully for one of them to come in each day to make some food for us, though we intend to lead a very frugal existence here, all porridge and hard work. I know you have told me to not be carried along by Archie, coming as he does from a very different background, one with a certain expectation of life, whereas I am mindful that my own future relies upon much hard work. But it's thanks to him and his family that I'm here and able to collect the research I need. Archie has been a true friend through these past two years at Cambridge, and you can see how much the natives here love him – though they can scarce do little else since it is Archie's father who owns the place. Lord Macleod, who has covered all of my expenses in getting here, says he'll be happy just to read my geological survey of the island in recompense. His father has not said as much but I can see that this is where I am to return some of the favour, in trying to keep Archie's nose to the grindstone. Archie is to carry out an archaeological survey here for his dissertation, and if my task is to keep him out of trouble, I anticipate being rather busy.

There's a chance that you may see me back in Edinburgh before this letter gets to you, given how irregular the mail is going out from the island. And now here's Archie coming along the path with the woman who is perhaps going to be our maid this next few weeks, a slip of a thing – though from the way she's listening to him, arms crossed, eyes sharp on his face, I'd say she has the measure of Archie Macleod nicely, thank you very much. The native girls here are very scenic, rather fetching – ruddy cheeks, black hair – and they all wear the same homespun style of full skirts and turkey-red scarves that would not look out of place in Victoria's reign.

Now Archie is saying I need to get this in the mail sack. The Hebrides is due to return to the mainland within the hour, leaving us to our adventure as castaways.

I remain, dear uncle, more grateful than I can ever say for all the care and affection you have shown me over these years. My own parents, had they lived, could not have been kinder. I look forward to seeing you at the end of summer.

Your loving nephew,

Fred

CHAPTER 3

Rachel Anne
MORVERN, SCOTLAND, 1940

My mother says I am her whole world, and she is mine, but all the same I would still like to know at least the name of my father.

This much I know: that I was born on an island far from here, a place called St Kilda, although we left there before I could form any useful memories, so the island is doubly lost to me. My mother doesn't like to talk about St Kilda. 'There's no use in looking back, Rachel Anne,' she says. 'This is our life now and we must make the best of it.'

I was not much more than two years old when some thirty of us left the island. We had lived together all our lives in one village, sharing what little we had, but after the evacuation we were scattered across the mainland. It wasn't long before many of the old ones and the children faded away from TB or from broken hearts, among them my grandmother. So now the loss of the island and our dear ones is too great for my mother to brook any questions from me.

But everything is different since Hitler turned the world upside down. Since many of the men from round here have gone to join the 51st Highland Division, my mother goes off early each morning to manage the dairy on Brockett's farm. She herds the cows into the yard with a stout stick tall as herself, calmly counting them in. She knows their names, sets up the milking parlour and sees to the milk churns. When I went over with her on the first day, Mr Brockett came to make sure she knew enough about the beasts. 'You don't need to worry,' she'd told him. 'On St Kilda, we used to walk miles each day to tend the cows. Wasn't I raised on a croft where every stalk of barley had to be wrested from the weather?'

'Aye, and you'd had to leave there for want of food. Well, we'll give you a trial, Mrs Gillies, see how things go.'

By the end of the week she's laughing about how he's so keen for her to stay on. '"Never seen the cows give so much milk,"' she says, imitating his Morvern accent. '"What do you do, Mrs Gillies, to make such a difference?" What does he think?' she says. 'I know them each by name. And all of them different.'

So with Mother away I am left here alone through the long summer days, instructed to practise my piano pieces. It was my mother who first taught me to play, my hands on hers, walking me over tunes she brought back from the island. She learned by ear and she thinks it a great thing that I am learning to read sheet music at school, taking the grade exams and so on. But there's only so long you can play a piano in a day and so it is that I have taken to searching through the house for a scrap of information on my father, growing bolder in my search each day, until I stand on the threshold of her silent room. I walk in on the balls of my feet, as if she might hear me away on Brockett's farm, gently slide open sleeping drawers, turning over her folded clothes and linens.

Finally, I find something, hidden between the layers of an old rough blanket in her kist from the island. Pictures of antique-looking people in long, full-skirted dresses and men in flat woollen bonnets and thick mufflers, standing in front of a row of cottages – my grandparents and aunts and uncles from before the island was emptied. I think I may have seen these pictures before. I recognize my grandmother Rachel Òg, who came with us to this house. By her side, a man who must be my grandfather. I know well my mother's stories, how he was famous for his skills in dancing sideways across the faces of the highest cliffs in Europe, his brother above holding the rope firm as my grandfather caught the fulmars and gannets whose feathers and meat kept the islanders alive. In the photograph, he stands solidly next to my grandmother. I memorize each detail and put them back, but as I smooth down the blankets, I feel something else tucked away at the end, an empty cocoa tin gritty with spots of brown rust. When I shake it, something light and muffled moves inside. I twist off the lid. It's not been opened in a long while, the lid sealed with rust and damp. Inside, wrapped in a piece of pale ginger tweed and curved around in the shape of the tin, there's another photo. I've never seen this picture before. It's grey rather than the sepia of my grandparents' photo, a blurred snap of two young men, arms around each other's shoulders. Not island men, but visitors. They're sitting on a hillside, the breeze ruffling their hair, a dog alert and panting by the side of one of them. I sit back, wanting to glean every detail, for I know with a conviction, feel it in my bones, that one of these men must be my father. I'm the spit of my mother, with dark hair and blue eyes, but all the same I'm disappointed that neither of them look anything like me. The conviction remains, however. Why would she have kept this, hidden it away, if it didn't mean something?

But the one person who can tell me is the one person I can never ask. The afternoon is fading. She'll be back soon. My hands, like quick little liars, hurry to put everything away.

Desperate as I am, it's hard not to blurt out questions when she comes home. The ticking of the clock above the fire, the calls of the birds outside, grow louder and louder as she moves about the kitchen, saying little other than to ask about my day. More than ever, I want my mother to tell me about Hirta and the other little islands that make up St Kilda: Boreray, Soay, Dùn and the great rock stacs around them. But she won't. I know that much.

So I take my search elsewhere. Telling her I have homework to do in the library, the following Saturday I wait for the bus that twists and tosses over the narrow roads to Lochaline. And I am not disappointed. Is there anyone who has visited the island and not written a book about it? I read myself up and down the slopes of St Kilda, inside houses that are no longer homes, until I feel I must surely be remembering more of the island – though it is only the memories of Mr Martin, or Mr Sands or those who went to the islands in their fancy yachts, coming back with mouth-gaping tales about the last hunter-gatherers in the British Isles. 'The natives are dirty but hospitable and wear bird skins on their feet. . .' or 'St Kilda, a simple utopian community from another century where money is unknown. . .'

I go back week after week. When I've read everything I can from the shelves, then I ask for books mentioned in the bibliographies that the library does not stock but must order in from Edinburgh or Inverness. As the librarian stamps a two-week lending date in yet another book, I glimpse the pity and curiosity in her face. She knows. She's realized I was one of the ones taken from the island, displayed for all to see in newsreel cinemas across the land, the last of the savages. I bend my head to hide my burning cheeks and I hurry away.

At home I carefully hide my finds away under my bed. My mother hates to have the island pulled about by visitors and tourists in the books they write.

But above all, when I want to feel I am back on the island again, I play the old tunes she taught me, trying to call up faint and jumbled memories from a small child, yellow irises by a deep stream, the silky coat of a puppy, of creased and kindly faces, of a lamp carried across the grass between dark bothies. I run my hands over the keys, over the hills and the slopes of Hirta. And sometimes I think I see those two smiling boys from the photograph, sitting there on the hillside.

And I wonder, where are you now? Do you know about me?

I'm listening to the wireless in the kitchen. We listen to every BBC bulletin about the war. Terrible news of late, the British forces pushed to the sea by Hitler, the men trapped on the beaches. My mother comes in and I'm about to tell her but she walks over to the wireless and turns it off, her face like stone. In her hands, I see the faded reds and greens of the library books.

'Why are you reading these?' she shouts, her face white. 'These people know nothing about the island. You are taking these back to that library.'

I've never defied her before, never raised my voice, but now I shout back. 'Why should I? I won't. I might as well have been found in a ditch for all I know about where I come from.'

She holds the books against her chest. The back door is open and she suddenly goes out as if she needs to breathe the cool air. I follow, standing a little way behind her. She sinks down on the back step, the closed books on her knees. In front of us, the forest is already turning dark against the last brightness in the sky. I sit beside her on the stoop. A swift is swooping back and forth across the meadow, sewing the air together with its flight. I can hear the shushing of the pine trees beyond the paddock. She stares at them for a while.

'Do you recall when we first saw trees, Rachel Anne? We'd never seen a single tree before we came here. You were afraid of them.'

'Perhaps,' I say, begrudgingly. More a feeling than a memory. I sit very quiet and still. Something is beginning.

'Rather, it's the bigness of the sky I miss. The island never felt small to us who lived there. Up on the cliffs, you could look out across the sea to the very beginning of the world. Or at least, it seemed that way to a child.' She turns and looks at me so sadly. 'You are right, Rachel Anne. I should tell you all the things that will be lost if I do not. Our people. You remember my mother a little perhaps, but my father, you never knew him. Such a kind man – though I gave him enough trouble. Just like you, I was never a child to be told.'

The evening falls, and the step is cold. But we are no longer here. We are a hundred miles out into the Atlantic.

CHAPTER 4

Chrissie
ST KILDA, 1910

By evening, the whole village was searching for little Christina, calling her name against the wind that had risen up with the darkness, voices hoarse with the hope of finding her. She must be found, for it's an island that has already lost too many children. No trace of a child in a blue woollen dress, not in the Village Bay, not in the Great Glen over the hill. Her mother even began to ask herself, could it be that a small boat had slipped in unseen at the edge of the bay, taken the child from where she slept as the women worked and gossiped?

She didn't want to think of a child being blown by the wind from the cliffs, the long drop, a small body flying like a bird, the sea below, so far away.

'Christina,' she called out on the top of Conachair's cliffs. 'Christina.'

And her father yelled her name into the wind on the hillsides and as he lifted his lantern to peer into caves hidden in the slopes beneath Mullach Mòr. The stones echoed back nothing but a muffled thrum, her name erased by the wind.

All afternoon her grandmother had stumbled among the shore rocks and along the burn race of Tobar Childa, looking for – and hoping never to see – the long black hair and the folds of blue cloth twisted into the water's flow that came down icy from the hills. She stood and prayed in Gaelic in the fading light, the old prayers against fairies and spirits.

Where had the child gone?

When Christina woke, some hours earlier, and looked out of the window she saw whirling flecks of white rising and drifting across the croft land. Snow or feathers? She'd only seen snow once before, little white clumps that drifted and rose against a blue light, the distance blurred by their swarm. If you stood out in snow it tickled your cheek, like Mother's eyelashes when you held her tight to kiss her nose. Snow you could catch on your tongue, feel it sharp and melting, your hands pinched by the cold.

If it was feathers, on the other hand, then the sea and the sky stayed solid and bright. Feathers made you cough and smelled burned and oily. The sun was coming warm through the window glass, the grass a deep green. Feathers it was then, the downy little ones from the breasts of fulmar petrels. The women would be sitting with Mother somewhere plucking at the fledgling birds, the beaks and soft heads dangling from the women's knees as they worked in a cloud of down.

Christina knew she should wake Granny in her chair so they could go to the women now, but it wasn't fair: the men had gone to get the birds from the cliffs and Father had taken Norman with him. The first time her brother had been allowed to join in with the climbing.

'And me. I can come too,' Christina had said, running to fetch her shawl.

Father had smoothed her hair but he had left her behind and gone out of the door to discuss the day ahead with the other men. She saw them talking in a group on the cobbled path. They were up by number three, Neil Ferguson's house, some of them sitting on the low wall with their backs to the bright sea, smoking pipes, sharing out the rough horsehair ropes, the jute ropes and the tackle, Norman holding a coil. Christina had sat on the step and burned to know what they were saying until Mother came out with a tin jug to tell her to fetch water from the pump.

When she came back with the jug, the men and Norman were gone and now she had to go and find them up on Conachair, never wanted anything more, so fiercely could she see herself roped along with Father and Norman, bringing home fat armfuls of white birds. 'Why, Chrissie, you've enough here to feed the whole village all winter,' Mama would say.

Granny was still asleep on the wooden chair by the peat fire, her chin fallen into the roll of woollen shawl around her neck. Christina lifted the door latch. Outside the bothy door, she didn't turn right along the wide paving cobbles towards where she could hear the women's voices singing as they sat together out on the turf, hands snatching at the white down fast as the wind. She turned the other way, walking past the old byre where featherless puffins had been left to dry in the wind, their beaks slotted between the stones of the walls, others hung in twos and threes from the ropes holding down the hump of thatched roof on the byre. Their wing feathers had been left on at the tips, fluttering in the wind as if the birds were dreaming of flying. She paused to watch a darting wren on the grass but he disappeared. All that was left of him was the whirr of his song. She'd always liked how a wren was so much louder and braver than their tiny body. A few more doors along and she'd slipped along the flagged path between a bothy and a byre, stumping determinedly up the hill. No time today to stroke the calf with his milky hay breath and his lumbering mother with her long ginger coat and horns wide as a boat.

Above the peak of Conachair she could see the birds rising, white ash over a green mound of fire, the grasses not yet cut for hay, rippling green under the hot wind. On the far side, she knew, the cliffs sheared off the back of the hill like a loaf sliced by a jagged bread knife. That's where the men would be hunting for fulmar petrels, where Norman would be close by his father, moving along the ledges and fastening the birds he caught around his belt.

She'd watched as Father gave Norman his climbing lessons. She'd followed them to the little cliff face at the back of the village at the base of Mullach Mòr. Father and Norman roped together, Father going up first, his bare feet on the rocks like two more big hands, his toes gripping and pushing. Father said St Kildans were famous for their strong feet, their long toes. His face turned to Norman as he called, 'Up there, to your right. No, the other right, Norman. See yes, pull up now and find where your foot can lodge. Only ever let go one point at a time.'

Christina thought she would be asked to join in this game when she was big enough. When there was no one about, she had tried climbing up herself. She never got stuck. Not going up. Not coming back down. But after a time she saw that the women and the girls had different work to the men. The women went to milk the cows in the Great Glen, or chatted as they knitted and carried the peats, or sang as they turned over the earth to lay the seed potatoes. Or they sat with their red scarves flickering in the wind at the top of the cliffs, plucking a storm of white feathers while the boys wrung the birds' necks and handed them to the women. They had plenty of work. But they never did go with the men to climb the wind-filled sweeps of Hirta's cliffs where the birds sailed on the air in dizzy towers, filling the air with their cries.

But Christina would go with her brother and the men. She made her way up to the summit's crest with her short, determined legs. It took a long time, as it always did. Behind her the village became a toy, and then it was gone as she went over the brow of the hill and began the descent on the other side, her legs going faster now. There was the sea beyond the hill's curve, bright blue against green, but no sign of Father or Norman yet. She'd had stern warnings from Father not to come here on her own, where the hillsides' slopes were suddenly broken off into a fall of over a thousand feet, the ink sea fringing white against the rocks. But he didn't need to worry because Chrissie was always good and steady on the hills. She'd only ever felt safe on the island, the sea below a blue quilt on a bed.

But the slope was pulling hard on her now, making her legs run. She slipped, grasped to hold on to the grass that tore away in her fingers, a bird flew low above her, startling her with its cries as she felt the earth tip and she was rolling and sliding down towards the edge of the land. She twisted in the air, flying with the birds, too fast to feel any fear, the sea washing over tiny rocks far, far away. Then she felt the blows of the earth hard against her side as she struck and bounced and fulmars exploded from their nests in a frenzy of harsh jabbering.

The last streaks of a red sun were going down into the ashen sea, a blanket of grey cloud smothering the last red flames.

The men were all back from the cliffs, but the birds lay forgotten in a pile of soft bodies. Where had Chrissie gone?

Dusk was falling. Lanterns all over the island, and you might think God would have helped with a bit of moonlight, but all he'd sent was his minister with his small lantern and his wife with another, calling for Christina because she's out on the hillside awfully late. But there was no sound or sight of her. Too dark now to search but the men carried on. The women gathered back in the village, not speaking their fears, hoping that first light would not show a small body floating on the water down at the foot of the cliffs.

The tides around St Kilda, as they knew too well, could keep a body close to the cliffs for days.

Down on the cliffs looking out towards the long isle, something has disturbed the fulmars and their precious one chick of the season.

They should be roosting in the dark, but they cluster in a flurry of dark wings in the air. Something they don't like.

Caught in a cleft between the crumbling cliff and a protruding rock, a blue cloth fluttering, matted hair. A bare child's foot hangs in the wind.

Christina opened her eyes. Why hadn't they come for her yet? Darkness filled with wind all around her, just enough faint light from a clouded moon to see that she was in the wrong place, the sea too loud, and no sign of Father or Norman. She should get up and go to find them, climb back up, but she can't move.

It began to dawn on Christina that she was very alone. That it was very dark, and no one had come to find her.

No one knew she was there.

She began to cry. Fear is as big and lonely as the black sea soughing below. Perhaps they would never find her. When she could sob no more, she lay still and empty, staring up into a darkness that had become complete.

Then a whirring in the air above. One small bird darted past in the dark air, a small body in flight alighting on the rock face. And then another, and another until the air was filled with a soft whirring sound, purring and fluttering, little home calls as the shadows of birds disappeared into their roosts between the cracks in the rocks. Storm Petrels. The little dark birds that dance on the waves like shadows and only come home to sleep when the dark falls. The air was alive, singing with the blurring of wings. The birds had come to keep her company, whispering their stories of the sea, crying out their tiny greetings. Lulled and mesmerized by their soft sounds and the little calls, she was no longer afraid.

The dark was at its blackest, the air quietened, the birds home and sleeping, her fear gone, for she could feel something she had not understood before. She was not alone: there was someone or something who would keep her safe, who bided with her, would always be with her. Ah, but her leg hurt and she was so weary. Her eyes closed.

The dawn had drawn a ruby line along the bottom of the dark when she woke, a grey light beginning to dissolve the night in the east so that she could see the fulmars falling from the cliff above and sailing out on the wind, and oh, lanterns, coming down the cliff. Voices calling her name. She yelled back with all the force left in her, a poor dry sound. 'Here, I'm here. It's me, Chrissie.' The lanterns moved closer, and she could see men with ropes, calling out to her as they descended.

'Don't move. For God's sake don't move, child. She's here, by God. Thank the Lord. She's alive.'

So here she was on the cliff with the cragsmen, tied against Father's chest, and sorry for it now. The men above held him steady with ropes as he climbed back up the great ladder of cliff ledges. She lay against his chest, in her body the sensation of how he carried her home down the hills to their village, floating in his arms through the indistinct early light past the circular wall of the graveyard with its many unnamed little stones of babies sleeping deep among the grass and the nettles from the long years of the island losing their children to the ten-day lockjaw.

He tipped her into her mother's arms that held on so tight. They forgot to scold her as they bundled her into the box bed in the cottage and piled all the blankets on and round her. She had to promise. Never again. Never do that again.

For Chrissie was that rare thing on the island, a baby that had lived. She was, Mother said, a Reverend Fiddes baby. Old Fiddes, the missionary who had lived in the manse in the years before Chrissie was born, had grown weary of the grief of burying so many babies, each ten days old, their little jaws clamped shut, their bodies arching and rigid until their crying stopped and they went quiet for ever. The mothers could not bear to name a child until they saw they would live. Oh, those mothers knew how to weep. It was the will of God, they repeated back to the minister as they always had. But he'd doubted it. He'd left the island to go back to Glasgow, put on an apron to train as a midwife.

Three times he had to go back there before he learned how to solve the plague of lockjaw that came down on the babes in their second week, and all the while more little souls flew up like birds into the air. He came back with a nurse. She had a tin of antiseptic powder to sprinkle over the cut cord, and carbolic soap and hot water to make sure that everything that touched the baby was innocent of germs.

The villagers had resented such intrusion on their privacy. The nurse had a hard time stopping the knee woman from anointing the baby cord with a rub of oil stinking from the fulmar's stomach as she always had done, but the proof was in the loud cries of living children and finally they listened.

Christina's mother had lost eleven of her own brothers and sisters, all of them sleeping now within the little planticrue walls of the churchyard, bulbs without flowers, a whole host of unknown family members that had left the village population too small and lonely in the middle of the sea.

But Christina's forehead was live and warm under her mother's hand, and her mother breathed in the earthy smell of curdled milk and sheep wool oil that was Christina.

Christina looked up at her mother's wet face. She wanted to tell her that she didn't need to be afraid. For she knew now, she has felt how He bided close with her, comforting her through the dark night. She put her hand into her mother's rough palm. Chrissie, being small, did not have enough words to comfort her mother, only this hand to tell her that someone loved her closely.

For even a small child can know a very great thing.

★

The story is finished. My mother is looking into the evening with its greenish sky and black trees, somewhere far away from me.

'Well, that's enough for today and long ago.' She squeezes my hand but my fist is clenched. She can see in my face what I'm thinking, what I don't dare to say. I wanted more, stories of him.

'Bide patiently, Rachel. You must be patient.'

She goes in and fills the kettle, puts it on the range and turns on the wireless that uncle Callum sent us from Glasgow. He works in the shipyards there, turning out ships for the navy. We drink our tea and listen to the big-band music from London, waiting for the news to come on. At last. She turns up the volume. Hundreds of fishermen and pleasure boats have sailed all the way across the Channel to the beaches of Dunkirk. They are bringing back the thousands of our soldiers trapped there at the edge of the sea.

'Thank God,' says my mother. 'Those boys are coming home.'

It's a few days before my mother picks up her story again. We're washing the supper dishes, her hands in the water as she looks out at the hills with their dark green forests. I'm drying a plate with a teacloth and it takes me a moment to realize she's back on the island again.

'It's hard to explain if you never lived on the island, how cut off we were in winter. How very much we longed for a boat to come by,' she begins. 'We could smell it in the night if a boat came into the bay, that's how much we waited, especially that year of the great storms. I must have been about eight, I think. We were so glad when the winds let up at last and a fishing trawler from Aberdeen finally came to shelter in the bay. The men were straight down to the shore to launch our little boat, rowing out to her. How were they to know what would come of it?'

CHAPTER 5

Chrissie
ST KILDA, 1913

The wind was raw as we watched the men row out at a fast pace to the Aberdeen drifter. It wasn't just that we were short of provisions after such a long spell with no visiting boats during the long storms that winter, the men were hungry for news. There was always a fear that the world might have changed during our months of isolation – a new war started, the government overthrown. The islanders had prayed for the health of Queen Victoria long after she was dead and buried. A brass band came to announce the new king but it had not made up for us being in such a foolish position for so long.

The women wailed that morning as we watched our small village boat bump against the side of the ship, the unsteady swell whipped up by the raw wind. We knew what the men would be shouting up to the crew. 'What's the news?' And then Finlay with his second great priority, 'And have you tobacco?' The men were already reaching for the ladder down the ship's side.

The face peering back over the rail had been grey, reddened nostrils, a hoarse voice, they told us later. 'You don't want to come on board,' the sailor called back. 'Everyone's got a terrible cold.'

But after such a long winter, they didn't hesitate. We watched them in the bitter chill, catching hold of the ladder firmly, balancing each other out as they stood and climbed up from the rocking boat.

After all, a boat cold was nothing new on St Kilda. It would pass through the village and we would shake it off. The men stayed on ship a while, no doubt sharing a hot toddy. They came back cheerful, with gifts from the captain of a little tobacco and tea and potatoes, sacks of coal, enough at least to last us until the next boat came by in a few days' time.

But that night the storms got up once again, the island swept even further out into great black waves, howling winds that stole the breath even as you drew it in. Father started coughing, and then Callum and me. Finally, Mother too. She collapsed in the kitchen and Father had to carry her to their bed. An influenza more severe than any we'd known travelled into each bothy along the village street. And in the gales no boats came by with their welcome supplies of fresh bread or milk – things an invalid could stomach, perhaps. Nothing left for us to eat but the bitterness of salted fulmars and no one left to prepare it.

Then people started dying, three old ones and a child. Four coffins needed and only a half-recovered Malcolm MacKinnon to try and saw the planks, soak them and bend the ends round to fit an old lady's shoulders. The shivering nurse and two of the feverish men forced themselves to the top of Conachair to light a bonfire and signal for help, but it was lost in the darkness of clouds and sea spray.

When the storms dropped and a boat finally sailed in to the bay there was only silence, not a soul moving. 'Surely,' the captain told us later, 'I thought you had all been evacuated someplace else, or died in your beds.'

Such an outcry in the newspapers: that the last savages in Great Britain had been left to starve and suffer. Mr Selfridge, he from the big London shop, along with the man who owned the *Daily Mail* newspaper, they got up a charity collection and sent an entire ship of supplies – the publicity from it didn't harm their sales, no doubt. And along with it came newsmen hungry for a story, wanting to film us islanders being grateful and scenic as sacks of meal and tins of butter were loaded off the ship. And grateful we were, though my mother and the women covered their faces and turned to the wall to hide the shame of being such a spectacle.

Mr Selfridge had also sent a radio mast so that the islanders might keep in touch with the modern world. It broke down as soon as the minister had learned to use it. So weren't we just as cut off again all the following winter, the government and Mr Selfridge arguing over who should pay for repairs?

'All we needed was a regular mail boat from the mainland,' grumbled Father. 'Why can they not route the lighthouse ship past us every once in the while? Too expensive, they say. Same story if we want to cast our votes. Must we be the only people in the British Isles, along with the insane and the criminals, who may not vote? In this day and age. And they call themselves modern.'

Usually it was the laird's steward who came out to collect the rents, but that year the laird himself came on the first trip of the tourist steamer, the *Hebrides*. He made it clear with his curt way that he was very put out by all this fuss in the papers. Starved indeed. Didn't we have sheep enough to kill if needed? Seed potatoes to eat? Hadn't he overlooked half our rents for years?

There was always such excitement, such combing down of hair and putting on of Sunday clothes when the *Hebrides* came in with the first tourists, the village women with knitted socks dangling from their arms and apron pockets as they waited by the jetty, the boys with boxes of white and brown-spattered guillemot eggs, the men shouldering bolts of tweed ready to roll out a length to be admired and even purchased.

The truth was, by then we islanders depended on the tourists to buy the tweed and the knitting we spent all winter making. A few years earlier, the island had sold many tons of fulmar feathers to the army quartermasters, their medicinal oils being proof against fleas. Hundreds of pints of fulmar oil and thousands of salted gannets went over to the mainland. But no one wanted to buy them from us any more, not with new petroleum products so cheap and with even cheaper imports from the Empire on the rise.

But we children understood little of that as we waited on the shore among the barking collies and golden-coated setters to watch the *Hebrides* come in. The thing that interested us was the boy being carried up from the boat. We had never seen a child like it, a creature who had long missed the sun, dipped in milk with hair the colour of grass at the end of winter. The tide was a long way out that day so the only way from the boat was across the slippery rocks with their blanket of seaweed. He was a tall child, ten years or eleven, long past needing to be carried, but since a stranger does not know how to place a foot in the bare rocks and hold fast, so he must submit to coming ashore in the arms of Malcolm MacQueen, that burly red beard making the child hold himself away as if there were a bad smell about Malcolm. Which there most probably was, oily fish and peat smoke, tobacco and sheep wool, though we did not notice it then being of much the same atmosphere.

Malcolm set him down on the beach and the boy squirmed in his pale suit and high collar as if adjusting his dignity. Left alone on the beach, the boy looked around as if waiting for someone to come and fetch him or attend to him.

But it was only us children there, watching from behind the stone dyke, for the steward and the men were all at the boats unloading the sacks and boxes and the women were going up the slope with loads tied to their shoulders, bent double under the weight, all the flour and potatoes and tea and butter that we had been waiting for so long. And at last each home would have its sack of sugar again, along with all the admonishments that the sack was not to be touched, not opened and not a finger dipped in it, since the bag must last the year entire.

The unloading and loading would go on for another hour. The boy was kicking at the sand in anger at being forgotten. We knew we were looking at the son of the laird who owned the island, and were consumed with curiosity at what sort of creature this was, more than a normal human being, perhaps, but certainly less than God himself. We crept out through the breach in the dyke, making the sparrows between the stones chatter and flurry up, and we sat ourselves quietly a little closer to see him better. Then my little brother Callum waddled even closer, in a squatting position, as if being so low he would not be noticed, and we all moved in behind him. The boy turned and scowled at us. The moment he looked away we came a little closer still, and so on until we had crossed to where the grass becomes sand and were ranged in a half circle not so far away from him. There we settled. With no other attendants, and rising to the occasion, he began to put on something of a show, all the time pretending not to see us. Taking up the largest sea boulder he could lift, staggering under its weight, he threw it into the sea. Then he found a kelp stalk, the kind that makes a good walking stick when it is dried, and began to thrash a pile of sea brack, beating it into submission though it was hard to see how it had offended him. Bored with that, he turned to us, hands on his hips, and told us he was Archie Macleod and so we must do his bidding.

Now on an island that had never seen a dictator, our ways always being those of long discussion and democratic agreement, be it when to cut the corn or where to harvest the sea fowls, this was a novel game and we jumped up, eager to follow behind our new general with his milk-white face and pale woollen suit.

He had us march up the glen behind him, a tall feather-haired child leading an assorted row of stocky children in make-piece twice-used breeches and skirts cut simple and bulky from ends of tweed, wind-blown hair and red cheeks and red kerchiefs well fastened round our necks by our mothers to keep out the wind. We were, he told us, a gang of pirates come up from the sea to raid the island and steal all its treasures. Which was willingly endorsed because had we not heard from Allie MacCrimmon tales of a time when the village had to run and hide in the cave below Mullach Mòr since pirates had indeed once landed in the bay.

We dammed the stream in front of the manse and we flooded the glebe field, sailing on it boats made of twigs, and then Archie declared we must send out a party to raid for food. Marching up to the factor he got cheese and bread enough for us all, which is what comes of being a pirate of the upper classes. We ate ourselves full on the hillside, watching the gannets dive from nowhere and explode in white plumes of water in the blue sea, some giving themselves away by the flash of the sun on their wings before they folded into blades to cut the water. I chewed my bread and watched how the white clouds on the mountain made the blue above us bluer, just as Archie being there made the day seem brighter, how the cloud like a soft scarf along Conachair's heights was taken away like breath before it could begin to roll down to us, and I felt a little shiver, for Conachair has its own ways, a stern sort of atmosphere that must always be respected. And so I was telling Archie a story of tourist ladies who had come from their yacht, in great big hats covered in silk veils and birds' wings, who had climbed up the hill in the sun, when a thick mist had come down of a sudden and the ladies had all stepped off those great cliffs eaten into the back of the mountain, unable to see the chasm that lay before them. How they had never been seen again.

Archie decided that he should go up and look at the back of the mountain for himself.

I told him we must not go up Conachair, not with the little ones with us. But Archie was already walking up the slopes leading to the place where the hill becomes sky. I told the littlest ones to go and play outside old Allie's house as she would watch them, and the six of us who were left followed Archie. My brother Callum at six years old was too little to come with us but he came anyhow.

We followed the path worn in the grass between the store cleits, those round stone huts with a thatch of green turf, a square door like a mouth and one eye above it for a window, watching all we did. I was shouting out stories to Archie, how the cleits were the heads of buried giants with green turf hair and one eye, how they came out of the ground at night to eat children – one of my best stories. He told me I was making up nonsense so sharply that I knew I had him a little bit scared.

It was not easy for Archie to stay ahead of we who climb the hills around the village or across to the glen where the cattle are each day, but he would not give in.

He stopped, holding up his hand so we all stopped.

'Ha,' said Archie. 'See how the people look like little beetles, and my father nothing but a big grasshopper.' Which was a clever observation, I thought, since his long-legged father strode around in a green tweed suit with the top of his head covered in a brown tweed hat with big ear-flaps blown out by the wind, making him look like a big insect. And we were awed by Archie's boldness in speaking of the laird so, which did certify to us the special powers of being Archie Macleod. We saw the houses were a row of black-roofed matchboxes set along a green cloth, each house facing the sea to watch for storms, or for the boats that might bring dear ones returning from the lands they left for. The waters of our little Village Bay looked like an old green penny, dark and oily.

When we reached the glen of The Gap we stopped to breathe, sticky sweat on our faces. Callum's was bright pink, the hair wet on his little round head. The sweaty damp cloth of our tweed clothes was smelling like lambs in the misty rain, of old butter and meal, of memories of days past. The village was all gone now. It was only us children, sitting in the shade of the wall of the sheep fank, the land towards the cliffs rising up each side of us. I pointed to the slope of Oiseval that rears up into the sky like a great snub-nosed whale, cut off cleanly by cliffs all around. The turf there was poor and thin, studded with humps of stone cleits that looked in the distance like barnacles on the head of a leaping whale. So I told them all that Oiseval had indeed once been a giant whale, far, far bigger than any that the Norway men leave in the bay to take to Bunavoneader in Harris. How the giant whale came to St Kilda meaning to eat up little Stac Levenish, but Hirta saw the whale just in time and cast a spell from the waters of the hill of blessings and just as the whale rose up it was turned into stone, its great open jaws turned to cliffs. Grass grew on its back, and the sheep went up there to graze, but if you looked sideways with your eyes half closed you could still see the barnacles on its back and the shape of its big head as it opened its mouth wide.

'I can see it, I can see it,' said Callum, and the others were agreeing.

'And one day a year, you must be careful not to climb it, for it will turn back to a whale and eat anyone who climbs it.'

'What day, Chrissie?' Callum asked earnestly.

But Archie said, 'Really, you natives do speak such nonsense,' in his Gaelic that has an English sound to it, and I was cross then because I saw that Archie likes to be first in all he does.

We drank from a stream, bright glass in the sun, and ploughed on through the nodding pinks and the silver-green plantain leaves, and the long grass with its brown butterflies tumbling across in the swift breeze.

At the top, the wind reached us cold from the Arctic, even in the full sun. Below us you could see how the back of the mountain was eaten away by the sea. We huddled down on the ground, arms around ourselves in the cold. Even Archie was lost for words by the greatness of the cliffs, how swiftly the land ended in a violent drop, how far we were above the seas below. We showed Archie how to creep forward, down on our bellies until our heads were all in a row in the air, taking in the skin-tingling sight of the sea below, dizzy with how far away it was.

'Father says the cliffs are a thousand and three hundred feet high,' I called out.

'One thousand three hundred and two to be precise,' Archie called back.

The sea was darkest blue and shining. We watched waves breaking on the pink rocks below in a frill of white surf. Fulmars sailed level with our heads, rising and falling on the currents of the wind, gliding and then breaking with a few flaps before gliding again. You could see their steady black eyes and little grey beaks. No words now, only the birds' secret calls and creaks, the sounds of the distant surf so tiny and far away, and the softness of the wind across our ears.

Then Archie said, 'Don't you people climb down the cliffs?'

'Aye,' said Donald. 'St Kildans are famous for being the best cragsmen.'

'Show me then. Show me how you do it.'

'But we've no rope,' Donald told him. 'No one goes down the cliffs without a rope and a man to hold him steady.'

'A rope,' said Archie. 'I knew you'd find an excuse not to go.'

'Archie, it is true,' I told him. I thought of the night I had spent on the cliff with only the storm petrels for company and shivered. 'No man, not even big Finlay MacQueen, would do it without ropes and a second man.'

'But I want you to,' said Archie, a strange gleam in his eye. 'This is my island and I order you to go.'

I was going to point out that it was his father our island belongs to, but I heard a shifting and a scraping behind me, and turning my head saw my brother Callum sliding round, his legs already over the cliff edge.

'I'll go for ye,' he called out cheerfully. I froze, could feel the fall of his body through the empty air, a bird not yet learned to fly, and it was me, flying across the grass to throw myself down and grab him by the arm.

Too late, for I felt the pull of the bones in his hand slipping out of my hold, and I lunged and clamped my other arm on his wrist, holding on, his round face surprised by the feeling of his legs dangling in nothing. Oh, but he was too much for me to pull up again. Then Donald was there too, leaning out to grab his shirt by the neck, the sound of the cloth tearing as we hauled Callum up, scraping over the edge of the broken turf so that we raked the earth up with him and you could hear the pebbles under it rattling away down the cliff, the fulmars on the ledges below crackling and sawing their calls.

I dragged him yards inland, him crying to me to let go for I was hurting him. I shouted all the while, how stupid he was.

The one I wanted to shout at was Archie Macleod, though I did not dare.

After the crying had stopped, the air was not the same as before. All the respect for Archie Macleod had blown away, a foolish boy sat on the grass with green stains on his pale breeches. And he felt it for he burst into tears. 'I never meant that. I'm sorry. I didn't mean it. A joke. I'm always doing something bad, I know it.'

We felt sorry for Archie then, his white face streaked with dashes of grey as he rubbed at his eyes, for he did not know the island as we did, and he surely hadn't meant to kill Callum.

And wasn't it Callum who had porridge for brains?

We went down the hill, children together, following behind Donald, the past moments all but forgot as he shouted back how he would show Archie where to get the guillemot eggs on the rocks out by the skerries.

We came back to the village, the people grown back into their proper size. The laird was with Archie's brother, who was almost as tall as his father, and favoured by all since he was the heir. The laird saw Archie with his dirty face and grass-marked suit, hand-knitted socks stiff with peat stains from wading in the stream, and said, 'Can you never stay clean for a moment, boy? You might have some concern that I would worry with you gone for hours.'

Archie looked beaten down by these words. I saw how he turned himself away, anger over his face lest he cry again. I slipped away back to the hills, herding the others before me so that Archie would not feel shamed by all our eyes upon him.

I pondered as my mother filled my plate with mutton stew that evening, on how the mothers and the fathers on St Kilda are strict and never let us get away with mischief or play games on the Sabbath but only read the Bible or go to the church, but how they are kind and cossetting in the welcome of their eyes, how they think that children should have sweets if sweets are to be had, and how they do not chide us with unkind words to make the heart give up, always being glad to see the children in the village.

Supper done, a lingering brightness outside, I stood at the foot of the hills and turned around, seeing our home as if with new eyes, the bigness of the hills and the wideness of the silver plains of sea, a land you could walk across to reach the other side of the world. I knew we were poor and insignificant but I knew too that I would never swap with Archie Macleod in his castle in Dunvegan.

At that time of year, it is still gloaming at nine o'clock, a greenish and purple last light over the sea. No one minded that we children were still out as we gathered on the slopes at the back gate to the factor's house, waiting until Archie saw us there. At last we saw a fair head and narrow shoulders down in the back window, a pause and then he came out in answer to our frantic beckonings.

Donald showed Archie a tin cup of sugar concealed beneath his jacket. 'This way now,' he whispered to a suspicious Archie. Over the croft lands, the evening air smelled fresh of grass and burn water. Sea spray on a wind that carried the calls of birds thinking about going to sleep. We folded Archie into our midst and led him to the fairies' house, Donald leading the way with the cup of sugar under his jersey.

In the near gloom of the souterrain, we lit a fire of dried grass and peat and sat an old iron dish on top, pouring in the sugar while I said spells. We watched it melt and turn brown, adding a piece of stolen butter as I stirred and stirred fast with a stick. Out on the grass, to the cracked bells of sheep calls, we showed Archie how to tip the mixture onto a flat stone so that it cooled. Then we sat around it, peeling off the toffee, chewing the heavenly substance slowly, all the while telling the worst stories we could think of from the island, of great birds who became witches, pirates who were cannibals, spiteful fairies who made you drop down dead for refusing them a drink of milk, of children stolen by the Devil because they did not know how to say the Lord's Prayer. We forgot that Archie was a Macleod of Dunvegan, and Archie too had forgotten it, lying back on his elbow and laughing with the other St Kilda bairns at Donald acting out the part of a witch.

The *Hebrides* sat calm in the bay as we left for our homes, the sun setting behind her. In the morning, Archie would be leaving. I felt sad then, for who knew how many months or years before he might return?

And I wondered if I too might like to go on that boat and travel to Dunvegan or to lands beyond. But curious though I was, I could not think how I could ever leave one day and give up my home here on the island, any more than I might tear out my own bones and leave them behind me.

It would indeed be a while before I'd see Archie Macleod again. For by the next year we were at war with the Kaiser, the Great War. A grey steel boat sailed into Village Bay and fast as you liked the navy men were building a row of huts down by the feather store, the radio mast finally mended. A full dozen men were stationed on the island to keep lookout over the Atlantic for German U-boats. We'd never had a time like it, for suddenly there was paid work for all the men on the island, digging trenches, putting up the wooden barracks down by the shore, or sitting up all night and day on Mullach Mòr as lookouts.

You could see the realisation on the faces of those young men, so this is how it is on the mainland: people would pay you to do simple tasks, and no need to risk your life wresting a living from the cliffs and the sea. There was a shop to spend their pay in. A boat came every week bringing letters. All the things we ordered came right back in a few days, new boots and pretty fabric and marmalade and sweets, because we had the money, you see.

It always was the way of the village to welcome strangers. Some of the young sailors would come to ceilidh by the fire of an evening, telling tales of how life was on the mainland, film shows and cars and great cities, and our ears lapped it all up like fairy tales.

So when the war ended and the navy men went and took it all away with them overnight, the young people never really settled back into their old life again. They knew how it was now, knew they were poor. Two of our island's girls had gone away with the navy men as wives, and then came the cruellest blow. The entire MacDonald family decided to follow their daughter to Stornoway. The first time we ever had one of the cottages left empty.

The sound of how good life was on the mainland was a bell sounding the end of our life, calling the young people away, one by one. And go they did, a handful, and then a flood.

My older brother Norman got up one morning, saw there was a boat in the bay and told Mother he was leaving. Went that same day. He lives in Canada now and we live for his letters though they come but rarely. Morning and evening we prayed for him at family worship, and we prayed for him to come home and visit us one day.

A few years after the Great War ended, there were barely fifty people left on the island, but those that were, they were determined to stay. There was no other life for them. And hadn't there been St Kildans on the island for two thousand years, and probably before that, so why would we not stay?

The tourists had started to come back on their summer visits, and we sore needed them to buy our tweed and souvenirs, but I'd begun to see how they must see us, backwards and poor, and to understand my place in the eyes of someone like Archie.

When Archie finally did come back to the island, he'd grown so tall, a gawky sixteen-year-old. I'd heard he was away at school in London for most of the year, and I don't think it was a kind place. My Archie had always been proud in himself, just as the stones and the sea know well who they are, but he'd changed. This tall, lanky, out-of-sorts Archie had a sly, watchful shame in his eyes.

Archie's older brother, the apple of his father's eye, had been lost at Passchendaele in the Great War. So now Archie had to measure up as heir and it didn't look like the laird thought he was doing too well, Archie loping after his father, the laird's attention elsewhere, then turning to bark at Archie to not look so lifeless. Disappointment on the human heart is like the tap, tap of water that can wear away even granite. You could see the hope in Archie, that his father's hand would rest easy on his shoulder, but his father's hand was on Neil

Ferguson's shoulder as they discussed the barrels of ling to go back to Skye and Glasgow. Archie set to tallying up the rolls of tweed, his father angry because Archie had made a mistake and now they must start over.

I found Archie down in the feather store, which we did not use any more to store the goods to be shipped out, not since the war, when the German submarine came up out of the bay like a great seal and smashed holes in the walls and roof. Archie was in the corner, sitting on a barrel and throwing stones at the broken wall. He did not hear me come in until I was there next to him and able to see the tears. As soon as he did notice me, he sprang up, shook his head back ready to be proud Archie, but I put my hand in his, quietly, and he turned to me surprised, hungry eyes. Then he said, fierce and determined, 'I'm going to stay here with you, Chrissie. No one will miss me back there.'

'I wish you could, Archie.'

'I'm not going back to that damned school. They can't make me.'

We both knew they could do just that.

'I will come back. I'll come one day and marry you, Chrissie, and we'll live in the factor's house.'

I nodded.

'You won't forget?'

'I won't ever forget.'

Out in the bay, the *Hebrides* sounded her whistle. There was a noise in the doorway and the steward came in. 'He's looking for you, boy. We need to get on the boat before the tide turns.'

Archie squeezed my hand. 'Don't forget, Chrissie.'

But it would be a good many years more before Archie came back to the island, a grown man then. And who remembers the promises of children?

★

We're sitting at the kitchen table. She's gone quiet again, her hands folded, her face regretful, pained.

I've so many more questions. It's best not to interrupt her or she may give up altogether, but I can't restrain myself.

'So did he come back to the island? Where is Archie now, Mother?' Has she heard me?

Frustrated, I blurt out, 'And that other boy in the photo. Who is he?'

'What photo?' She turns furious blue eyes on me. 'Rachel Anne, you've been going through my things! You'd no right.' She rises up, fists on the table. 'You can get up those stairs now, and don't let me see your face again. That you could be so sly.'

'Well, it's you that makes me so because you never tell me anything.' I clatter up, slam the door to my room under the sloping eaves – though it doesn't make a very satisfying bang since the damp makes the door stiff. I drop onto my mattress with a creaking of iron springs. Surely she can hear the thundering of my heart below after my daring to throw out such naked words.

After a while I hear a noise downstairs, small cries like a muffled bird, and I creep out to the top of the stairs. My mother is crying. I go down, trying not to let the stairs crack and startle her. She's sitting at the piano, weeping quietly into her hands. I kneel by her, put my arms around her waist.

'Oh, I loved that boy, Rachel Anne.'

Archie? Did she mean Archie? But I dare not ask.

It's early, but I leave her and go up to bed, relieved to be alone and with my thoughts. When I wake a little while later, I hear her downstairs still, the faint sound of the English broadcaster on the wireless. My mother listening, leaning forward, as though expecting a particular message from the newsreader. Turning over in my bed, it strikes me, of course, those boys in the photo, not boys any more, would surely be well of an age to fight in France.

Then I realize what my mother is listening for and go cold.

For even though there has been all the triumphant news of the boys brought back from Dunkirk, everyone here in the Highlands knows of a brother or a father or a neighbour who has not come back from France. The BBC doesn't seem to want to talk about the thousands of Highland men still missing. All through the villages and glens, people wait for news of the 51st Highland Division. Are they prisoners – dead? Where are they?

CHAPTER 6

Fred

NORTHERN FRANCE, 1940

After Tournai, I was sent to a prison barracks in Bethune. And as soon as my health was good enough, I began to make plans to escape again.

Bethune prison was overcrowded and filthy. We slept on musty straw that came alive with lice at night. It was a holding station for escapees and men left behind in northern France before they were moved on to camps inside Germany. From the rumours coming back, it seemed that thousands of the 51st Highland Division had already been shipped off that way. At least the guards were nothing like the police Gestapo at Tournai. These were regular German soldiers and not without some fellow feeling. Overwhelmed by the numbers, they struggled to feed us, but at least they turned a blind eye to local people passing food through the prison gates. It must have looked harmless enough, girls, or old women with baskets, broken-hearted for all those boys. That's how I got talking with a Belgian teacher who agreed to help with some essentials.

On the third day she passed me a small loaf, told me to eat it with care. Inside, a map of France. I studied it carefully. With the coasts so heavily patrolled by German troops, our only hope now was to go south and try for the border into Spain. The following day she managed to pass through some civilian clothes.

This is what the start of resistance looks like, I thought, girls in pretty dresses passing discreet parcels of their brothers' and fathers' shirts through the bars while our boys make sure the guards are distracted.

I'd noticed a washhouse around the side. Once you were on the roof there'd only be a few feet more to climb to the top of the massive flint wall. It was a long drop of twenty feet on the other side, but not impossible with some luck.

It was just the two of us, me and a boy from Uist called Angus Maclean, tall and thin with sandy hair and a pale, freckled face. We counted a five-minute gap between patrols, enough time to get up on the roof. Others would follow if we got away.

In the small hours of the morning, the moonlight much brighter than I would have liked, we climbed up onto the washhouse roof and lay on the tiles, waiting to be discovered at any moment, every breath far too loud. We heard the patrol passing below. As soon as the sound of their boots died away, I was up on the wall, hung from my fingers and then dropped. A jarring jolt through my bones, but I staggered up with nothing more than bruises. Angus dropped next, tears to his trousers but no more.

The barracks were on the edge of town. We dashed into the cover of some bushes, ran a few hundred yards through a back street then across the fields. As soon as we were inside the forest, I signalled to Angus to stop. Stood with hands on my knees, head hanging down for a while. We weren't in the best condition after months on meagre prison rations.

Angus took out the map, copied out by hand onto a thin sheet of paper.

'If we strike out that way we should hit the road into the next town, perhaps get there by the morning.'

It was a clear night with enough moonlight to carry on through the trees, then across fields of corn ready for harvest as the dawn began to break. We walked until the singing of the birds became deafening – a while since we had been outside in the open like this. But the light brought another problem. Our friend at the gate had given us civilian jackets and berets but we still wore enough army kit to be instantly recognizable. Passing along the edge of fields of potato plants we came upon a farmhouse set back in a copse, workmen's clothes on the line. Swiftly, we pulled a couple of pairs of trousers down. We buried the khakis at the edge of the wood nearby and carried on. The boots were still a giveaway but we'd have to hope they'd go unnoticed if dusty enough.

By noon we were on the road, better to walk in daylight like two labourers with nothing to hide than get caught in the dark and shot out of hand for breaking curfew. We acquired a hoe and a shovel to look more the part and covered sixty kilometres over the next few days, walking south through the vast, open fields of northern France. There were still signs of the massive displacement of refugees towards the coasts during the invasion. Streams of refugees had blocked our army vehicles with their high-sided farm carts loaded with bundles and a flotilla of prams and wheelbarrows and bicycles. People had started to return home but you could still see the faint chalk messages on barn doors or walls: *famille* Mercier passed this way; lost, boy aged six called Louis. They had gone back to round up the animals that had been turned out into the fields to fend for themselves but in places the endless fields of corn were now scarred and ruled across by the brutal lines of parallel tank tracks.

And there were still scars from the Great War only twenty years before. In the middle of a cornfield we found a stone cross surrounded by flint walls. We slept with the rows of fallen soldiers that night.

Back on the road the next morning, a convoy of German troops passed us, but we carried on at a slouching pace, better than to run and raise suspicions, holding our nerve, missing the rifles we had handed in at St Valery. We left the road again as soon as we could.

For the next few nights we slept in barns or hen houses, eating carrots or cabbages from the fields, or asking for food at farms, looking more and more like tramps, unshaven, filthy, blisters on our feet. If I mumbled, my schoolboy French could pass for a Belgian labourer looking for farm work. Most guessed who we were, sometimes they gave us a few francs with the food they brought to the door. We walked through a village where more Germans were milling around, walked straight on as swiftly as we dared. You couldn't avoid them. Northern France had been battened down and overrun with Reich troops. We needed to get over the border into France *libre* where there was nominally less chance of being recaptured.

I felt for Angus, only eighteen but on the run through a country where there were people prepared to kill you. Out of prison, but not free. An intensely lonely feeling.

Sometimes, the longing to be home again was overwhelming. But where was home now? With my uncle Lachlan passed away, there was nowhere for me to go back to.

I thought of you, Chrissie. It was you I was walking towards, hoping to get home to, one foot in front of the other.

But I'd always seen you back on the island, in the bothy next to where we once lived. If it was true that the island really had been cleared, then where you were now, I could only guess.

Parched from a day's march through dry countryside, we walked into a small village one afternoon, a few houses on the bend of a road, dust gritting the breeze. Ahead, a small *estaminet* with faded red lettering. The idea of a cold beer had never seemed more enticing. In our berets and blue workmen's trousers, I thought my French, gruff and mumbled, would do well enough. We still had some francs left from the money given us.

We sat down at a table by the door. I ordered two beers. Immediately the girl gave us a hard look. Whispered, 'English?'

So much for my French, then.

Before I could reply, two German soldiers came in, went across to the zinc-topped bar. They stood with one foot up on the rail, helmets off, at ease and talking loudly.

Angus had half risen, ready to scarper. I put my hand on his firmly, stared at the girl to see what she would do.

She leaned in, rubbing the table with her cloth, and muttered, 'Finish your beer then go around to the back door.'

We were shown into a small storeroom off the kitchen. The girl brought us two plates of fried eggs, potatoes, hunks of bread and small cheeses. The best meal we'd had in weeks. We were tucking into it, sitting on wine crates and saying how much kindness we'd been shown by people who were risking their lives to help us, when the door opened and two French gendarmes came in to the room, rifles slung over their backs. I saw the girl behind them in the doorway, arms folded. Was it she who'd betrayed us?

The French police force was now officially under German command. No other way out of the room. I couldn't believe we were back to square one. And my own fault, for hadn't I'd gone against my own rules? Always stay on your guard. Never be too quick to trust a smiling face.

CHAPTER 7

Rachel Anne
MORVERN, 1940

It's that time of year when the cold ambushes you each time you go out no matter what you wear, burning and burnishing the skin, leaving you weary in the warmth on coming home. Mother gets back from Brockett's farm and falls asleep by the fire after supper each evening. She's not young any more, into her thirties, but with her face soft in sleep, cheeks blooming from the cold, I can see that girl back on the island. I tuck a crochet shawl around her.

Her eyes open, startled, as if she expected to see someone else, in a different room.

'Was I singing?'

'No.'

'I was singing in my dreams.' She pulls the shawl higher over her shoulders.

'What were you singing?'

'Oh, some nonsense from we used to waulk the wet cloth. Feathers and eggs, feathers and eggs. That's how it went.'

We listen to the fire shift and rustle, the cry of some bird out in the dusk. 'Do you remember it, Rachel Anne, when the birds came back at the end of winter? That was spring for us, the birds coming back to the island.'

I shake my head but I see, or feel, a sensation of being held up in the air, wings flying over and my hands stretching up to catch something far, far away.

'We'd had such a long winter of it once again, waves five hundred feet high hammering on the cliffs, winds that made the bothies shudder and rock like boats at sea for nights on end. The storm so loud it drowned out the thunder, left us all deaf for a week. It wasn't until May that the storms died down, and then, at last, the first puffins started to arrive. Just a few little sea parrots to begin with, their funny way of landing with a rush and a bump on the grass – for they're made for water, never truly at home waddling on the grass. Then more and more, hour upon hour, until the whole sky above us was a whirling of little dark wings, the great wheel of feathers dipping this way and that around the island heights. I would lie on the grass on the hilltop and feel the birds flying over me, the shushing of their wings like a whisper.

At past twenty, I was too old for the schoolroom, of course, but I used to go there from time to time to help the minister's wife, Mrs Munro. She was a short, self-contained woman, who wore a narrow, straight up and down dress and a long cardigan she'd hold close. She preferred her own way in everything but she was always kind.

I was hearing the little ones read from their English books, helping with the sums on their slates, when we heard the whistle of a boat at last. Even Mrs Munro couldn't hide her excitement, the hope of letters from home lighting up her face. The children's thoughts, of course, were gone out of the window straight away, to the bags of peppermints and lemon drops that the captain might bring them. Rodderick MacKinnon, the oldest boy, tall as a man now, was half standing at the back, trying to see out through the glass. The little ones in pinafores and mufflers ran to the window, calling out, 'It's the *Hebrides*. No, it's one of the Aberdeen trawlers.'

My cousin Tormod had stopped dead with his reader, waiting for Mrs Munro to declare the end of school, as often happened when a tourist boat came in.

'We'll carry on, I think, Chrissie. Running down to the shore in a rabble won't make the boat come over any faster now, will it? If it does stop here today.'

There it was. The pain that mixes with hope in hearing a boat's call, for not all boats stopped by. Even the ones that whistled to us might sail straight on to the fishing grounds at Rockall.

Poor Mrs Munro. She'd told me how she'd cried when the call came for her husband to be minister on St Kilda. They'd told God they were ready to go anywhere in the Highlands to spread the word, expecting at the worst a little manse by a sky-mirrored loch, a garden to tend and a neat bevy of crofters, a town nearby for the shopping. They'd never pictured St Kilda.

'Chrissie,' she said to me one drear winter's day as she looked out on a thick fog sealing the village off in a low, grey space, a cold dampness in everything, the dark near at four in the afternoon. 'I do not think I can do another winter here. My own dear piano, that's what I miss most. That and some company.' Which was hard to hear since I was standing there with her. But I did understand her loneliness.

The children were back in their seats now, hope tamped down like a fire under ash for the night. Rodderick sat back down on the child's bench once more. Tormod laboured on with the story of the English ant and grasshopper, all eyes going back to the window again and again.

She wasn't being unkind to make the children's shoulders droop, Mrs Munro. Out here in the Atlantic, it is necessary to learn to defer hope of any contact for months on end, although this winter had been terribly bad for feeling cut off, with the storms never ending.

A second blast of a steam whistle sounded jaunty across the water. All the faces looked up, Rodderick back at the window in three strides. 'Miss, the reverend's down there on the jetty, and I can see the men putting out the boat.'

'We will end school early today,' said Mrs Munro, excitement in her voice. 'But first we will finish with a hymn.' It was our custom, and nothing else to be expected that we must sing all the verses entire before she would open the school door, but 'There is a Blessed Land' did seem interminable long that morning. Another blast and the children were out of the door like spring lambs let out of the sheep fank.

Everyone in the village, some forty persons, were walking or running down the grassy slopes to gather at the jetty. The men were already out on the water in the little village boat, shipping out with great briskness, oars beating the water in time. Even the breeze was all a flutter, flying a hundred flags of cheerfulness for being back in contact with the outside world again.

Mrs Munro had pulled on her new tweed coat woven and sewn by Mr MacKinnon, and stood eyes screwed up, the cold, spring wind taking liberties with her hair. 'Yes, it is the *Hebrides*. News from home. And the orders we placed. A whole wheel of cheddar and salt beef I put down. And blacking for the stove. And new boots at last.'

Something big was being winched down from the *Hebrides*'s crane, a great wooden box, slowly lowered into the small village boat. The women on shore set up a wail each time the boat rose up in the water, sure the rowing boat would topple over with such a precarious load. We could see the men were standing and holding on to it and untying the ropes fast as they could.

The boat made its way back slowly, tantalizingly. And plenty of time to make out as it neared that it was weighed down not only with the great flat box, but also with something else: two strangers. One was standing with his fists on his hips, his long coat held back, fair hair.

'Bless my soul if it isn't Archie,' cried out my grandmother. 'The image of his father. It's him, the laird's son.'

I narrowed my eyes to see something of the fair-haired boy who had half killed six-year-old Callum by teasing him on to go down the cliffs – until I had put a stop to it. Or the tall, tearful boy hiding in the feather store. And yes, surely this creature was Archie Macleod himself. I smiled at our fancy we would wed one day. Chrissie, he'd say, such ideas we had when we were children. Or perhaps he'd say nothing about his old promise but I'd tease him anyway.

I wondered who the man sat next to him was, getting out of the boat as it ran onto the pebbles, shorter than Archie, thick dark hair, a small ruddy face with a little brown beard, a boy being a man, his trousers rolled up to his knees, bare legs in the icy water, laughing as he gave his lankier, fair friend a lift on his back through the waves to the shore.

We all ran down to the beach to meet them since the wooden box was too heavy a thing to be lifted onto the jetty and was being manhandled out of the boat onto the sand, the dogs, collies and retrievers and all mixes in between, running in and out of the surf in a happy frenzy.

With everything so windy and busy, I could only take in Archie Macleod in snatches, like gusts of wind blowing me against my will, knocking me off step, for he had become a creature handsome and glowing. Taller, a long narrow face cut fine as white china, shades of blue under the eyes. I caught a clean-cut nose like a bird beak, round blue eyes, a mouth that would not stop smiling. And I could not stop the gladness inside me to see him again, filled to bursting as I waited for his cheery, 'Chrissie, it's you,' his face bright as he saw me again.

But no such thing came about. He was past me and gone up the village in a few strides, waving to all like royalty. I felt angry at myself for such foolishness in expecting him to remember the child I was, but all the same, my heart was away with the children and the dogs following Archie, and nothing I could do to stop it.

And why should he recognize me, for there I was, the same plain blue dress and apron that all the women wear, the same square checked scarf over my hair and tied around my shoulders? So why should I expect Archie to pick me out or remember me among all the others? Oh, but I did want him to notice me and remember the boldness of the girl who had led him across the wind-blown hills. But we stood in a quaint row, just like one of those photos the tourists liked to take showing the St Kildans as picturesque and backwards remnants from a bygone age, a relic, while the rest of the world had hurtled on into a new century.

I followed the villagers back up to the pier where a handful of tourists were now alighting. Among them were two girls, narrow coats with fur collars and hats shaped like bells close on their heads. The taller one, her coat made of a soft lustrous leather, raised her arm and called out, 'Archie, yoo hoo. Come and give a girl a hand, would you?'

I saw Archie running down to the jetty, handing her up from the boat while she clung on to him and giggled, though she was tall and strong enough to manage on her own, in my opinion. The second girl made her own way. Archie's friend went to offer a hand. She did not take it.

The tall girl had the simpering, amused look of one who has done something daring in coming to see such a place. The children were delightful, and the dogs were delightful and so darling, and oh look at the houses. Goodness, do people really live in such small places?

They made their way over to greet Mrs Munro and the reverend – easy to mark out since he was the only one with a wide white band round his neck – while my mother and the other women at the jetty's end started carrying up the sacks unloaded from the second boat, the men roping them to the women's backs. I picked up a small box and drifted nearer to the manse. There were introductions, Archie, Fred Lawson and also the misses Flora and Sylvia, who were just there for the day and absolutely had to buy some of the marvellous tweed here. 'And socks, isn't it, Archie, that one really should buy here?'

'The best walking socks.'

'First you must come and take tea then we will show you the village. And what a lot of things have arrived with you,' said Mrs Munro. 'All our orders I think.'

'It's as requested,' Archie replied. 'But I'm afraid the men will need to make a second trip to bring in the things Fred and I have brought with us for our stay. There's quite a lot.'

'You'll be staying a while, then?'

'You did get my letter a few weeks ago? We'll be staying through the summer – if that's not an inconvenience.'

'No letter came,' said Reverend Munro, 'but it's always the way here. Nonetheless, you're welcome. More than welcome. It is a great pleasure for us to have visitors. We can put these gentlemen in the spare room, can't we, Margaret, in the manse?'

A quick look of bewilderment on Margaret Munro's face as she thought of the stores she kept in there. 'Of course. And if I may ask what it is that is in the large box, Mr Macleod?'

'That is something for you, Mrs Munro.' He was beaming with mischief, and if I thought before that Archie Macleod could not get any more handsome, then that smile changed my mind.

The village men had set the box on logs, rolled it up to the grass and left it in front of the manse garden. The minister, who was the son of a crofter and not averse to working his glebe with a spade himself, took a crowbar and helped them carefully lever a side panel away. His two young children were running around asking to help and being denied it, boys of ten and six in beautiful knitted jerseys and thick ribbed socks with turn backs, boots laced up firm well above the ankles and polished to a shine. Archie and his friend were equally well shod in good leather. I looked down at my own battered shoes and all the bare feet of the children from our village street.

The sides of the crate were off now, the children coming close to see a second wooden box inside, but this one polished to a glow, standing in the middle of a great envelope of crate sides laid on the ground. The minister's wife went over, lifted the long lid jutting from the side and tapped some of the white keys that lay like a run of whale's teeth. Then she put both hands to the board, paused for a reverent moment, and began to play a tune. I did not know what it was – now I know it well: 'Nearer My God to Thee', one of the great Sankey hymns. Her husband came and stood beside her and began to sing. Back in Berneray where he was raised, the minister was known as a great singer. Then he began a Gaelic song that we do not know here, but it was about a sailor lost to his sweetheart and how she waited for him on the cliffs day after day all the same.

The piano was a beautiful thing with its deep voice, the wood golden like butter fried in a pan and giving off with a sweet, vinegary smell of varnish and polish – the second time I fell in love that morning. There were small flowers inlaid in the front in ivory and darker woods, and below them two brass candlesticks in case you wanted to play in the winter evenings and needed to lighten the dark.

Mrs Munro had tears in her eyes. 'Mr Macleod, I can't thank you enough. But I don't understand. How is it here?'

'The Lady's Benevolent Fund in Edinburgh took the news very much to heart when they heard how bereft you were without your piano and so I was charged with making sure it reaches you safely.'

I felt so proud of my Archie then, that he had done something so kindly for Mrs Munro. It had been a long while since we had a family living in the manse cottage, which had stood so lonely away down by the sea. Some had said that since there are so few of us left on the island we wouldn't get a new minister again but now that Mrs Munro had her music, perhaps they would stay a while longer than a year. I was ready to run over to Archie and tell him what a good thing he had done – if I thought he'd have known me from Adam.

Mrs Ferguson took the two young ladies off to look at the socks and guillemot eggs and tweed that they might like to buy. I could hear the sharp voice of Miss Sylvia as they went off up the path, declaring how very darling everything was, and so unspoiled and should we all just live like this, Flora dear?

'I can see you, doing without taxis and gin and the Kit-Kat club for about five minutes,' Flora replied.

An hour later and Mrs Munro was greatly grieved. The piano was too big to get into her sitting room, the turn between the front door and the parlour proving too narrow. For the first time, I saw the resolve to make the best of everything crumble and sag in her long face before she could remove herself a few paces to keep her tears private from the village women who had come to help. But she soon came back brisk and determined and said, 'Well, are there no other rooms at the back of the manse we might try? Or am I to come out here in all weathers each time I want to play?'

'Would it be such a bad thing to play hymns here in God's own church?' said Archie, taking in the hills and the bay with a sweep of his arm.

She did not stop to listen to such nonsense, but went off in the hope of finding a wider door entrance. We all knew she would find no such thing.

Old Finlay MacQueen, six feet tall, with his long white beard and thin wind-dried face, regarded Archie with a long stare. 'They'd be playing amid the storm of God's judgements, the wind and waves coming in fifty feet high out there on the shore.'

'We'll house it somewhere, Mr MacQueen,' Archie reassured him.

'So long as you comprehend it's not to go in the church,' Finlay replied. 'We can't allow that. There's always people who see fit to try and change our ways. I recall back when widow MacDonald was a girl about to be wed to Donald MacDonald, God rest his soul. Didn't the papers get heed we was short of a vicar and send one out from the main land? And with him a whole boat filled with nonsense, hair oil and fish knives and health salts and a giant pork pie and a fancy dress that didn't fit the girl and a great church pipe organ for the marriage, when we never in our church praise the Lord other than with our God-given voices, our only songs the psalms from the Bible. And a host of newspaper men came too, wanting to take pictures. Poor Annie, she was so mortified and embarrassed to think of the whole world knowing she was about to get married. We sent the boat back, pork pie and all, never unloaded a thing. They wanted us to have a minister from another denomination but we waited until a minister from our own Free Church could come out to do the marriage. So remember we'll not have any piano in the church here. We will make a joyful noise in our old way.'

'Indeed you will,' said Archie pleasantly.

In the end, the schoolroom's door was the only one the piano would fit through. Then Mrs Munro fussed about and checked it, letting each key sound through the room. 'Well, it's almost right, Chrissie, if you didn't know any better. It will have to be left like that till it settles then my Duguld will tune it fully.' She gave one last look at it before leaving to see about the visitors at the manse, wistful because there would be no evenings playing music in a warm parlour with the family gathered round, all singing her English hymns.

I was meant to hurry behind her to dust and unpack but I did linger a moment in the quiet, only the wash and suck of the waves falling on the beach for company, lifted the lid and tried out a few notes before I hurried to follow her.

Out on the grass I found Mrs Munro standing in her doorway watching a small fortress of sacks and boxes being carried up to the manse.

'All these things they've brought,' she said, her hands on her hips. 'What's to be done to store everything? And the back room not ready. And where's Kate?'

No sign of Kate the housekeeper nearby, no doubt down on the pier still helping unload the boat. Mrs Munro looked grateful as I told her I'd see to what needed to be done to make their room ready. I called out to Lachie and we had the meal bins and sacks carried out to a cleit nearby and the room swept by the time we heard the Reverend Munro and the boys on the path, Mrs Munro showing them in and giving a description of our quaint and none-too-clean, it seems, ways. A last few sweeps of the broom and they came in. 'And this will be your room,' she told Archie and his friend. Not like this, with a broom in my hands, did I want him to recall the girl I was. I stood turned away and I was only too glad that Archie still showed no recognition.

'May I give your girl a penny for her trouble?' the dark-haired boy with the little beard asked. 'I'm sorry, I don't know her name.'

'We don't like to spoil the villagers. Please don't feel you should do that,' Mrs Munro said.

I decided I'd leave Mrs Munro to help herself then, and I put the broom away.

'You'll have a hard time of it learning their names to begin with,' I heard Archie telling his friend as I left. 'They're all a Gillies or a MacKinnon or a MacDonald. Confuses newcomers no end.'

I could see the misses Sylvia and Flora coming up the path arm in arm in their long coats, like two seals barking away in English.

'Honestly, Sylvia, why would you need walking socks? When would you ever use such a thing?'

'Somebody might ask me to his estate, darling, you know, to shoot things.'

'Oh, Sylvia.' And in they went, though their strident voices still drifted out over the manse garden. 'Cooee, just us. Mrs Munro, such a darling house. . .'

I stood outside on the grass, wondering who these girls were who knew Archie so well. There was much still to be taken inside, a chest with the initials A M, a box with a trumpet attached – a gramophone – a crate of bottles, boxes of books. So many other strange things Archie Macleod and his friend needed to endure the harshness of a few weeks on St Kilda.

I thought of the dirty-kneed boy that I'd once shown how to catch a puffin in a snare. Archie had insisted on setting it free again, no matter how much I scolded him that we depended on the puffins for much of our sustenance.

I had realized something that day, that though Archie might speak the Gaelic from his nurse, his Gaelic words meant different things. Archie was from another world to mine. And as to a promise he had made to a girl long ago, that was blown away on the wind between our worlds.

My mother called to me to help with the carrying down at the jetty. Lachie from next door roped a sack of potatoes on my back. I walked bent forward, the sack weighted secure on my back. It is always an amazement to visitors to see how we women on St Kilda think nothing of carrying such loads. But wasn't it Archie and his friend coming down the slope with the two English girls? I pulled my scarf over my face and tried to hurry by as fast as I was able, but the boy with brown hair said it wasn't right to let women carry such a load and didn't he try to take the sack? He all but toppled me, since it was well secured. I scurried on, best I could, with my scarf pulled down around my flaming cheeks to hide the shame of being so pitied before Archie.

Archie and the brown-haired boy waved while the ship left the bay, the two girls leaning out over the water, waving and blowing kisses. Then they went back up to the village jaunty, boys let out for a holiday, and no signs, I saw with sharp relief, of any broken hearts in the parting.

But it wasn't any help to me, for I had understood now what a girl for Archie Macleod and his ilk looked like, and she did not look or dress anything like me. They dressed like the drawings in Mrs Munro's magazines, while I wore clothes plucked from wool off the back of our wild little sheep, spun by my mother and sewn by my father to a pattern his grandmother might have worn.

The villagers were gathered together in front of the tin hut joined on to Neil Ferguson's bothy, the St Kilda Post Office. He passed out the mail – two whole sacks for the Munros. The village fell quiet that evening with the reading of letters from loved ones. I crept back into the schoolroom where Lachie and I had carried in the two tea chests filled with old books donated by the ladies of the SPCK. In books you may visit places that you will never see with your own eyes. Although this is the great lesson I have learned from such books, there may be grander, or more modern places than our island, but there's no guarantee that any of them is happier. I found *Treasure Island*, and I picked it up for I knew that Mrs Munro would not mind if I took it away to read.

There stood the piano, a stranger beneath the familiar shelves of nib pens, chalks, and the buckling map of the world with its new islands of black mildew spots from the damp sea air – no sign of St Kilda on our school map. I raised the piano's lid and pressed one of the white keys, a voice that came out loud and deep like the knock of a memory deep in your chest. I ran my fingers across more of the white keys, the sound growing more silvery, wishing I could call up the tune that Mrs Munro had played. I would one day, that was my resolution, but now the room was growing dim and cold. I put the lid back down, the wood smooth as the curve of a wave before it falls, and left the piano to its silence.

I walked home thoughtful through the evening, the bothies darkening into the hillside's shadow, the square windows at the side of each door casting oblongs of slanted light across the flagstones and grass. It was always sad to walk past number two, the MacDonalds', the windows dark now, the door locked. Their eldest girl, Mary Anne, was one of the ones who had fallen in love with a navy man in the Great War. He'd visit almost every night there by the fireside, spinning stories from his home in Lewis. When the war was over, and Mary left to marry him and all the family followed, they took with them four grown sons, which made it all the harder for those of us left behind to do all the work we must, in order that we might live. Old Mrs MacDonald and the MacDonald cousins still lived in number eight, but the old lady had never recovered from the loss of her son and his bairns.

I could see the light of my father's pipe glowing outside our home at the far end of the village street. He was watching the lingering of a pink stain between the darkening sea and sky, listening to the creaking and cawing of the sea parrots settling in their burrows on the outcrops of Dùn across the bay. He'd had a good day, selling off a full length of tweed to one of the tourists come out with the boat.

'The air is lightening. We'll have all the fulmars back soon,' he said. 'Who knows the map they follow, but they always know the way home.'

'It is lonely here without the birds,' I said.

I glanced beyond to the last cottage, number sixteen, also in darkness since the death of Angus Mor. Beyond the unlit bothy lay the darkening land and the deep gulley where the stream lay hidden. And after that, the stony land rose and broke off into vast rocky cliffs, then nothing but air above water.

With us all standing around the table, Father made worship with a reading from his worn little Bible and a prayer. We shared a meal of boiled mutton and potatoes. We had tea with sugar and a tin of sweet biscuits from the boat – all the little gentle habits that could begin again now that we had the summer boats in each week and tourists to buy what things we'd woven and knitted over the winter.

Fortified by such a meal, I felt less troubled by the thought of Archie's golden beauty here on our island, and golden he was. After all, he was away over on the other side of the bay where I would like as hardly see him. And surely there was no reason for him to ever come into the schoolroom when I was with Mrs Munro.

'And, Chrissie, you'll come and help tomorrow,' my mother said. 'We've to clean out Angus Mor's place. It will be good to have a lamp in the window at nights again.'

'Who is taking it?' I asked, wondering if there might soon be news of a wedding – though who it could be from our small pool of young people I could not imagine.

'The laird's son and his friend will bide there. The minister's feared it will be too much for his wife to have the boys staying in the manse for months on end so he has asked me to sweep out the bothy and get it ready and I'll be glad if you can help me.'

And all night, I could not decide if this was terrible news or very good news.

The next day, I volunteered to go up over to the glen to find fresh grass for the cows. Soon the cows would be out on the summer shielings and I'd be going over each day to milk them. That would be my saving, I thought – though the other half of me wanted nothing but to come upon Archie as I walked along the path and see his face finally light up – Chrissie, is that you at last?

It was years since the lonely bothy at the end of the village had seen so much company, every woman along the village street popping by to help clean a window or sweep out the floor or shake out the curtains on loan from the manse. The house was watertight but it had been used to store the climbing ropes. They hung from the rafters like vines. There was a mess of ash and a rusted kettle in the fireplace used by passing sailors or by the young men from the village who came to escape their little homes and smoke their tobacco when they had some.

From halfway up the slope of Mullach Mòr I paused to look back at the goods being carried from the manse along the village street. I could hear the barking of the dogs small and clear from down below, someone singing. Above, snow-white gannets were circling around the bay, narrow wings outstretched like bent knives. I waited to watch that moment they fold into a dart and fall so swift that you lose sight of them until a white star of foam blooms silent on the sea. There were hosts of fulmars too, hanging steady on the up-currents from the cliffs. I could hear them calling to each other down on the rock faces like wooden hinges, with the puffins and the guillemots, the great cacophony and riot of seabirds that is our full summer chorus here on St Kilda, an ever-present storm of creaking, chattering, ack-acking, laughing bird song.

When I came back with the bundle of new-grown docken and hay, so many things were still out on the grass like an excess of playthings. What, for example, was the need for the great wooden tripod with the box next to it? And a telescope, and more parcels of books than I had ever seen in the schoolroom. Untold tins, sacks and bottles.

Someone should have reminded his lordship that we were safe from famine here over the summer. I pulled my young cousin Tormod away from the unguarded telescope and hauled him home with me, along with a stern and whispered warning about touching any of those things which if broken we would never be able to replace.

'Ah, Chrissie, but they said I could,' he protested as I shut him inside.

'They did no such thing.'

'They did, Chrissie,' said Mother. 'They are good boys.' She was arranging tins of salted beef and butter inside the cupboard. 'All this, and they have done the same kindness for every home in the village.' She was smiling at all her stores like a harvest gathered in from the croft. 'And it behoves us as Christians to return the care and keep an eye on those boys, see they fare well for the sake of their mothers.'

'Just as their mother Lady Macleod would for me if I were to go and live next to her,' I said.

'As she would, Chrissie dear. As she does for all those who work the laird's lands.'

I shrugged my shoulders. If the laird cared for us so much where was the regular mail boat that should come to us all through the winter? What if, during the last bad winter, no one had found our scraps of paper in their tiny wooden floats calling for help when we were hungry and sick? What if the winds and the tides had not taken one of the tiny boats to a beach in Norway where a man had opened the tin with our message inside and contacted the admiralty for us? The boy who had already found the letter washed up in Taransay had not been believed and our message ignored as a childish trick. That was how precarious it was for us in winter. But I kept silent, for there is always only kindness in my mother. It was ever the way of the St Kilda folk to think kindness and duty both first and last, and to see any bad in people, whenever they find it, as a rare and anomalous condition.

As was his custom, Father went out with his pipe to watch the last of the setting sun. I wanted to go out with him as I often did, but I could hear the English-sounding voices of our new neighbours outside, talking between themselves, calling a goodnight to Father. So I kept by the lamp with the book brought over from the schoolroom.

It was an almost full moon. Perhaps that is why I slept so badly, my mind whirring like the constant cries of the birds as they flew around the stacs, never still and never completing their circle but starting off on new angles and arcs. Perhaps it was reading so late. My grandmother, Rachel Òg, held that too many books damage the brain and ruin sleep. She trod only the steady path of her Bible, end to end, twice a year, in her old black house at the back of the village, and she was indeed a most sharp-minded woman for all her eighty years, a living encyclopaedia of all our stories and the old songs the people used to sing. But I knew what the problem was. It was the picture of Archie's bright face and hair before me in the darkness.

Giving up on sleep, I left my bed and, wrapping the blanket round my shoulders, went outside. The moon has a soothing effect on a soul that cannot sleep. There she was in her almost perfect roundness over the bay, and the insubstantial silver line that she throws to us across the sea wherever you may stand, that disappears before it reaches the shore. I felt so restless. I wanted to go down and pace the beach. None of my thoughts made any sense, and all around the same topic.

I thought of Archie in the bothy next door, sleeping on the oat-chaff mattress we had brushed down and covered with the sheets from Dunvegan Castle. Someone would fall for him one day. Probably half the ladies in London already had. And seeing him standing there with his fair hair, even I hadn't been able to stop myself being powerfully struck by the beauty of his tall frame and his open blue eyes.

I told myself off then, for I was not like the silly girls in London. I surely had a stronger mind than to be swayed by worldly glamour and charms. A smile that promised secrets, a face proportioned just right. That laugh of his. A new creature. He even smelled new, like leather and wind and clean sweat. It was a mystery to me why I should be so fascinated in my thoughts by this new Archie when he was surely the same fretful boy I had always known.

I went back in, sat down on the deep windowsill and drew up my knees. It was the chill part of the night now, the sky a luminous grey, black clouds bleeding across the moon, turning the sea to black then silver then black again. I watched the drama of the sky until I had all but forgotten my own small one, my eyelids finally drooping. I returned to my bed, but even in my sleep the thought of him stayed strong in my mind like the pull of the moon on the sea.

CHAPTER 8

Rachel Anne
MORVERN, 1940

Mother's stories made me very curious about Dunvegan Castle on Skye, the seat of the Macleods. I'd managed to find photographs of it in books, looked up the family history. I could not find a picture of Archie Macleod, boy nor man, but I recalled well the photograph in my mother's drawer and the tall blond boy, so I already knew what he looked like, at least as a young man.

In my less sensible moments, I came up with a plan of how I would go to Dunvegan with its turrets and servants and knock on the great oak door and tell them, I'm Rachel Anne, your granddaughter. Perhaps. Though I knew I never would, even if I was cast-iron certain that such was the case.

I've heard the very bad word that people use when they despise someone or think they have bad character. It's the word for someone with no father to claim them. The worst of swears and insults. I know enough to understand that if your mother never marries the father, then you are nothing. You are legally a bastard.

My mother lets people think my father passed away, Mrs Gillies, widow – but I know she's a Miss. And it makes me feel very small to think that people could rightly come up to me and shout that bad word in my face. So I don't think I will ever go to Dunvegan. Instead, I feel glad that we live far away from the world, lost among the hills and pine forests of Morvern, with neighbours too polite and discreet to ever suggest that my mother is anything other than who she lets it be known she is.

So I put all thoughts of finding Archie Macleod out of my head.

But then I see a copy of the *Free Highland Press* in the library, large letters across the front, Archie Macleod, heir to Dunvegan, presumed missing at St Valery. I know I shouldn't but I put the newspaper in my bag, run home with it to show Mother.

She goes white when she sees it, sinks down onto the chair.

'Oh my poor boy,' she whispers.

I'm beside myself. 'But he'll never know now, never know about me. I was going to go to Dunvegan Castle—'

My mother takes me by the arms, shakes me till I come back to my senses. 'Oh, Rachel Anne, dearest, dearest girl. What are you thinking? No good could ever come of you going to Dunvegan.'

Then all the fight and the anger goes out of her and she holds me close.

'Mother, do you think they will come home safe?' I ask.

I can feel her shaking her head. 'I don't know, Rachel Anne. All we can do is wait, and pray. Pray for all those boys so far from home.'

No more words from her now. She sighs. Is it Archie she's thinking of now? Why is she so reluctant to spell out the name of the man who is my own father? I can't bear to be with her then, pull away from her and go out into the lane, walking alone until my anger has faded and it's only my hunger and lack of supper that send me back home again.

I won't answer her when she speaks that evening, go to my bed angry still. And worried too. Just what is it that stops her telling me plainly? What is the secret that she keeps so close?

Late into the evening I can hear the muffled sound of the wireless. She never turns it off until she finally goes up to bed now. I picture her hunched nearby with the sewing left forgotten on her lap, listening and listening for a bulletin from the BBC with news of our men so far away. So many women across Scotland like my mother. There was no victorious return home for our boys from the beaches of St Valery. It wasn't trumpeted in the papers, but we know now that many of them have been taken prisoner, thousands of them. So across the glens and the cities of Scotland, across the mountains and the islands, women wait for news, hoping the worst they'll hear is that their men have been taken prisoner, and not lost at St Valery.

CHAPTER 9

Fred
FRANCE, 1940

Locked inside the prison van, I realized with a sinking heart that
we were moving north again, erasing any small progress we'd made
towards the Spanish border and the hope of getting home. No chance
of getting away from the Channel coasts with them so heavily guarded
and patrolled. I expected to hear the noises of a city after a while, for
us to be taken inside a regional prison, but the van began to pitch and
rock as if we were travelling along an unmade track. Finally, it came to
a halt. The doors opened and we found ourselves marooned between
endless beet and cabbage fields, blinking at a view of nothing but sky
in every direction. One of the policemen uncuffed us. He pointed to
a farmhouse set back in a spinney. '*Là-bas. Frappez à la porte. Et vive la
France*' He gave a salute. Speechless, we watched as they drove away.
Then we turned towards to the farmhouse in the distance.

'What d'you think?' asked Angus.

'Looks like the French are already fighting back on the quiet.'

The day wouldn't last much longer, the sky fading to an ominous
blue black, the last of a low sun slicing through the clouds like glass.

The door was answered by a middle-aged man in a bulging waistcoat
and blue workmen's trousers, bulked shoulders, grey stubble, a resigned
chin set on a heavy neck, eyes that had seen it all and expected no better.
He appraised us then gestured with his head to come in.

In a dark kitchen, a woman in a summer dress and cardigan, a stained apron, was at the stove. She gave us a harried nod and sat us down to vast plates of duck eggs, bread and pâté. Tumblers of red wine. Half dead with fatigue, we were taken to a hayloft over a barn and left to fall asleep amid the champing of goats, the sharp scent of their coats rising from beneath like the cuddy smell of a byre back on the island – in the clean days of early summer, before what Archie did in his anger and everything was broken for ever.

I woke, still half in a dream. Longing for you. Watching as you sat spinning before the bothy, your foot pressing the lever, your hands pulling the thread towards you and releasing, pulling to and fro as the spindle filled in a blur. I was a way off, across the grass, your song a hope that I could reach you again.

I became dimly aware that I could hear the shuffling of goats below in the barn, the dust of the hay acidly sweet. You were far away although I felt the hope of your song still with me in my breast. The rank smell of the goats brought me fully to my senses. A voice was calling us from below.

'*Monsieurs, venez.*'

I shook Angus awake. He stared at me with a scowl, rising up in a rush, straw stuck all over his clothes.

'It's just the farm woman.'

Relief on his face.

We went down the ladder, springy under our weight. She turned away, arms crossed as if we were not really there, and we followed her like shadows past the goat pens out into the glare of the morning, the sun promising a day of good weather.

She led us back into the gloom of the farm buildings where the farmer and two other men were waiting to talk to us. The younger of them had good English.

They told us that we were welcome to stay at their farm until they could arrange to take us further south towards the Spanish border. I felt intensely grateful to realize that a network resistance was already beginning to take shape, helping the trickle of stranded soldiers who were trying to get back home. But it was still piecemeal and fragile. The plans for us to move on uncertain.

For the next few weeks we were two farm labourers, demobbed after occupation, helping the farmer with the chores. The Tissiers were more than glad of the hands, Monsieur doubly impressed when he realized I could milk a goat – not so hard after watching Chrissie milk the little cow and the black-faced sheep.

But every nerve in my body was telling me we should keep moving. We needed to keep crossing off the miles. And yet, for now, to stay seemed our safest chance of making it back.

We began to get visitors from the neighbouring farms, two girls bringing food and clothes, smiling at Angus. Then a boy and his mother arrived with gifts of food for *les Anglais*. It can't have been easy feeding two extra when rationing was beginning to bite, but the lack of security due to our local fame worried me, and not only for ourselves.

Our standing further rose when Angus noticed deer in the woods nearby and set a wire trap. Monsieur Tissier was amazed I knew how to gralloch the carcass into sections – skills I'd learned from the gamekeeper's son on the estate where my uncle Lachlan worked until he retired to the little flat in Edinburgh.

A long table of friends toasting the venison and *les Écossais*. An old man began humming a ditty, making his fingers dance as if playing the bagpipes. Bemused, I recognized a marching tune, 'Miss Drummond of Perth'. A girl leaned forward. 'My grandfather wants to tell you that in the last war, we hid soldiers from Scotland. Many men. And now we do it again.'

The goodwill and the risks these people were running left me without words. I raised my glass. 'To friends,' I said. '*Les amis*. And the old alliance.'

But looking around the room at the crowded table made me deeply anxious. Weeks had gone by and still there was no news of a contact to help us move on towards the border. 'Soon,' the farmer told us, each time I asked. 'Soon. A few problems to sort out, and then you will move south.'

I slept uneasily after supper that night. Should we make a move on our own, risk it? I woke with a headache from the cold. The frost had settled on the small window of the grenier. The water in the washing bowl had a thin glaze of ice.

Angus and I were helping tie the last stooks of wheat in the fenceless fields when we saw the small figure of Madame running across the uneven ground, carrying a bag. Out of breath, she delivered her message. The Germans were searching for abandoned war equipment and guns. They'd caught wind of something and were in the next village asking about escapees. No time to go back to the house. She'd brought what spare clothes we had, the compass folded inside a map torn from a calendar, boiled eggs and bread, a little money.

Down a bank on a side track, a man was waiting with bicycles.

There was barely time for a goodbye. They took our thanks gruffly. It was simply what decent people did, to help someone. To resist *les Boches*. We followed the man ahead, pedalling through the countryside, the first signs of changing colours in the trees.

I had no idea where we were headed. No idea what lay before us. All I knew was, I was ready to travel the length and breadth of France if the world would give me the chance to spend one more hour with you. To say I'm sorry.

CHAPTER 10

Chrissie
ST KILDA, 1927

What should I see as I came out of my door in the morning but Archie's companion stood facing out to sea, a mug of water and a mirror on the low wall that runs between the path and the potato rigs below. He was still in his long-sleeved undergarment, his braces hanging down by his trousers. Quite at home, feet planted apart, he was neatening round his beard with a razor. Hearing the rattle of the pump as I filled the bucket, he turned and waved at me, calling out a greeting in English. I bent my head and made as if I had not noticed him, embarrassed to meet him as he carried out so private a task.

Seeing the bucket was filled, he came over, the shaving soap still on half his chin, and took the handle. 'Here, let me,' he said in his awkward Gaelic. But I did not let go.

'There is no need,' I told him in English. 'I am as capable of hauling a bucket of water as you, I think.'

He put up both hands. Nodded his head. 'I cede to the fairer sex.'

And then I felt badly for him because he was not a tall man. 'It's not that you couldn't. I wasn't implying.'

His eyes widened as if here was truly the beginning of an insult. I gave up and hurried away.

'I'm Frederick by the way, Fred,' he called after me. 'And you must be?'

'I must be who I am,' I told him. 'I'm Chrissie Gillies,' I added over my shoulder.

If I had to leave the house that day, I made sure to look out and check that they were not there, quickly cutting up between the bothies and going along their backs so that I might not see him or Archie again, annoyed that my freedom on my own land should be curtailed so.

'Chrissie,' Mrs MacQueen called as I passed behind her bothy where she was out seeing to her hens. 'I've an awful bad back today and I need to take Ewen Ian up his bite to eat where he's with the sheep. You don't have time to run up the hill with it, do you? There's a good girl.'

Climbing up, I heard a thin and imperious voice calling my name, all but carried away on the wind, and there was Ewen Ian waving to me – something of national importance judging by his face.

'Is that my strupac there, Chrissie?'

I took him his cheese and oatcakes, a flask of tea, and he nibbled and chewed slowly, his eyes on the shimmering water of the sea. It always looked calm at such a distance. At the end of the Great War, when the U-boat came up in the bay and bombed the radio mast, the navy sent us a gun. No one expected such a thing now any more, but the navy still paid Ewen to keep their gun in order. Far more useful to us would have been for them to come and repair the radio mast. Full of the importance of his task, Ewen tended to the gun every month.

Ewen Ian's long face jutted out against the sky like one of the cliff rocks, a fine, great nose that had surely came off the Viking boats, handed down as an heirloom. A full beard, a narrow, querulous mouth. Try as I might, I could not think him a husband for me one day, no matter how much his mother or my mother recommended him. It was no help that he'd taken to wearing a wide cap on his long head like a mushroom on a stalk, which he never took off, much as he never took off the great importance he assigned to being Ewen Ian MacQueen.

And just as I was being so uncharitable in my thoughts, he turned the kindest smile on me and said, 'I thank you, Chrissie, for the trouble you have taken in climbing the hill to bring such a fine strupac of cheese and oatcakes yourself while I am here with the sheep. Quite peculiar in its fineness.' Ewen Ian's eyes were bright blue and filled with his blinkered good will. And wasn't there a lot to admire in the efforts he put into learning new words from the books he borrowed from Mrs Munro's little library in the schoolroom? And you know why he does that, don't you, Chrissie? my mother says. Words he must find occasion to use irrespective of whether they are in the right place or not.

I stood for a while looking out towards the curve of the horizon and America beyond, leaning a little into the wind as if I might be a sail on a ship going who knows where on these highways across the seas of the world.

Ewen Ian's voice cut in. He tipped his head towards the mainland. 'Your cousin Marion went away on a boat, all the way to Glasgow.'

'Aye, and lived in the house of our great-uncle Alexander Ferguson.'

We lapsed into silence again, thinking of my great-uncle who left the island years back. Now he sold some of our tweed on the mainland for us, much to the annoyance of Lord Macleod.

Ewen Ian sucked in the air through his teeth, shook his head in disbelief. 'That's an awful busy place, Glasgow. People running around everywhere in crowds. I was there. Makes your head spin. All I wanted was to get home again. Marion too, when she went there. She had the new shoes and dressed like Sunday best every day to work in the big shop, but isn't she back in her mother's cottage again now? Came home as soon as she could.'

His eyes met mine, a lesson in there for me.

'Don't worry, I wouldn't go to live in Glasgow.'

He nodded.

'America, or Australia perhaps.'

'You wouldn't, would you, Christina?'

'And why not?'

'Because you have your old ones to take care of, like me with my mother and her legs so bad.' He folded the empty cloth and gave it to me. 'There you are now.'

'It is an honour to carry it down the hill for you,' I said, taking it in both hands with a bow.

He did not see any sarcasm or humour. He gave one slow nod. All was as it should be.

Walking back down to the line of bothies that sat around the bay like a tide line, it pained me to admit it, but Ewen Ian was right: I could never go from here. For Hirta was a part of me and I was made from her. Nowhere more beautiful, nowhere else home, though the winter was long, and what could we do but sit round the peat fire carding, spinning, weaving – and hoping that our stores would last long enough to bring us safe to a new spring. Often, we went hungry in the long dark. How keenly we looked for the first lessening of the blackness in the morning, for the first hints of the day staying with us a little longer. And we listened out above the wind for the birds' return, the first shearwaters, the fulmars on the cliffs of Hirta, the great gatherings of gannets on the fastness of Boreray and the myriads of little puffins wheeling around the island until they settled on the grassy slopes of Dùn and Cambir once again. For each of the little sea parrots came home to the same burrow, faithful to the same mate.

I could never follow the young people who left, tempted away by memories of the lives we lived in the Great War. I was a little girl then but even I could hear how amazed the young people were: so this is how it must be on the mainland, to have the shop nearby and paid work and the money to buy what you fancied.

There were so many things in that navy shop that we had never known we needed. I recall my grandfather sitting by the fire translating the English words on a blue and yellow tin into Gaelic. 'Custard powder,' he read out slowly. 'So what is that now?' He put a finger into the pale yellow flour and tasted it. Shook his head. Not to be trusted. He preferred the same reliable dish every day, boiled oats with a salted puffin for flavour. My mother, however, adored the thick yellow pudding, and so did we. Long after the army men and their shop were gone, we kept the last tin for storing buttons, the label worn and the lid rusted in the island's damp air.

My grandfather had got up and fetched the bag of barley sugars from the dresser that day. Everyone was in agreement that it was good the children could have sweets. But once you have a taste for sweets or cocoa or tea, it is hard to forget such things. And since we cannot grow tins of treacle or bags of peppermints here, then we must wait for the boats to come and bring us such necessities – or not.

Walking home along the back of the village I saw two figures moving about on the croft land near the fairies' house. Archie and his brown-haired friend.

A second thing caught my eye. Two small boys lying flat on the turf roof of an old cleit, the soles of their feet and the behinds of their baggy old shorts proud to the sun, their chins on their fists. They were watching the laird's son and his friend measuring out the ground around the fairies' house with string and posts. I trod softly, coming up the bank until I was standing head and shoulders by the cleit roof.

'And what is it you think you are doing now, Angus and Tormod MacDonald?'

Angus turned his little flat face to me, brow wrinkled, shorn hair standing up shock in the wind, his waistcoat front pulled up to his eyes as though it might hide him.

'Ah, will you get down, Chrissie. They'll see ye.'

'And why should they not see me, standing here where I live? And why is it that you are spying on them?'

'It's them that's the spies,' whispered Angus. 'Get down, Chrissie.'

I sighed and waited a while, no time for their games of make-believe, but curious as to what Archie and his friend were trying to do.

'All you are looking at is the laird's son and his very ordinary friend,' I said.

The shorter figure, in baggy blue trousers turned up to the knee and a white roll-neck jersey, unfurled a reel of string and pulled it taut between two posts.

The tall one with the pale hair, a grace in his confident movements – he that made my silly heart go a little faster each time I saw him – held a long stick steady while Fred Lawson hammered it in with a mallet. A pole at each corner, they tied on cross poles and then pulled over canvas tarpaulins like a makeshift dwelling.

The sun was warm at last under an open blue sky, the wind gentle across the grass. Fred pulled off his jersey, rolled it in a ball and placed it by his canvas bag, looking towards us for a second, his hand shielding his eyes.

The two boys ducked down fiercely, heads pressed to the turf. I too shrank back, wondering if he'd seen us but he merely turned his back, looking out at the wide view of the bay and the sea. When Angus and Tormod dared to raise their heads again, the two men were sitting below with their backs to us, committing the suspicious act of looking at a piece of paper.

'Is it a map, Angus?' asked Tormod. 'For treasure?'

'No, there are messages for the spies on the paper,' said Angus in a whisper. 'Secret instructions from the Kaiser to blow us all up again.'

A missile flew low over our heads. Landed on the turf behind Tormod. That made us jump right enough.

It was an apple. That's all it was. But my heart was thudding and the one with the dark hair had turned his head up to see if his target had reached us. I could see him laughing, pleased with himself, which made me more than angry. Were we so poor and backward they may toss us food like animals? Throughout all my childhood we had had to endure the tourists. Their boats had brought us income but the price had been too high for the island. They came to study us, the last savages of Scotland, took home our tweed and the socks we women knitted in winter as if they were artefacts. And they wrote stories in the papers of how we were picturesque but ignorant and always in need.

I had read the newspapers that the minister keeps in a pile.

I rose up now to my full height, such as it is, and walked back to the village, never once looking behind where those men were still laughing at their trick, no doubt. I marched down the slope towards the stone necklace of bothies laid out lonely along the grass at the foot of the hills.

CHAPTER 11

Chrissie
ST KILDA, 1927

'It's not the first time men have come to dig up the fairies' house,' said my grandmother. 'No good came of it then, and no good will come of it now.'

My grandmother had the second sight, but it took no magic to see that her prophecy would come true. Out over the jagged fortress of Dùn's rocks, grey giants fifty feet high were rising up, bent on vengeance, the wind blowing spray off their tall crests like the white hair of ancient gods.

I do not have the second sight that has blessed – or cursed – my mother and her mother. Perhaps it is fading from us as the years go by. Pure superstition, said Mrs Munro. It's a sin to believe in things like that, Chrissie. The minister, however, had other things to say. An Uist man, he reckoned many Gaels carry a remnant of second sight, that there are far more things in the world than we can comprehend. 'I've had more than one person tell me that they foresaw a death, Chrissie. A man I knew saw his uncle in Australia come to him even as he cut the hay on the croft. Came to say his last goodbye. And didn't that man get a letter some months later from Melbourne saying that his uncle had passed away on that very day he had seen him? It is because we on St Kilda spend so much time in the Lord's silence that there are those who can hear and see such things.'

Cooped up in the house because of the storm, my father fretted about the sheep we had just let out, wily little half-black-face, half-Soays, but even they could not survive a full blast of the gale if they wandered close to the edge of the cliffs. 'We'll maybe lose one today,' he grumbled, 'if they've gone over to the slopes of Cambir. And what do those two boys think they are doing?' He peered out of the side window towards the back of the village where Archie and his friend, dressed in baggy oilskins, were yelling and trying to hold on to the canvas panels. 'Who is it that thinks to try and build a wood and canvas hut here in the Atlantic winds?'

'Poor lads,' murmured Mother.

I squeezed myself next to Father to see. The gale was demolishing the shelter that the boys had rigged up over the entrance to the old underground house in the middle of the potato rigs at the back of Donald Òg's croft. There was Archie, struggling to gather the stiff canvas fabric in with his friend. His friend ran up the slope and launched himself on top of an escaping sheet of plywood, holding tight, but the wind flipped him over and spun the sheet away like a giant mis-made bird, the boy left sprawling on the grass, clutching at his arm. Village men had come running now from all sides to help secure the flailing structure. My father grabbed his hat and jacket to join them.

'Christina, no. . .' cried Mother, but I'd already gone out of the door, wrapping a shawl around my head as I ran, bare feet on the icy wet grass. It surely was a wind to blow the sheep straight off the cliffs.

We fought the squalls to catch the rest of their escaping house, roped the sheets down in a roll too heavy to be blown away and Archie and some of the men carried it down to the cleit.

'What a welcome,' a voice yelled. I turned to see Fred in a baggy oilskin jacket close to me, his cheeks stung red by the wind, eyes dark as a new calf. His brown hair stained darker with rain. He was holding his elbow with his hand, face strained. 'I don't think the island likes our intrusion,' he shouted above the wind, nodding at the vengeance of the waves.

'That's island weather. What else did you expect? Now you had better get yourself away to the nurse's house.'

The boy was led away by my father to the old factor's house where Nurse Barclay lived. 'Thanks,' he called back as they left. 'For your help, Chrissie.'

'My little Chrissie, I should have known you would rescue us. Always you leading the charge in all our escapades as children. I hardly recognized you, you're so grown. Quite the lady. I see I'll have to mind my manners.'

There was Archie beaming down his smile on me, water running down his face in spite of the yellow oilskin hood. Blue eyes like drops of summer.

Then he hurried off to where someone was calling him to the factor's house to see Fred.

I walked back home slowly, my hands hugging my elbows, all my soul dancing in the roughness of the wind. All along he'd recalled who I was. He had, I knew it, been teasing me not to say a greeting before.

And in spite of myself, I was smiling all through supper and through prayers because Archie Macleod still knew my name.

CHAPTER 12

Fred
ST KILDA, 1927

Fairies are clearly more spiteful than we realized. The moment Archie and I began work on the long souterrain roofed with slabs that they call the fairies' house – a structure possibly from the bronze or medieval age, date to be confirmed – then gales set in. Giants of dark waves up to sixty feet high, streaming with white spindrift, crashed against the cliffs or folded themselves into great molten barrels of water as they thundered towards the Village Bay. One truly felt what it was to be up against the wrath of the elements. And it was sobering to experience the island's isolation in bad weather. Imagine a hill farm of some four square miles dropped in the middle of an Atlantic swell that even the sturdiest boats would think twice to sail and you have the situation of St Kilda.

Old Finlay MacQueen and Finlay Gillies told us – after the event – that they could not understand our thinking in trying to put up a tented cover when we did. They said they could smell a gale coming from a change in the air. So not the work of fairies then. 'Why did you not tell us?' I asked Finlay Gillies, the shorter of the two with his folded-in, battered face. Finlay MacQueen, on the other hand, is one of the tallest men I have ever met with a bushy white beard and a very long stare.

'We didn't like to assume that you didn't already know,' he'd replied.

'Please,' I assured him, 'I promise not be offended by any advice you want to give me in the future.'

The winds were like nothing I'd experienced before, strong enough to whip a plank out of your hands and whack it into the man next to you. Soaked as we were by driving rain after we battled to save any equipment not sent spinning over the hill, we were never so glad as to accept the invitation of hot tea and scones from our neighbours.

Apart from their rather inconvenient modesty in failing to warn us about the weather, we couldn't have had a better welcome than the one we have had from the people of St Kilda. Oh, they were sorry for us, those old biddies. They fed us up like we were missing sons come home. Decent, that's the word that comes to mind when I think of the families that made up the village. No one went short while they had something to share. The warmth in those little houses you'd be hard-pressed to match anywhere. You couldn't miss the fact that they were poor, though. The swept-clean bareness of the cottages where there's nothing upholstered, furniture made from logs that have washed up on shore – no trees here. Adverts from magazines posted up as pictures. All the signs of a house where there's not much to spare.

But you'd be mistaken to think they were cut off in their outlook. Eager for news from the mainland, ready to mull over any topic, well read some of them, all know the Bible end to end, well-versed theologians. Although, I have to say, some of the things they asked could make them sound a bit unworldly – simple, even. I worried how easy it would be for someone to come in and trick the villagers.

I thought, the people here, this place, Fred, you've got a chance to be a better man here. A new start. Archie and I had been a bit wild at times as students, I had to admit. Perhaps I'd followed him too easily, for he had the shine of glamour about everything he did. We'd not always done things we might be proud of in Cambridge. It would be important to have something academically strong in our chosen fields in order for us to be welcomed back next term – especially in Archie's case, though as to the girl in question, Archie assured me that she'd exaggerated out of all proportion.

As for me, I have apparently blotted my copybook with the lesser – or greater – sin of always being ready to argue for the new way of thinking. But how can one not? I should, Archie says, keep such debates for the student common room since most of our professors have been teaching since long before the Great War ruptured every certainty. Their minds remain stuffed with the fragile china of Victorian ideas. They are still happy to recite the creed and the Lord's Prayer in chapel while their God has allowed millions upon millions to perish in a barbaric and futile war, my own brother and Archie's brother among those who died. Died before they saw twenty years. And who could believe in any God who sent the Spanish sickness that killed my own father at the end of the war? Who took my mother away while I was still small? And Christian forgiveness? If there were a God, I doubt that I would forgive him for all he so carelessly lets happen. No, we are alone on this earth, and we must do the best we can in this darkness.

And yet, there is still goodness, in the kindness of my uncle who took me home to live with him in his cottage on the Dunvegan estate where he looked after the laird's cars, kindness too in the help that Archie's family has given me, and a natural kindness in the people here. There was, I found, something about the island that cleansed the soul of bitterness.

I truly was full of all good intentions to make a better stab at things as I left our door and passed before the line of houses and lamp-lit windows on my way to Nurse Williamina Barclay's house to have my arm checked and, I hoped, the bandage removed. The evening wind was keen and cleansing, the sky was filled with swirls and marches of clouds in palest rose and ashy violet, behind them a light beaming from the sea as if it were dawn rather than sunset. A dog tied outside a cottage lay lop-eared, nose burrowed into paws ready for sleep, and I felt the pride of him not being bothered to bark as I walked by – not a stranger any more. I could hear the burn full with the spring rains, its gurgle and splutter under the flagstone bridge in its path towards the sea. There was the whirr and scuffle of the secretive wrens that nest between the boulders of the old houses that still stood between the smooth-rendered newer bothies, where more birds nest in the roofs of old byres with turfed roofs on top. A thick smell of cow dung on the evening air mixed with the tang of peat smoke, undertones of paraffin or petrol, took me right back to the garage and my uncle.

My father was a good man. After Mother died, he transferred to the Edinburgh branch of his bank, rose to become deputy manager, well respected and an elder at the church. But he was not an approachable father. At mealtimes, he orated and I listened. I thought of my father, eating his meals alone in that cold dining room in his frock coat and stiff collar. And I thought of him when I entered the poor homes along the village street here, homes crowded with the warmth of parents and children who were content with each other. No lone wolf cub setting out into the world could have known a more trenchant and atavistic longing for the warmth of belonging than I did those evenings as I listened to the old mothers and grannies and their unlikely tales of second sight and hauntings, one them always spinning wool by the glow of a peat fire that never went out.

I began to develop a passion for recording their stories, their customs, the whole life here on St Kilda, conscious of how I might be watching a unique culture slipping away before my eyes. No detail too small to go down in my diaries. I feared for what the future held for the young people. Chrissie, for instance, who watches me from the corner of her parents' kitchen when I go to take a cup of her mother's very strong tea, who is as bright and intelligent as any girl you might meet at Cambridge, and generally a lot more sensible.

How many times have I sat down to make notes on this place, and ended up writing about Chrissie? I would begin to write about the qualities of the rocks, the proportion of salt and calcium, of smooth olivine-gabbro and sparkling black feldspar, and it is Chrissie's qualities I saw, those dark sparkling eyes and her suntanned arms as she walked with a basket on her hip, the way her red scarf fell from her hair. It seemed to me that to understand this place you'd need to understand what makes a girl like Chrissie, just as much as you needed to understand the layers and fissures of the ancient rocks that band the hills and cliffs and the sweetness of the minerals that produce the flowers of spring and the tiny overlooked alpine gentians and the sweet common daisies.

I pictured Chrissie's eyes now, dark as blue gentians. But they did not look back at me. They were always turned towards Archie, though he chose not to see it.

CHAPTER 13

Fred
FRANCE, 1940

As the three of us fled from the farm, cycling as fast as we could along the tracks between open fields of stubble and ploughed earth, Angus began to drop behind. I stopped to let him catch up but his bike wobbled and he dismounted, leaning over the handlebars. I rode back to see what was the matter. He looked yellowish, sweat around his forehead and lips.

'Is it the stomach cramps again?' I asked. He'd been complaining of them on and off for a while but I'd assumed they'd worn off since he'd stopped mentioning them for the past few days.

'Bad,' was all Angus could manage. Then he vomited over the handlebars. He crumpled up and, letting the bicycle fall, curled up on the ground. By now, our guide had also wheeled back. He looked around frantically in case anyone should pass and come to investigate with awkward questions.

'He can't go a little further? We're just a few miles away.'

No reply from Angus. He was out cold.

We dragged him up the bank to the edge of a field where a thicket would give us some protection from the eyes of any passers-by.

'What do you think is the matter with him?' the guide asked.

'From his groans, I'd say we needed to get him a doctor as fast as possible.'

Clearly panicked by this change in plans, our companion pulled his cap lower and sped off to see what he could do, the bike jolting with his frantic pedalling. I sat by Angus as the day's cold intensified, put my jacket over him, wondering if the man would ever return. Couldn't blame him if he'd given up on us and done a runner. I tried to feed sips of water from my army flask between Angus's dry lips but the response was a worrying retching and more groans.

It must have been almost two hours later by the time I heard a voice on the track below us. I looked out through the bushes to see a sight from medieval times, a mule and cart driven by a small woman in a grey habit. Her head was covered with a grey veil, a band of white wimple showing. Close by, at the foot of the bank, she stopped, called out again, '*Vous êtes toujours là?*'

I stayed silent.

'*Je suis venue pour le malade. Montrez-vous s'il vous plaît.*'

She'd come for the sick man. So this was our ambulance. I slid down the bank and helped her up to where Angus lay. She knelt down heavily, her rosy face showing the signs of early old age, an authority to her manner that brooked no discussion. She felt his forehead and examined his stomach gently. A deep moan from Angus when her fingertips pressed to one side.

'It is appendicitis. I'm sure of it. We must not delay.'

We carried Angus as gently as we could down to the cart, laid him in the back and covered him with empty hessian sacks, the smell of string and dust and Angus's vomit mixing in the air. How he'd breathe under there I didn't know.

It was an agonizing journey as we made our way through the country lanes in the frigid air. The mule objected to the extra load and stopped every few hundred yards, refusing to move again until it suited him. Her range of French to encourage the beast was surprising for a woman in holy orders. I followed at a distance on my bicycle but soon abandoned it and took to pulling the mule by the reins, holding handfuls of grass out for him to walk towards in the way I'd seen Chrissie do to encourage the cows.

We'd another couple of miles to go, she said, almost there, when an open-topped car appeared on the road ahead, two German officers in caps with black bands and silver skulls. The same moment the mule chose to stop again. They drew up alongside us. One of the officers got out.

He asked if they could be of any assistance to the good sister. His French was very good. His charm impeccable, benign.

'Allow me,' the officer said with a courteous smile.

He took his pistol from his holster, raised it into the air and fired. The mule shot forward, the sister jerked back in her seat but managed to hold on to the reins. I ran beside her, eyes down, a lumbering farmhand – hoping that Angus's groans couldn't be heard. Behind us, the slamming of car doors, laughter, the engine roaring away.

The convent hospital was a two-storied building with tall windows that adjoined a grey church on the edge of the village square. As soon as we were through the archway and in the back courtyard, nuns in hospital armbands and white headdresses ran down the steps to uncover Angus from his sacking and roll him onto a stretcher. Our nun, giving orders as she ran, disappeared with the stretcher and a younger woman came down to take me inside.

'Can you find out what is happening to Angus?'

She came back a while later to say that he was in surgery. They hoped for the best but she had to warn me that Angus's condition had been left too long.

An hour later, perhaps less, and the nun who had collected us came along the corridor, removing her bloodstained apron.

'We will know in the morning. And the sisters will pray for him through the night. Now, tell me, do you know of an address where we may send news to his family?'

I wrote it down hastily on the notepad she held out.

'He is from Scotland. *Écossais*. And you, Monsieur. . .'

'Lawson. Fred Lawson. Also Scots.'

'You also must have family you wish to contact. We can send a letter.'

'There is no one,' I told her.

She examined my face for a moment, a look of pity?

'Know that we will also include you in our prayers tonight, Mr Lawson. You have a family here.'

I was given a bed in a side room that was not being used for patients. I lay sleepless, thinking of Angus, willing him to get better. At intervals through the night, I could hear the faint singing of women's voices, the sisters in the convent chapel keeping the offices of their order, or sometimes the quiet-soled shoes of sisters passing along the hospital corridors, answering the calls of the sick.

In the morning, Angus was awake, groggy and sore but cheerful. But with no memory of the cart ride or any German officers.

It was going to be another two or three weeks before Angus could be moved. His scar gave him a bone fide reason for being in a hospital, but I was a liability and needed to be hidden. By day, I became a mute labourer who worked for the sisters. I donned a hessian apron and set to digging in the convent gardens at the back of the hospital walls, alongside an elderly gardener with two brown teeth and a cracked smile. He was in fear of the sister who had rescued us, the Mother Superior, probably because of the brown bottle he kept in his pocket, and a habit of falling asleep in the barn when the sun warmed the afternoon.

In fact, I found the sister very good company. She loved a cigarette and a small glass of sweet wine in the evening, and she played to win, as I soon found out when she challenged me to a game of chess.

At the end of two weeks, she came rushing into my room with serious news. Someone had informed German authorities that she was hiding English soldiers. Angus, with his post-operative scar, was possible to explain if he kept quiet, but I would have to hide. And there was very little time. She shut me into her study. I crouched behind her desk, listening as she spoke to the German officer in the corridor.

'You have my word,' she assured him. 'There is nothing to this rumour. We have no English soldiers here.'

'As a woman of God, your word is enough,' he replied, and I heard the sound of boots retreating along the corridors.

A while later she came in, shaking.

'They are gone,' she said. 'With a little white lie. After all, we have no English soldiers. Only Scottish ones.'

Our original guide returned and I set off with him by bicycle once again, leaving Angus to follow in a day or two – hidden in the boot of the midwife's car since she had official permission to drive between villages and a modest petrol allowance. I hated to leave Angus, feeling as responsible for him as I would for a younger brother.

'But can't you tell me where you're going in case something goes wrong?' he asked, reverting to Gaelic in his distress.

'You know that's not how it's done.'

He bit his lips together, tried a joke. 'Just not sure how you'll manage without me, that's all.'

I embraced him, promised we'd meet up again in a few days' time and set off following the stranger on the bicycle ahead, a slanting sun rising, the fields blanketed with a white mist, no end or landmark in sight.

CHAPTER 14

Fred
ST KILDA, 1927

Late afternoon and I still had notes to write up on my survey of the rock formations west of the village. But with a clear view of the bay from the bothy window, my attention had wandered to the whaler that had just anchored. I could see people clustered at the jetty, welcoming the captain like an old friend. Captain Olufson always took the trouble to ask the villagers what he could bring from Harris and he had arrived with a dinghy of provisions. Later, I would understand the debt of gratitude that he owed to the village and get to know the odour of whale carcasses stored in the bay between hunting trips.

Back to my geological paper and the western slopes' high preponderance of olivine-gabbro with a small sill of dolerite, the east side being mostly granite. The outlying islands and sea stacs were also a mix of gabbro and dolerite, but scoured out by the full force of Atlantic waves into fantastical dark towers and castles.

Archie, too, had been making progress of late. Some interesting shards of beaker pottery, possibly of Neolithic origin, had been unearthed with the help of Lachie and Callum, the two boys he was paying to help with the dig, but he had left his notes on the table and headed down to the jetty to see what was afoot.

The twilight began to deepen. I lit the oil lamp to carry on with my notes. A knock came at the door. It was Chrissie with a message.

'My granny says you should come ceilidh with us, you who are interested in history and these things. They are at all Allie MacCrimmon's house and she would have you know you are welcome too.'

I blotted my page and closed my notes while Chrissie stood by the fire, casting a critical eye on the pot hung over it. Even I had to admit the smell of our attempts at cooking did not suggest an appetizing meal. She lifted the lid and jerked her head away from the contents – burned offerings yet again.

'Perhaps your mother might help us with some cooking from time to time,' I suggested as I pulled on my jacket, my notebook in the pocket.

'I will ask her for you,' said Chrissie with a shrug. She had moved over to the small desk Archie used to write up his notes on the dig at the fairies' house. Her hand brushed the curling loops of his writing.

'So who is Allie MacCrimmon?' I enquired as I tied my laces.

'The oldest person in the village, and she has never left the old place she was born in.'

We walked out past the graveyard. The soil had been built up inside its circular walls since the island's natural turf was too shallow for a burial. It was studded with memorial rocks that floated white in the fading light. Most, I had noted on a previous visit, with no names other than in the memory of the people. It was sad to see how many of the rocks were very small and almost lost among the abundant nettles.

A little way further still, standing quite alone, was Allie's dwelling, more like the old byres and ancient storage cleits than one of the newer cottages along the street. It was made of weather-worn boulders cut not by hand but by the wind and the sea. It was small and narrow with a roof made of thatch covered by a fishing net weighted round with stones.

Chrissie paused before the door. 'Now don't be surprised by how the whaler captain looks,' she said. 'His mother was an Eskimo wife to a Norwegian whaler. His father took his son home to educate him in Bergen but he still bears the tattoos of his Eskimo tribe on his face.'

She hesitated. I could see she was not wanting to offend me when she began, 'And I know you have the Gaelic, such as it is, but Allie is not always easy to hear and speaks a very old tongue so I will translate for you. You have but to ask.'

I was offended. I had learned my Gaelic from Lachlan after I went to live with him on the estate, where most conversations were in Gaelic, and it had been hard won.

It wasn't easy to see anything inside the smokiness of Allie's bothy. The fire was directly in the centre in the old way with an iron chain and a black kettle hung from the rafter. A hole in the thatch was the only chimney. Truly, Allie's bothy was a form of living archaeology. People would have lived thus in Viking times, before even. How many people, I wondered, had had the privilege of stepping back into antiquity like this? A smoked peaty smell was sharp in the nostrils, the surfaces of everything in Allie's house covered with a fine ashy encrustation and turned silvery grey, like ghosts of themselves. Grannies MacDonald, MacKinnon and Gillies were ranged along the bench on one side and Captain Olufson, a man in his sixties, was seated opposite on the largest chair, contributing his own small cloud of smoke to the dim atmosphere with his tar-stained pipe. I could see that Captain Olufson had been a striking man in his youth, still well built but now grey-haired, with long cheekbones and dark eyes that slanted in a long stare. In the smoky air I could make out three lines running from his lips to his jawline in a faded inky blue.

Several other villagers were squashed into the tiny space, on tubs or stools or seated on the floor around the peat embers that never went out. Archie was sat next to the captain, his face flushed by the fire under a tangled fair fringe, the very picture of a handsome man. Chrissie's eyes, as ever, were drawn to where he sat.

I've never been one to waste time on envy, but I did for that moment wish I were a taller man with the sort of magnetic power that Archie had to charm a whole room. A bottle or two of whisky from Archie's crate were open on the floor.

The noise inside was thick, with the three grannies cackling and a fast banter in Gaelic flying around the room like the harsh and inscrutable calls of the fulmars and the gannets.

I moved myself closer to Chrissie, who was laughing at something the captain had said, and when she had her breath again, I asked her to translate.

'It's nothing but silliness. The captain has been coming here for years and he and old Allie always have the same joke that she is finally going to say yes and be his sweetheart one day. So now Allie is saying that she would gladly take such a handsome man but she had heard that he already has a couple of wives back in Norway. And he says that for a girl like Allie MacCrimmon he is willing to forget all his wives and run away with her to live on a whaling ship.'

There was laughter around the room again. Then Allie began to tell a tale, the room quiet and listening as Chrissie whispered the English to me, her breath warm on my ear.

'It's the story of the girl who was away in the glen milking the cow and churning the butter. She met the fairy there, and he persuaded her to marry him and go away with him to his land. But the girl loved her mother and so she asked the fairy if she could go home for one more night to see her family one more time. So she went home and her sister could see she was troubled and she got the secret off her. As soon as the girl slept, her sister ran and told her mother who went out into the moonlight to find the henbane plant, which is a charm against fairies. So her mother wove a garter and she wove the henbane into it and left it with her daughter's clothes. And suspecting nothing, the daughter put the garter on and off she went to meet her handsome fairy. She went over to the hill, her arms outstretched as he came towards her, but he stopped. He could come no closer, for there was a magic circle around her that he could not enter, try as he might, and so he turned around and went away back to his people, and she never did see him again though she loved him until the day she died.'

Old Allie and Mary began to sing, in slow lilting incantations, the song of the fairy lover. The room fell even quieter and almost melancholic. Their elderly voices cracked from time to time and the words were hesitant, but you could see the loveliness behind it, adding a strange longing to a song that was already wistful for things lost.

In the quiet that followed, the captain tapped his pipe out over the hearth, and began his own story, speaking in slow Gaelic, which he had learned from his long years working from the whaling station in Harris. 'It's a story about an Eskimo princess,' Chrissie whispered. 'She met the prince of the fulmars with his dark eyes who promised she would live in a tent made of caribou furs and eat the finest food if she eloped with him. But as soon as she got to his home the prince shape-shifted into a bird and put her in a tent made of fish skins full of holes, with nothing to eat all day but fish. Try as she might, she could never escape this life she hated and even though she begged her father to rescue her, she couldn't return to the home she had loved.'

'You see I was well to be careful,' said Allie. 'You mark my words and be wise,' she said, pointing at Chrissie and the other young girls, 'no matter how tempting the offer, for you don't want to end up eating fish all day in the land of the great snow.'

'There is the truth,' said the captain. 'Never trust a shape-shifter, for they will always belong to the world they come from no matter what they tell you.'

'Oh my soul,' said Allie. 'Now he's telling me he's a shape-shifter. Don't they say that when a whaler captain dies, his spirit becomes a fulmar and he glides over the north seas for ever onwards?'

'The sea is the true home of a whaler captain,' the half-Eskimo man said with a shrug. 'So a better end for me I could not imagine.'

'You've had a narrow escape there, Allie,' said Archie, toasting her with his raised whisky bottle.

'Oh, but I was tempted,' Allie said, with a wagging of her chin and its white hairs, her blue eyes twinkling young as ever. 'We girls are ever so.'

The children wanted Allie to sing her birdsong then, a ditty in Gaelic mimicking their calls. And as she sang, the fire-lit room echoed with the melancholic brooding noise of the puffins calling their fledgling chicks to leave the cliffs for the cold of the water below, and with the harsher calls of the gannets and fulmars, so that it seemed as though the birds themselves were flying among us. I closed my eyes to ride and hover on the sound, and felt myself a part of the rhythm of the island for a moment, a life dictated not by my own will but by the rhythm of the year and the beating heart of the land.

Then I opened my eyes. The sooty grey surfaces of the room returned, and the crowded humanity with its warm stink from the day's work. I wondered if the sip of whisky passed round by the captain had been stronger than I thought.

And all the while, the heat from Chrissie's arm radiated into my side. Whether she was sitting back against the wall, or leaning forward to tease the children, I could not stop mapping her presence, aware of her nearness.

The room emptied and people began to leave in the long June twilight of eleven o'clock.

'Come out to the whaler,' Archie said, leaning on my shoulder. 'We're invited to go back to the boat, carry on the yarns and have a few more drinks.'

'I don't know, Archie. It'll mean half of tomorrow will be lost. I've a lot to get done if the paper's to be finished before we leave. And you too, you need to get on.'

'We've oodles of time. You don't need to worry so.' He tripped a little on the word 'worry' as he pulled round to face me, his breath hot and purified with the whisky. His cheeks were florid as apples, hair spiked with sweat. 'Have it your own way,' he finished cheerfully.

'And be careful going out in the rowing boat,' I called after him, his steps not entirely steady. Perhaps I should have gone with him, but the captain was by his side, striding on solid and watchful in his quiet way. I knew Archie would come to no harm other than to fail to progress his paper yet again.

I walked back home, catching up with Chrissie on the path over the burn where even in summer the water ran ice cold under the flagstones.

'You're not going with them?' she asked.

'Not tonight.'

Above us the pale moon in a dusky sky, a line of light still lingering along the horizon of the sea even though it was almost midnight.

I thought of the evening's tales of falling hopelessly in love with a being from another land, and had the mad desire to take Chrissie's hand in mine, though I was sure it would frighten her if I did. Hopeless too, because I didn't doubt from the hungry way her eyes had followed every movement from Archie in the dim room that her thoughts were still back in the smoky cottage with him.

'Well, I will leave you,' she said as we came to her door. 'No doubt I will see you both in the morning.'

'In the morning?'

'In church. It's the Sabbath tomorrow. You haven't yet been to the chapel of a Sunday.'

A small laugh escaped me. 'I'm no churchgoer, I'm afraid. Not for a long time. Too many impossible things to believe before breakfast and all that.'

'But what do you believe in then if not in the creator?'

'Logic. The material world. Reason. I tried with the church stuff, but I'm afraid university tore down my last superstitions.'

'I see. So you are telling me that if I were better educated I would understand the foolishness of my superstitious ways.'

'Of course not. I wasn't judging you. I understand, completely. It's simply what you've all been taught here.'

'So it's a communal foolishness? Well, you're not the first one coming here knowing better. We've had the tourists at the church door sniggering and laughing at our Gaelic singing before now, saying how it sounds so peculiar and caterwauling. Perhaps it does to them. But we understand what we sing when we raise our voices to God together. And since no one in the village is asking for your opinion, Mr Lawson, I will take my foolish weak mind away to bed ready for another day of my superstitious beliefs. Good night.'

I stared at her closed door as if it might open suddenly and I could reply. If there was a girl with less in common with me than Chrissie Gillies, then I would like to meet her. And there was something disturbing about that sort of mindset in a girl so young, as if she had decided to limit the entire world to one belief, one place, to make the world no bigger than this island. It seemed a pity. A mind from another time almost, before the war tore everything apart and left us with the task of reassembling a modern word we could live with.

You had to fear for someone on the brink of life who was so willing to live down a hole like that, refusing to see the future.

No sign of Archie in our bothy other than the lights glowing from the whaler out in the bay and a thread of accordion music intermittent on the breeze. I shook my head with a smile. Archie had the gift of making friends. Didn't everyone love Archie?

I went to bed in the small back room, determined not to think of Chrissie any more. But the impression of the warmth of her sitting close to me remained, disturbing my sleep.

At dawn, I rose from my bed to watch the black outlines of Dùn Island, a ruined castle or a giant's jawbone across the bay. As the light gathered, the land began to take depth and dimension, with hollows and outcrops in dark greens appearing in a dark land outlined against a blanched sea. All this I watched, as a realization came to me, something I already knew in my skin and in my bones: I was in love with Chrissie – a love that was as unfeasible and impossible as declaring my love for the cliffs or the sea and expecting them to return it. And it was true that the island was provoking a response that was far more than any ordering and categorizing of minerals and elements. Two loves – the place, the girl – had somehow become intermingled, in a fleeting mirage of something ungraspable. And yet, there it was, love, like a strange bell from the deep that must be answered. And at that moment I would have gladly given up all my ambitions and all my plans had the world offered me instead just this place, this girl.

This girl called Chrissie Gillies with her narrow outlook, a mind that had never left the island.

So it is, we fall in love with the impossible, break our hearts pining for a dream. I went early to my desk to finish writing up my finds.

CHAPTER 15

Chrissie
ST KILDA, 1927

Sabbath morning, and everything had been prepared the eve before, the buckets of water by the door, the porridge and the mutton stew ready to place on the fire. No sounds in the village except for God's sounds, the birds and the wind, the sheep calling to their lambs.

The house still slumbered but I was seated in front of the little mirror on the chest, my father's tailoring scissors in one hand, contemplating my wayward black curls with vexation. Was it any wonder Archie overlooked me, my old-fashioned hair bun no different from my mother's or Mrs MacKinnon's – she who was worn out with her eight children? With a feeling of dread and liberation I held out a hank and began to rasp the blades through it. I was thinking of the girls I'd seen in the journals the reverend's wife got sent to her. They had short sleek hair, long narrow dresses and pointed shoes, each girl elegant as a gannet as it dives into the sea.

What I got was hair springing up in its shortness around my head like a black lamb, the fringe a mistake, I could see, but at least it curled itself up to hide the choppiness of my cutting. I put on my new Sunday dress, a length of flowered cloth from Glasgow cut straight up and down in the new way. Chrissie's flower sack, my brother Callum called it.

It was no help when my brother began laughing over his bowl of porridge as I came in to the kitchen and sat down at the table.

My mother told him to shush but said, 'Oh, Chrissie, what have you done to your hair?'

The ship's bell down by the chapel called out but we were already halfway across the grass, Father holding the Bible, the whole village going with us, the men in their hand-tailored tweed suits that would not shame a laird on his estate, the women with their Sunday turkey-red scarves and polished hair tied down tight. It was a gift of a day, the sun bright on the fresh grass and on the pale, feathery green of the barley and the deep green of the potato rigs, a grey sea that the sun turned to silver and brightness.

We waited in the chill of the building – my new dress none too warm – the great ship of a pulpit before us. The people who sent it forgot to measure the chapel for size. Mother and I sat with the women on one side of the benches, Father and the boys with the men on the other so I did not have to turn my head much to see Archie a little way in front of us. The minister came in the side door, prayed and then the precentor who was yesterday dipping the sheep on the hill offered up the first line of the psalm in his sinewy voice anguished in its calling, a man drowning in the storms of the sea and calling out to God for help. The people all sang the line back, braiding and embellishing the tune with their many solemn voices as they saw fit, just as the singing of many waves makes the sound of the ocean. Line by line, pleading for the help of our Saviour to save us in one breathing out of song.

I, however, was not thinking of the psalm that morning, but of a pair of pale blue eyes and a long rosy face with fair hair brushed to one side that was still a little tangled from the pillow at the back. For the first time, I had no condemnation for Lot's wife, turned as she was to a pillar of salt for not being able to refrain from casting her eyes back to the city of sins. I tried. I stared hard at the minister as he preached, almost mouthing the words along with him, but all I could think is – he is near.

But then, I thought, only old widow MacDonald who cannot walk is missing from our congregation, and of course that boy who thinks so highly of himself that he can ignore the call of the Lord on the Lord's own day. And it was this anger for Mr Fred Lawson that saved me from my thoughts about Archie, for I found myself paying close attention to the service, imagining what Fred would think if he were here, which bits he would find ridiculous, which parts might stir his soul, and I almost forgot that Archie was so close as I listened to the singing and sermon as if through the ears of that most annoying boy.

Stepping out of the church with the women, I waited for Father. But there was Archie with him in his plus fours and toffee-gold corduroy jacket. He was shaking the men's hands as they went by as if they would wish to thank him for the sermon. I bowed my head as we came near to, resigned to the fact that Archie thought only of his English girls now, but he dipped his head to catch my eye. 'Chrissie, good morning. I hardly recognized you, you look so splendid with your new hairstyle. And such singing. I could pick your voice out anywhere, you know, lovely as ever. We really should kidnap you and take you back to Dunvegan to sing for us.'

I nodded and hurried away. Scolding myself for having nothing to reply – perhaps the only time in my life this had happened. But my heart was full and rising like a lark. He said he would like to take me away with him. Foolish that I am, I wondered then, does he remember the promise he once made – nothing but a child's promise – and everything to me?

CHAPTER 16

Fred
ST KILDA, 1927

From under my burrow of blankets I heard someone moving about on the other side of the partition, pleasant smells of porridge, eggs and tea floating through. By the time I was up and out of the wooden box that made up my sleeping quarters in the middle of the bothy, she was gone, leaving behind an unusually tidy table and dresser, the peat fire burning bright in the hearth. It was Chrissie's first morning helping with the cooking, her mother being too busy. I could see that I was going to have to set my alarm forward if I was going to find Chrissie at her morning work.

I called Archie through. He had the pitiful, greenish look of a man who'd stayed too many hours late into the night, sharing one of the bottles from his rapidly diminishing supply over at Lachie's house.

'It's great they are giving you such a hand with the digging but you know the boys here like Callum and Lachie they're not used to strong drink. Do you think it's a good idea to be so free with it?' I said, attempting some casual lightness in my voice.

'My God, does anyone get used to strong drink?' said Archie, hands on his head. 'Do see if there's an aspirin on the dresser somewhere, would you. And yes, point taken, I shall never drink again. Not a drop. My liver, it would seem, forbids it.'

He stirred his porridge rather than ate it. Drank two cups of coffee and smoked a cigarette while I finished up his share of the eggs. Before setting off with my canvas bag weighed down with tools and notebooks, I made sure Archie was out of the door and on his way to complete his work on the souterrain.

'You'll see,' he said. 'I'll have this done and dusted and then I'll be over in the glen working on my next project, the warrior queen's house. I'm sure it's another Neolithic site. After all, if the island belongs to someone else this time next year, I might not even get permission to come back and work on it, so it's now or never.'

Archie's news that his father might have to sell the island disturbed me as I walked along the bothies towards the schoolroom. The men had gone up into the hills with most of the dogs to collect some of the sheep, ruaging they called it, for most of the week, and the village felt quiet and bereft, one old lady outside number eleven sat at her spinning wheel. I'd followed the debate in the newspapers over the past couple of years on whether it was time to evacuate the island. You had to wonder how much longer they could manage with so few able-bodied men to do the hard and often dangerous work needed to keep themselves fed. I stood and looked around the village bothies, so much a part of the hills, homes of a generous-hearted people unspoiled by the grasping city, and my heart felt a contraction of pain to think that this unique little settlement might one day be relegated to a footnote in history.

The minister had not been any more reassuring when I'd spoken with him over the past few days. He'd shown me a pile of letters that he'd received from various government ministries in reply to his requests for a regular mail boat. 'A regular boat isn't worth it, they say, for the few people here. In the government's opinion, the costs of supplying a school and a nurse for a mere forty people are already too high. I'm afraid I don't see how the village can hold on through another bad winter unless something substantial changes in the mainland government's attitude towards the mail boats.'

'But if the seas are impossible in winter, what can they do?'

'They could get the lighthouse ship to call in on her way to the Flannan Isles. Nothing impossible about it.'

The school was tucked alongside the flank of the church. I found myself in a room directly from the Victorian age, high wooden desks in a row, cast-iron inkwells and a ledger high desk for the teacher. Mrs Munro was marking names in a register, its pages wavy with sea damp. In the corner hearth a peat fire cast its unique scent of ancient oils from bogwood and long preserved roots – necessary even in summer in an attempt to keep the damp at bay. A wistful feeling lingered in the room that it had once been far more crowded. I'd seen a photograph of the crowded rows of Victorian children. Now just eight children sat at their desks, hair neatly combed, clean pinafores, faces expectant.

I was heartened to see Chrissie there, evidently one of her days when she came in to help the minister's wife, but she gave me the briefest nod in greeting, no smile.

Still cross with me for being such an atheist, then.

Mrs Munro closed her register. 'Thank you so much for coming, Mr Lawson. The children are very fortunate to have you here this morning and we are so interested to hear what you might have to tell us.'

The slanted desks were no good for laying out the rocks, so we agreed to hold the class out on the grass, the minister's son running to fetch a blanket on which to display the specimens.

'I'm more than glad we are out here,' I told the children sitting along the edges of the blanket, 'because the lesson is all around us. Does anyone here know what a volcano is?'

Mrs Munro was pleased to see that the children could explain a volcano.

'Excellent. And did you know that you are sitting inside the crater of a volcano right now?'

Children always love a safely scary story.

'The bay where the boats are calmly sitting on the water, the beach, this grass where you are sitting, were all once a deep hole, with red-hot molten lava shooting up from deep inside the earth, and huge billowing clouds of dusty gas above us.'

'Will it go off again, Mr Lawson?' asked Mary MacDonald, looking at the water doubtfully.

'No, don't worry, Mary. That was six million years ago, and the land is cold and completely sealed off now. The molten lava is all safely hidden away deep, deep inside the earth's crust. But it was a very good thing that the volcano went off all that time ago, because those great fountains of molten rock piled up as they cooled, and eventually they made the hills we see now. The islands are the result of a series of volcanoes in fact.'

I let the children look around at the ring of hills and take in what they had just heard. The adults seemed no less impressed. I had a feeling they did not have many encounters with pure science in their lives.

Tormod raised his hand. 'So that's how God did it. First the earth was covered in water and then he made dry land, and it was with the volcanoes he did it. Just like in Genesis. I always did wonder how he did it so fast.'

'Well done, Tormod,' said Mrs Munro.

'Well, actually. . .' I began.

I glanced over at Chrissie who was staring down hard as if she knew what I would say next. I decided to avoid the more philosophical side of geology for the morning.

'The thing that has me very interested about the island, and may interest all of you, is that the volcano, or volcanoes perhaps, must have gone off several times because I am finding quite different areas of cooled magma across Hirta and her islets.'

I stood and pointed to the shale slipping from the side of Conachair. 'You see, over there to the right, the rocks are cream-coloured granite, the hard stones we use to make the bothies and the storage cleits. But if you look on the left side of the village, the patch of shale coming down the side of Mullach Mòr has a bluish tinge, especially in the rain. That's dolerite. Then, over towards the Cambir and the isle of Soay the rock is a dense and greenish olivine-gabbro. It's a sort of rock that's so hard people used to make hand axes from it. In fact, Mr Archie Macleod found just such an ancient axe inside what you call the fairies' house, made by the people who lived there over a thousand years ago. But what I want you to do now is to look at these rocks on the blanket. Pick them up and feel how heavy they are.'

The children handled the specimens, discussing their various colours and textures. 'They are different, you see, because each of the eruptions produced a different mix of chemicals. Some have just salt and calcium, others, these yellower ones, have more potassium in them. And can you feel that some rocks are smoother than others? That's because the faster they cooled, the smoother the rock. These very grainy ones now, they would have cooled down slowly, do you see? And the result is the different kinds of rock that make the island archipelago we sit on.'

'For great are the works of the Lord,' said the minister's wife

'Or a question of chemistry and physics,' I said, a mite apologetically.

Mrs Munro gave me a hard look, dolerite at least, and I did not pursue my corrections. I glanced over to where Chrissie sat on the edge of the blanket in her blue dress, her tanned feet and ankles bare. She still hadn't spoken. I could tell from the heightened colour in her cheeks that she was still angry with me.

'And you are very sure the volcano will not be exploding again?' asked Mary, pressing on the grass as if to test its reliability.

'Absolutely. I promise. You are safe as houses here on this island.'

I spent some time letting the children examine the rock collection and answering their very intelligent questions. They agreed to help me by bringing back any interesting specimens they found on the island, being careful to note where they had found them.

I soon realized how thorough children are.

'More gifts from your little ants,' Archie would say as another child appeared at our bothy door holding an offering. Some of the specimens they came with were quite beautiful, polished smooth by the sea to show the quality of the rock, green olivine-gabbro veined with cream, pink granite flecked with quartz, sparks of blue feldspar layered inside rough gabbro, even a rare lump of black volcanic glass. We filled the surfaces in the bothy and then began to place a line of them along the low wall in front of the door.

I wonder, if I were to go back there now, would those stones still be there along the sea wall, keeping vigil in front of the empty cottages?

CHAPTER 17

Chrissie

ST KILDA, 1927

It was my own curiosity that ruined my peace of mind. It was wrong of me to steal a look that first morning I went to help at Archie's cottage, and there was no undoing what I saw.

Archie slept in the larger room at the far end of the cottage with a desk under the window and a hearth on the far wall to keep the room warm. His finds from the fairies' house, however, were laid along the kitchen windowsill. A piece of brown pottery with patterns pressed into it as if with a stick. Animal and bird bones, chalk-white shells of limpets, which we call famine food, for we eat limpets here only if we must. A smooth round stone that was once an axe, hard and greenish, used perhaps for smashing shells held fast to the rocks. All things the fairies had put there, or rather, the ancient men and women who once lived beneath the turf, safe from the gales and spray of the winter storms. I ran my hands over the objects and wondered if those people had looked like we St Kildans do now, what they thought about and prayed for.

The porridge was ready, the table set, a pan of mutton and potatoes ready for the boys to put over the fire for their supper later. What else to do? Fred had the smaller bedroom in the middle of the bothy, so his desk was in the kitchen, his stones ranged along the back like the pieces of a game whose rules I did not know. I picked up a rock filled with glassy black layers shimmering like a dark sea, weighed another in my hand, green as moss but hard as iron.

Then my eyes went to the notebook lying open. No harm in looking, just dull notes about rocks. Some notes on the ceilidh at Allie's house. I smiled, for hadn't he written down the song of the fairy lovers from what he recalled of my English telling, though he hadn't it all correctly – I could see that much. Curious, I glanced through more, turning the pages back, notes on rocks interspersed with passages about the island and our village ways. Pleased to see that he thought well of our old traditions and our kind community, I read on. Surely I had the right since it was us he was describing, and then I stopped, my cheeks on fire. For I was reading about me, words on how I was lovely to look at, on my dark hair. How he thought of me often. How much I loved my own opinions. I stepped back like I'd been burned.

I was so embarrassed I could have melted on the spot. I touched the back of my hand to my hot cheeks. Why ever was he going on so much about me? And then I saw in a moment what I had never imagined or suspected: Mr Lawson thought he loved me.

But what a nonsense. And how sorry I was for him, for how could he be so mistook as to think like that of me – who cared for him not at all?

I turned the pages back, smoothed them down. I hurried to give the porridge a last stir, making sure the fire was hot enough to keep it warm but not burn it, checked the room was tidy, and then took myself away as quietly as I could.

Much good it was going to do me, since in a village like ours there was no hiding. I'd be back there the next day and the next to set their breakfast. And wasn't he coming down to the school today to talk to the children? Oh, but I could never let him know I had read his secret pages – I would die with the shame of it. Poor man. To imagine himself in love so. How could he be so mistook? And he was very mistaken – for wouldn't I love him back if his love were a true thing?

So many other thoughts crept in, as if I had never before noticed this Mr Fred Lawson on our island. Such as his eyes were merry with a quiet mischief beneath a thick brown fringe that had grown too long. How he could be as bashful as a boy at times. How he was a good friend to Archie. Though he was ever galling with his superior thoughts, I reminded myself.

When he came down to the schoolroom that day, I was cool but kindly distant. Never so glad for the breeze on my face outside, and never so glad when it was over and he went away with his satchel of rocks.

'He has a thoughtful way with children,' Mrs Munro said after school was dismissed. 'I do think that Mr Lawson would make a very good teacher if that were the path he wished to take, don't you agree? As would you, Chrissie. Remember, if you ever wanted to come away with us to finish your studies when we go, I could make sure you had employment after in a good school.'

I thanked her but both she and I knew that would never happen, for all my future was here on the island. The very thought of ever leaving the island was like the news of a death to me, a blow of loss in my heart.

I decided that I should show myself in my worst light when I was with Mr Lawson, so that he might be quicker rid of his illusions. But I did not get much opportunity, for the next day the tourist boat came. My great-uncle, old Finlay MacQueen, might have been more than eighty, but he was still the tallest man on the island, and the proudest, with his white beard spread over his chest in the way that all our grandfathers wore theirs. But since Finlay and his generation never had the English lessons that we were all made to have as children, it was difficult for him to talk with the tourists and so he often got overlooked and failed to sell his tweed.

I found myself sitting by Fred on the wall, watching as the tourists gaped and twittered around Mrs MacKinnon's front door as she demonstrated her skill with her spinning wheel. I was making sure to make a display of scratching my side, slumping in an ungainly way. But Fred was looking over at old Finlay who had spent all day carrying his roll of grey tweed to and fro among the tourists.

'Don't you think it sad,' said Fred, 'that Finlay was the pride of the island in his youth, famous as the greatest of the cragsmen, and look at him, so rudely overlooked by these silly tourists?'

'I see you have been listening to Finlay. But, aye, it is true. Finlay, even now, is never afeared on the cliffs, never dizzy. They say he was the last man to balance by his toes on the edge of the lover's stone that juts out above Soay, heels in the air with nothing but a thousand feet of wind beneath. But these fools see nothing of all that. He will be sore disappointed to have no pennies to buy his tobacco. Though Finlay always finds someone who will give him a little as a present of it, that's how canny he is.'

Finlay also had been carrying a gannet that he had skinned and stuffed, a tall startled-looking creature, its long neck stretched up and its beak to the sky, which would have been handsome were it not for the crick in the bird's neck. We watched two city ladies giggle and shake their heads when Finlay offered it for sale.

Coming into the cottage the next day to start the porridge, I saw the very same bird leaning lopsided at the back of Fred's desk. For the rest of the week Finlay went about like a sea captain on the bridge of his boat, smoking away at his clay pipe, or happy as he sat on the log outside his cottage, watching the evening sun take its leave in the west.

'That's a fine-looking bird,' I said to Fred as I left that morning.

'I was always very fond of taxidermy,' he told me. And there was a smile in his eyes, an understanding between us of what he had done.

'And there's a message,' I said. 'Lachie says they are rowing out to Boreray to catch the gannets if you want to go with them.'

CHAPTER 18

Fred
ST KILDA, 1927

I had begun to give up any hope of getting over to the island of Boreray, that tantalizing deep-blue shadow four miles out from the main island of Hirta, so was more than delighted when Lachie told me they were taking the boat there. With the number of able men so depleted, it was no longer a trip they made often.

'But you can swim, can't you, Mr Lawson?' Chrissie had added after she'd told me about the trip. Worry in her eyes. I remembered then that Chrissie had lost two uncles in a boat accident off Boreray as a child. Plus a cousin who had died of appendicitis, stranded there in a storm before they could get him off. 'And you know how sharp gannet beaks are?' I listened to her as she described the birds, as erudite in her island knowledge as any book-learned naturalist.

Seen from far away, the gannet is a sleek creature of feathers and air, gliding on the winds or streaking like an arrow into the water. They float above the volcanic towers of Boreray in battalions, narrow wings held wide to ride the air, black silhouettes or dazzling white depending on the angle of the sun. But for all their elegance, the gannet is a dangerous bird, always at war with its neighbour for its few inches of rock. Gannets can only be taken from the rock at night, and even then you must first kill the sentry bird so he does not wake the colony, their sword-like beaks sharp as any gutting knife.

There were eight of us in the boat, old Finlay, Chrissie's brother Callum and the boy Lachie who also helps Archie from time to time. Archie, myself, Neil Ferguson, Tormod Òg and the eldest of the MacKinnon boys. We rowed out just after dusk, the night above us a great tent of luminous blue where the stars were beginning to make themselves known. The sea shelves away thousands of feet as soon as you are away from the island cliffs and you could feel the power of the rise and fall of the Atlantic swell, lifting the small boat up and down with its deep, steady breathing. How tiny a speck we were amid such grandeur and strength. Never once was the sea at rest lest we should begin again to consider ourselves the captains of the world as we might have done on land. The navy skies darkened, slowly revealing their depths in a knowledge hidden to the eye by day, a host of lights in the darkness, singing in silence above us. The stacs and Boreray, dark and ancient fantastical shapes against the stars, looming and dipping with the horizon, approaching us and swinging away with the progress of the boat. Some four miles away from Hirta, the men began to set the lines, leaving buoys to mark their place.

The plan was to land on the rocky outcrops at the foot of Boreray for a few hours to catch some of the little sheep out there, gather eggs or young birds, and I was hoping to collect various samples of rock, but the men began conferring in Gaelic, their tone serious. My ears picked up a frisson of alarm that entered my soul, a fear that was atavistic and numinous, for here we were all but alone, at the mercy of the deep and the mounting swell. The force of the boat's pitching had become uncomfortable and alarming. Tormod Òg explained in his slow, lilting English that since they had decided there was no hope of landing that night with the swell so high, we were best to try and shelter in a cave among the abrupt precipices at the back of the rock.

Cave does not describe the vast cathedral of black rock we entered, an unseen hand pushing us up and down the height of the walls. We shipped the boat into the middle, far enough from the rock sides to lie at anchor in relative safety, and sat listening to the echo of the water slopping against the cave wall. The entrance held a view unparalleled, the great night of stars and the universe's deepness framed by the dark sides of the cavern.

We had some of the oatcakes left from an earlier meal, a little of the home-made cheese, the men expecting by now to be on the field that tops the rock, lighting a fire to make a meal of roast mutton for the party. After eating, they removed their woollen caps and one of them produced a small, black book and began to read from it in sonorous Gaelic. Tormod murmured to me the number of the psalm, and although I cannot in retrospect recall which one it was, I would recall its purport as clearly as though I had heard it in English.

The lector began to sing, one pleading voice, a powerful nasal tenor rendered small and lonely by the sea cave, crying out in a strange, gnarled language; the men answering him as one, line by line, the call and answer of ancient text, till the cave filled and amplified and echoed back the voice of their combined wailing, deep and strange, not beautiful, but a thing of dignity and wisdom and tears, until the hairs on my arms and the back of my neck stood up. Something beyond mankind came near to us. It was not an hour that I will ever forget as the sea bore us up and down and we seemed to launch out among the deep of the stars.

Archie was more familiar with the island's ways of doing things and had made a pillow from his coat, quickly unconscious in sleep. I too slept with my head on my coat, my boots in the wet of sea slop at the bottom of the boat, my soul still reverberating with this half glimpse of something near and far off.

At first light we left. I was able to examine with my eyes the cave walls and the layers of black gabbro of the back of Boreray, the fantastical chimneys, precipices and petrified castles rising up out of the sea, the gannets pouring off the cliffs in white, feathery waves. As the boat pulled away, the outlying stacs swung round before us like Neolithic tools spearing the deep, black and cribbed with the runes of lines of nesting birds.

All the men's efforts were now to bring in the ling caught overnight. I helped haul in the garlands of viscous brown and silver creatures, the muscular fruit of salt water. The boat lay low as we rowed for Hirta once more, the men quiet as the waves lapped at the boat's rim.

We reached the bay at noon, the women on the jetty greeting us as though they had feared for their men's lives – which they had indeed.

I returned with not a single solid specimen, and without ever setting foot on that place, but I had brought something else back. The lifting of the boat on the water, the impression of that vast cave of night resonating with the men's song, I held in my mind, brooding over that experience many times as I lay near to sleep.

And it was that singing in the stars that stayed with me, years later, in the long afternoons of hiding and fleeing in northern France, trying to keep at bay the cold fear and depression, or as I lay burning with typhoid in the Spanish prison camp in Ebro through the frozen nights of winter, calling me back from feverish dreams to rise and try and find you once again.

CHAPTER 19

Fred

The garage down a side street of Lille didn't look like the most likely place for us to stop. A man was stripping down the engine of the type of black Mercedes favoured by the German officers.

He straightened up as we approached, looking up and down the street for anyone watching. Tall and elderly, shoulders stooped, grey hair and an anxious, furrowed brow, he wiped his hands on a rag. The pungent smell of engine oil and petrol took me back to that boy in Uncle Lachlan's garage.

'*Le soldat Anglais?*' he muttered to the guide.

'*Écossais,*' I said.

We wheeled our bikes through to the back of the garage into a courtyard stacked with tyres and rusting car parts, and parked them against the wall. Up a set of rickety wooden stairs on the side of a workshop and we came to an apartment, a long row of low windows overlooking a canal. A second elderly man, equally tall and lugubrious in blue overalls, was making coffee on a small wood-burning stove, the same deliberate way of doing things, the same watchful, unhappy expression, alert for bad news. They were the brothers Anton and Gilbert Lesage. We shook hands, cold and leathery. Gilbert poured hot coffee and cut slices from a dark loaf.

Our guide, a printer from the city, explained that we would wait there until a *passeur* took us on to Paris.

Leaving Gilbert some muttered instructions, Anton returned to the garage, a sad glance back at us before he left.

After we had eaten, Gilbert showed me a ladder up to a room at the back of the apartment. It had the dusty, faded smell of a place long unused. Two single beds. So they were expecting Angus to arrive. On the wall was a photo from the last war of two young men in uniform. Gilbert tapped the glass.

'*Les fils d'Anton*,' he said, shaking his head. I realized that his brother's boys must have been killed by the Germans in the last war. The bullet marks you saw on the buildings, the damage and the memories, it was all still there from the last war.

It was another week before Angus finally turned up. I'd never been happier to see his freckled face, gaunt and tinged with violet under the eyes after the hospital stay.

I could see what it cost the brothers to have us there, Anton especially, whose wife had not wanted to outlive their children. They couldn't do enough for us, quietly, no fuss or thanks wanted, because that's what people did, the right thing. They fed us, they found clothes for us, shared their meals of fried potatoes and eggs, sometimes a chicken, the sofa worn and their habits frugal. Some of the clothes they gave us, the mothball-embalmed long underpants and button vests, I suspected had once belonged to the boys who'd slept in our room, and were handed to us at great cost.

After a week, Madame Curtil arrived, a middle-aged woman with grey-blond hair, a rusty voice, and an avid pipe smoker. She was the contact who would make arrangements for us to be moved on. We talked around the table over glasses of astringent red wine. Her late husband had been an English teacher and she spoke it fluently. I had the feeling we were being interviewed for our reliability as we chatted – these people were risking their lives for us.

We had to wait for our next contact before we could go south, she said. It was arranged but there were some problems and we would have to be patient. But first we had to do something about our terrible clothes, and provide a photo. A couple of days later, two suits arrived. Angus turned in front of the shaving mirror to catch sight of his transformation. 'If my girl could see me now, looking like a Frenchman.'

'A Frenchman with freckles and red hair.'

Our first outing for two weeks. We were taken to the tall church with a copper-roofed spire a few streets away to meet l'Abbé, a priest in wire-rimmed spectacles and a woollen cardigan. He took our photos to produce beautifully forged *ausweis* passes. The walls around his study were lined with meticulous watercolours, the usual outlet for his artistic skills.

More long days with nothing to do but wait. The brothers, increasingly quiet, seemed to age before our eyes. We began to wonder how long we could impose upon them. I was longing to be on the move again, longing for impossible things like the chance to walk into Lachlan's sitting room one more time.

Angus spent his time whittling away at a piece of wood with his penknife, a bird that fitted inside the palm of your hand. For his girl. In the evening, we listened to Radio Londres, and watched rare smiles dawn over Gilbert and Anton's faces as news began to come through about the first successes of the British pilots, the first hope that the war might turn one day.

The two of us were sitting at the table one afternoon, a fly buzzing, Angus cleaning some spark plugs set out on newspaper. We had been chatting now and then in Gaelic when we realized a child had appeared in the room, a boy of eight, blond hair. His light steps had made no sound on the wooden stairs. He had a thin little face, quizzical. He looked at us for a moment, then turned and went back down to his mother. Spying sideways through the window in the door, I saw the woman. She had blond hair and a red dress, a tiny trilby hat. She was talking loudly in French with a heavy German accent. A cold sickly sweat sprung over my back. We waited for the boy to call out to his mother, for the ensuing ruckus, but as he tried to talk to her she brushed the child off impatiently. He gave up, kicking at an oil drum with boredom.

She was the wife of a Nazi officer. She'd dented his car and wanted it repaired without an official fuss.

We were going to have to move.

There were tears in Anton's eyes as he embraced me. Pain on his face as he grasped Angus – the same age as his youngest son – to his chest one last time. Now all our hopes of making it home were in the hands of our *passeur*, a tall, thin seventeen-year-old called Richard Leneuve.

CHAPTER 20

Fred

ST KILDA, 1927

I woke to the sight of two dead whales floating in the bay, tethered together at the nose. A steam whaler must have come in overnight. No sign of Archie in the bothy. I wondered if he had fallen asleep over at Lachie's, or perhaps he'd risen early to begin work somewhere over in the glen.

Buttoning my shirt and pulling up my braces, I went down to the shore to get a closer look at the beasts. I'd seen whales breach the water and slap back down in a magnificent plume of spray off Sunderland as a boy, but these whales were sad reminders of any such glory, two empty carcasses, pushed and bobbed by the waves with no reply.

Over on the rocks Callum was already casting lines for ling. I walked over and climbed up beside him. He wasn't a bit surprised by the dead beasts.

'Come the whaling season we get them here a lot. The captain leaves a couple here and then goes off to get another so he has a decent haul to take back to Bunavoneader.'

'But the warm weather,' I said, indicating the sun already bright and unchallenged. 'They'll start to smell soon, surely.'

'The whalers pay Lord Macleod for the rent of the bay. It's not always we can pay our rent, so we can't begrudge him the chance to make something from the Norwegians. Aye, the beasts'll not get moved until the whaler has at least three to tow back.'

'I hope to goodness the captain's back before the whale's guts split.'

'And did you know Archie Macleod was sleeping on the beach here? Came off the whaler this morning, a bit the worse for wear. Seems he was rowed out and had a good time celebrating the catch with the crew. The minister found him sleeping at the jetty and took him home to the manse to sleep it off.'

Archie was sitting at Mrs Munro's breakfast table. He wore my white roll-neck jersey, and was unshaven, his fair hair tousled. He looked like he'd slept in his clothes, as indeed he had, blue eyes smiling and as handsome as ever. She was ladling out oatmeal and judgement, not happy at all to have a drunk sleep off his sins in her sitting room. I was glad to see a bowl of porridge and a mug of strong tea set down before me too. And Archie was off on a new passion.

'Did you see the creatures in the bay? I'm going out with the whalers one day soon. You haven't lived, Fred, until you been on a ship riding the waves and chasing those beasts. I tell you, we got through the whisky I took out with me. But there's plenty left in this one in my jacket. Mrs Munro, this one should be for you, for your kindness.'

She took it from Archie, held it at arm's length. 'Thank you, Mr Macleod. I will put it in my medicine cabinet.'

'The question I have for you,' I said, moving my chair away, 'is when did you last wash?'

'That is the sort of question you would ask, my boy. Not the first concern for the men on a whaler.'

'Well, it's the first concern for those who have to share the air with you. I'll take him up to the cottage, Mrs Munro, and get some hot water on.'

'And I think I shall have quite a beard,' said Archie, his hand on the growth he'd been cultivating around his chin. It was fair and curly, almost pretty, giving weight to a chin that was slight compared to his wide forehead. 'I'm planning on becoming quite the pirate,' he said with a grin, and picking up a fork, created mayhem by challenging the two Munro boys to a duel.

Lachie and Callum met us on the way back to the bothy, grinning to hear Archie's story. Archie was never short of those who are mesmerized by him, over whom he casts the net of his friendship like a royal blessing.

The boys came back with us and stayed much of the day, helping Archie toast the whalers and much else. All the work I'd done and was looking forward to showing Archie would have to wait. The boys only left when Chrissie came to fetch her brother, the expression on her face as she pulled him out of his chair accusing and angry.

'You'd better not let Father see you like this,' she scolded as they left. Callum, who was full of smiles, put his finger to his lips, shushing her good-naturedly.

When Lachie had left, I let Archie know what I thought of him, suddenly angry.

'And the water's still hot,' I said. 'If you're still thinking of washing today.'

'Dear Fred,' he said with a smile. 'Always that middle-class anxiety for order and cleanliness.'

I turned away from him so he couldn't see how that had wounded.

'The people deserve better than to see you like this. They're not used to strong drink and it's wrong of you to set this example. With all you have. . .' I stopped myself.

'Thing is, Fred. People always assume I have everything, but it's an illusion. I have nothing for me, you see. The fact is I'll do what I have to do, and there's nothing to be done about it. I've agreed to go into law after Cambridge.'

'A lawyer? But your studies. Both of us carrying on at Cambridge, a dig in North Africa, together. A professorship one day.'

'I thought you understood. Having a large estate isn't always the blessing one assumes. The place consumes more than it makes. Has done so for a long time. So, there it is, Father may be the laird, but in reality he's working in a law firm in London most of the time. And from his last letter doesn't look like he's come up with a way to keep the island, but don't mention that here, of course. So there it is. We'll have to sell and I'll have to make my own way in the world like any other chap these days.'

'I'm so sorry. To lose the island, how could you bear it?'

He sighed, a what-can-you-do-about-it shrug. Got up and grinned. 'Now, bathing. There's an idea.' He left the house, pulling off his jersey and shoes and trousers, me running behind to gather them up from the grass and then the sand. Down to his underpants, he plunged into the sea.

Behind us, the villagers had come out to see the sight of poor Archie Macleod going mad. No one among them had ever chosen to plunge into the sea half-naked. He dived like a cormorant under the skin of the green sea, and moments later came up from the waves. 'Bloody freezing,' he yelled.

And there was Chrissie, laughing with the girls, their faces shocked and mischievous and admiring. And I thought, damn it, why not? So I stripped down to my long johns and ran in the sea to join him.

For that is the effect Archie has on people. You don't know what he'll do next, or why you will join him.

And shaking his hair like a dog, he towelled himself down with his shirt while the black-and-white or yellow mongrels ran in and out of the sea, spraying him with water again from their shaggy long coats.

CHAPTER 21

Fred
ST KILDA, 1927

The progress I'd made on my paper spurred Archie on to finish his own report. I'd been up early each day, gathering rocks, cataloguing them, telling the story of the island since its birth as a volcanic eruption from the sea. I'd row out early to trace the darker basalt columns along Dùn, the layers and folds of rocks almost as old as the world itself. In reply, Archie spent long hours digging down into the floor of the fairies' house, laying out the finds he made on a table in the byre, a piece of pottery, deer antlers on an island with no deer, masses of limpets from a human midden and another smooth-ended granite hand axe that confirmed that people had surely lived on the island since Neolithic times. That project completed, he began a survey of an ancient dwelling over in the Great Glen, a beehive structure known as the warrior queen's house, which he reckoned Norse or earlier from the construction and attached legends. Day after day, he went over there, digging and sifting through the soil, layer by layer, with young Callum and Lachie to help, though I suspected that from the amount the whisky was going down in the bottles that there was a fair bit of relaxing with a dram at the end of each day.

'Could you not excavate some other structure?' Chrissie scolded him when she met me and Archie and her brother Callum coming home on the path. 'Where are we to store the milk for cheese over there, now you boys are making such a mess?' But from the way she looked so cheerful and the brightness of her eyes you could plainly see how she rather liked teasing Archie.

Once or twice, I'd watched Chrissie and some of the girls catching puffins with long snares among the burrows of Dùn Island, but the puffin harvest was a mere entrée in the St Kildans' diet.

For the next two weeks, the island took on an atmosphere of expectation and focus as each man, woman and child got ready for the fulmar harvest – the birdmen's equivalent of a reaping of the fields and a harvest festival. If there were not enough birds put by, then the people risked going hungry in the winter, cut off from the mainland by stormy weather that might go on for months on end.

Chrissie and the women fetched the cattle down from the summer shielings in the Great Glen since there would be no time to walk over there and milk them each day. They spent long hours into the simmer dim of evening light grinding enough corn to last them through the next two weeks. Neil and the rest of the boys fetched out barrels and the sacks of salt laid up ready in the cleits and stacked them by the rocks.

All week the old ones clucked over the ropes and went with the men to examine the cliffs and decide who would be given which stretch of rocks to harvest according to their strength. I was touched to see the gleam in Finlay's eye as he parsed the guano-wreathed ledges among the grass and skeletons of sea pinks, pointing out any changes, the best ways down, longing to still go down himself.

Early in the morning as I came out to empty my pot in the piss bucket I saw the men already gathered. But today there was no leisurely filling of stained clay pipes as they debated between themselves how to share out the activities of the day. The men were speaking quickly, decided in their manners. Even the dogs were caught up in the atmosphere of seriousness and occasion. Every door was open, the smells of a good breakfast of porridge and tea and boiled sea birds drifting from cottage to cottage. The children running up and down in excitement, stirring the mongrel collies and retrievers into more of a frenzy.

Chrissie told us she'd not be in to help for a while. 'August the twelfth tomorrow, the day the men will set off for the rocks to collect the fulmar chicks and we will all be busy.'

I woke to see a line of small figures on the hillside, following the path towards The Gap and the cliffs beyond. Others were heading west towards the Cambir, some towards the far slopes of Conachair. Behind them were groups of women with heads shawled against the brisk summer wind, the children and dogs following.

Men had set off to cull the birds from the cliff since Neolithic times. Looking out at the sweep of hillsides, I could almost hear a whispering of hundreds of unseen feet setting off across the grass, all come back to join in with this one day on the island.

Chrissie was coming out of her cottage door, the red scarf tight over her head, her feet bare, a clutch of small ropes in her hand and a cloth with provisions tied inside. I ran to fetch my notebook and pencils, hauled my camera on my shoulder and set off behind her, treading where she trod as I knew she would pick out the best path but try as I might I did not catch up with her until we had breasted the slope leading up to the cliffs. At the top, the sea was a disc as wide as the edge of the world in a vista of unparalleled light and dazzle.

The first man had already gone over the cliff edge. Lachie Gillies was sitting on the turf at the top with the rope twice round his shoulder and chest, one foot braced against a rock, carefully letting out the rope, two dogs patrolling up and down behind him. A tall boy, Angus MacKinnon, stood to one side, watching, waiting for his turn to go down, looking over at me as if to say, what do you think of us now? On the other side stood old Finlay smoking, gauging the level of skill in the operation so far with a discerning squint to his eyes.

I was seeing the true kernel of the Kildans, the cragsmen, the birdmen. I sat down as close to the edge of the cliff as I dared.

Chrissie was standing on the turf a yard from the edge. Behind her the hazed blue of the sea and the endless dome of sky so that she seemed to be a thing of flight, suspended in air. She wore the short dress that all the island girls wear, her calves and feet tanned, her bare arms in a cotton shift tucked into her skirt. The red kerchief was tied to the basket she had brought up, her dark hair blown by the wind. She held a hand over her eyes to shield the gold of her face then turned back full of excitement and called out, 'Do you see? The hills of the long island are as clear as clear. Even the white specks of houses on Uist. And look, you can make out the hills of Skye sharp as teeth. It's a rare day to see so clearly.'

I went and stood beside her, not looking down to avoid the weakness in my legs from contemplating that drop of over a thousand feet down to the waves, and then something happened – for the fear left me. Standing with Chrissie's hand on my arm, following her pointed finger with my gaze, I saw what she was seeing on the horizon. I could even make out the distinct colours in the mountain slopes of Skye, the differing shades of blue and turquoise and cobalt. 'Like drinking the champagne of the skies up here,' I told her. She looked at me awry and said, 'Well, we don't know much about drinking champagne, but we know that there is no better place to know the beauty of the world our Lord has created.'

'I'll bring you back some real champagne one day,' I told her. 'Then you'll know.'

'Then you'd have to go away from here, and why would you do that?' she said, her eyes mischievous, and I swear she let her hand linger on my arm for a good few moments more than was necessary.

Standing by her, I thought, but isn't that the truth, that I would like more than anything to stay here in this day, with Chrissie, barely educated as she was, unworldly – guilelessly superstitious as if the last war and the twentieth century had never begun – and wise and glowing and alive and beautiful as the land around us? Nothing I would exchange for this moment, close by her, the sight of her brown tanned face and her clear blue eyes, her mischievous intelligence, and the sweet, sweet smell of her, of warm wool and peat and the grassy green of new cut hay and yes, a smoky hint of the sea birds and the fish that seep through every pore of this place. All the health and the beauty and the magic of that place distilled into the girl that was Chrissie.

I could not make out the details around her, here, or there in London or Cambridge, nor could I envisage any type of life that I could live here in such an isolated spot, and yet I saw her there, wherever I went, the centre of my future, my wife. I can tell you that it was a revelation that hit me out of the blue and made a nonsense of all I knew. St Paul on the road to Damascus could not have been more changed, or more certain, or more blinded by his thunderbolt from the skies.

She went to stand by an anchor man who was setting himself up along the cliff edge, Angus. He'd banged a stout wooden peg deep into the earth and fastened the rope to it, his foot wedged against a rock and the rope heavy around his shoulders. Donald, his feet bare but clad in his everyday trousers and shirt, had the other end around him, let himself over the precipice and began to disappear.

'You'll see better from over the way,' Chrissie told me and I followed her around the curve of the cliff where we could watch

Donald walking down the rocks as unconcerned as if he were going to buy a newspaper along the street. He pushed with his feet from time to time, swinging out from the cliff and landing lower down in a slow, graceful ballet, bare feet alighting off the rock ledges, the rope some two hundred feet long. Below him, a thousand feet more down to the sea, a rock skerry with a ruff of deep turquoise water breaking prettily against its sea-worn indentations like a flower on the sea. To fall, to hit those rocks, would mean certain death.

He was working on a ledge now, inching forward towards a narrow outcrop thick with scruffy nests, drapes of white guano runs fringing the rocks below. A row of huge fulmar chicks sat unguarded by parents who had left to glide out towards the Arctic sea, these smaller relatives of the albatross never more at home than when riding the wind over the ocean, only dipping down to scoop up the sand eels and herrings, digesting the rich silver treasure into a slurry of oil-rich goodness in a special gut sack. It was this oil that swelled the chicks with layers of fat ready to face the harsh times of fending for themselves. The chicks were now twice the size of their hard-working parents, swathed in a cocoon of white down with little nibs of black beaks and eyes.

The trick was, Chrissie said, to catch the chick unawares before it could draw back its wings and spray foul stomach oil over the cragsman. Donald soon had a row of chicks hanging from his belt. He pulled on the rope to climb back up and unload them, the rope shortening as he climbed.

'You can help now,' said Chrissie as Donald unloaded his tutu of birds and I wondered for a moment what she meant as she held out a short rope to me. Laughing. 'Don't worry, we would not let you loose on the rocks. Your feet are too tender.' She showed me how to rope the legs of a few birds to each end of a short rope, the wings hanging like hopeless prayers, and then hang it around the shoulders so that the bulk of dead birds was easy to carry. They were not as light as one might imagine, loaded with all the goodness the parents have been able to sluice down them in fishy oils. These birds would pay the sacrifice of being the main sustenance for the islanders during winter. Mrs MacDonald was helping squirt the ruby-coloured oil from the bird's beaks into a drum.

I caught up with Chrissie as she headed down the slopes. 'If the ladies in London could see you now, Chrissie, with your stole of fulmars, they'd give up those dead-eyed fox furs they wear round their necks and all want one like yours. Why don't you travel a little, to Glasgow, or down to London one day?'

'Me? All those people rushing round in their fancy clothes and those motorcars in the streets. I'm Chrissie Gillies from Hirta. This is where I belong.'

'Chrissie, you are a wonder. Honestly, if you could only see yourself, so pretty with your feather cape and your blue eyes. And you smell of the wind.'

She looked at me with a mixed expression, annoyance that I might be making fun of her – and hope that perhaps that it was a compliment.

'Oh, you do nothing but talk your nonsense. And I smell a lot better than you do.'

I turned my head to give a quick sniff to my armpit region. She had a point. And after that she was hard to keep up with as we went up and down the hill all day, carrying the birds. The sun shone down unabated, though a cooling wind made our work easier as an impressive pile of white birds grew on the platform of flat rocks down by the sea, a bounty contributed to by all the teams, and waiting to be divided between the families.

I stayed for a while and watched how the boys and the women were already taking off heads and feet, transmuting the creatures from birds to wing-shaped food. Some of the older women sat nearby on stools, plucking in a storm of down. Finlay MacQueen was gathering the down into canvas sacks. He shook his head as he opened the bag wide to let me see the treasure.

'Good enough for a bed for the old queen. And she'd not get any fleas in her bed with fulmar down. It's the oil that keeps the fleas away. But no one but us wants our feathers these days. Was a time too when the world wanted a bottle of fulmar oil to ease their aches and pains. You should take some too, Mr Lawson. If you run out of electricity, it's excellent for a lamp. I wove all this tweed I'm wearing by the light of a fulmar oil lamp.' Finlay stood tall so I could admire his workmanship.

'Oh, sit you down, Finlay, and shut up. Why should the young man want to take a bottle of our oil all the way to London?' said Allie MacCrimmon.

'I'd love a bottle to keep,' I insisted, though I had no intention of surprising my friends with a nice fishy reek in my rooms. 'Why don't I run and get a glass bottle to put a little in?'

I stoppered the bottle tightly lest any of the odour escape, and sat it in the bothy window. The low evening light lit up the reddish oil, my own bottled spark of ruby sunset. I pictured it on the sill of the mullioned window in my college rooms, a little foreigner in civilization, evening light illuminating it like a shard of stained glass, and there, in the background, in the shadows of the room, I saw you, standing in my rooms in Cambridge with your gentle smile.

I had a lot to write up that evening after a day in the company of the last true hunter-gatherers of the British Isles – at least in the way of men who must hunt in order to put food on the table rather than as sport. The St Kildans never take so many birds that the population cannot replenish itself. In truth, it was the birds that had the power to do away with the people should they ever choose to stop coming here.

But once again, my notes wandered off once into a long passage on one particular St Kildan. Chrissie.

I put down my pen, rested my head in my hands.

I saw myself back in the common room in Cambridge again, the fellows there pulling to pieces the cant of our tutor Canon Edgington. I tried to place Chrissie there, but all I saw was the confusion on her face as all the brutal speeches of truth that we'd learned from the terrible years of the war beat against her ears. I saw her clasp her hands over them and the tears of pain in her eyes. How cruel would it be to do that to her?

Chrissie, my love, I thought. I can never tell you just how much I love you, for I could never give you a future. And when the boat comes back, I will go and leave you here where you are happy.

I gave up on work and lay on my bed, the last of the light glinting in the bottle of oil, and from outside the plaintive cries of seals on the skerry rocks uncannily like the calls of lost children.

CHAPTER 22

Fred

ST KILDA, 1927

Archie decided he'd go and see for himself how the fulmar harvest was progressing. He was part of that set who liked to hunt and stalk, up for the challenge of bagging a few birds even without the aid of a gun.

'But listen, Archie,' I said as he left that morning. 'You're to stay in one piece and come back and do your essay. No heroics now.'

He gave that wicked little grin.

I watched him set off with the boys, a faint harr of mist across the grass that would vanish as the sun grew warmer, Callum and Lachie listening to Archie's prattle, clearly in awe of him, though he was the one going to learn from them; the boys in their old and well-worn tweed trousers, double patched at the knees and shoulders against the rubbing of the guide rope and the edges of the rock face, their feet bare; Archie in his plus fours, a tweed jacket slung over his shoulder, a white shirt freshly laundered by Mrs MacKinnon. They were joshing together, crowning Archie with the coil of rope. I saw him take out his hip flask, a quick sip, holding it out for the others to join him.

With the bothy quiet again, I took the chance to carry on with my notes, although the awareness that Archie was out on the cliffs felt like a dim figure of foreboding standing behind me. Eventually, I could ignore it no longer, gave up on work and glanced at my watch.

Almost noon. I noticed Chrissie and Mrs MacKinnon heading up the hill with the boys' strupac and ran out to join them, a kind wind at our backs as we rose up the flank of Conachair.

I wondered how these women coped with their men down on the cliffs so often. My nerves were in shreds after a morning of vivid imaginings. I knew Archie would have to try something risky. Combine that with my memory of looking over the long giddy drop to the water, and I felt an increasing unease even as we climbed. But then didn't these men go out on the cliffs all the time? I told myself. Didn't they come home perfectly safe?

Almost always came home safe.

Arm in arm, talking together, the women had summited the hill, a view across the slopes to where the boys were working at the cliff edge. I saw Chrissie raise an arm to wave to Archie and Callum. Then she stopped, began to run. I narrowed my eyes. Something wrong in the way Archie was sitting so near the cliff, his head bowed, Callum pacing up and down the edge. Something very wrong.

Both Chrissie and Mrs MacKinnon were running now. I broke into a run too, the sweet air and the bird cries filled with dread. Archie raised his head as we approached, Callum running to meet us, his eyes wide and brow wrinkled.

There was no sign of the rope on the grass. And Lachie? Where was Lachie?

A terrible keening sound as Mrs MacKinnon threw herself down on the turf and crawled to the very edge. Chrissie was shaking Callum, asking him what had happened. I too lay down, peered as far as I could over the edge, searching with Mrs MacKinnon for any sign of Lachie. Calling out his name into the din of alarmed birds. No sign of someone waiting on the ledges for a new rope to be passed down.

I heard another terrible wail, Chrissie pulling the woman back from the edge. Then I saw what Lachie's mother had seen.

A thousand feet below us, a small dark form was being sucked up and down the side of a pinkish rock, the dark seaweed plastered like hair each time the rock rose from the swell. A seal? No. Too long to be a seal. Arms flailing lifelessly.

Lachie.

The birds screaming and clattering, I searched and hoped for any sign of wilful movement, but the body rose and turned at the will of the waves. No sign of any life.

I hurried to help Chrissie as she held on to Mrs MacKinnon who seemed ready to launch herself over the cliff, crying out in Gaelic, cursing the sea.

Archie's face too was streaming with tears.

'For God's sake, what happened?' Chrissie shouted. 'How could he fall? There's no one better on the rocks than Lachie. How?'

Archie sobbed. 'I tried—'

'It was me,' Callum said, babbling fast. 'It was me. I hadn't pegged the rope. We were watching Lachie going down, and then the ledge must have given way. The pull was so sudden, the rope whipped out of my hands. We heard him shout but he was gone. And it was so quiet after, as if the wind and the birds stopped dead. And then we saw him below and we shouted and we shouted but there was no reply.'

Archie was standing wordlessly, face white, his weeping stopped. Mrs MacKinnon had crumpled down on the grass. She was so heavy when we tried to lift her back up, as though she would stay there for all her days. We led her away from the edge, away from the rising and the falling of the fulmars that watched us with their unchanging black eyes.

'Come away home now, Mrs MacKinnon,' said Chrissie. 'We'll fetch Lachie.' Then she said to me in a low voice, 'And we must tell the men we need to get the boat to go round for him.'

Mrs MacKinnon nodded. 'Yes. We'll get him from the water. For, yes, he may still be alive.'

What could we reply? Hope will carry on long after reason.

Mrs MacKinnon turned to face Callum. 'I don't blame you, boy, for what you have done. But you must always live with your deeds now. That is the curse you will live under.'

Callum stepped back, looked as if he had been struck by her.

'Archie,' I called. 'Help take Mrs MacKinnon down. I'll run and tell the village what's happened.'

The woman hung on to Archie as if her legs were gone, her wails filled with grief, one arm stretched back towards the sea as Chrissie and he guided her gently away.

Tears in my own eyes as I scrambled down the slopes. Trying to understand that we would never see Lachie again, so full of life, barely on the edge of manhood, the tousle of light brown hair never combed down, that ready grin, and always a dog winding round his ankles, a hand on its head.

And no place on earth that could spare a man less.

It took the rest of the day for the men to row out round the back of Conachair and rescue Lachie's body from the currents that had taken him right out towards Boreray. He lay in his bothy that night, his mother silent beside him. The villagers sat with her through the twilight and the hours of dark, the windows left open in the old way to let Lachie's soul take flight. But when the minister's wife came, she said they must be closed, for Lachie's soul had gone to the Lord, and was not floating outside homeless. She wanted his mother to have that comfort. As soon as the light from Mrs Munro's lamp was seen diminishing along the path to the manse, then his mother opened the windows again.

Lachie's mourning and burial took three days. At night, an owl was heard hooting over the slopes of Ruival, and old Rachel Òg said it was Lachie's blood calling out because he had died too young. The wretched owl was back the next night too. It sat on our roof, an eerie human timbre to its calls. I found Archie up, sitting at the table in the kitchen with the lamp lit. He looked like he had not slept, or woken from a bad dream.

'Bloody bird,' he said. 'I tell you I've had enough of this place, Fred. What I'd give to be away from here tonight.' I saw the hip flask was on the table, the monogram of Dunvegan Castle etched on the silver.

Over the next few days Archie appeared strangely manic in his efforts to do good in the village, or he would slump in a bleak depression, barely moving from the chair by the fire, staring into the glowing peats. The people in the village assumed it was the same grief that had swept over us all. But there was something else there, something that could not be assuaged.

As we were sitting by the fire with a dram one evening he said, 'I've noticed the way you look at Chrissie. You should be careful of that little moon calf. Don't get snared by a native girl while I'm gone.'

I ignored his more spiteful comment. 'You're leaving? When? But what shall I do with your things? Shall I get them sent on?'

'No, I will return and get the damned paper done, when I've had a break from here. I always finish what I started,' he said bitterly. 'That's the Macleod way. Family motto and all that.'

'But when are you going?'

'I don't know. I'll see. There'll be a couple more tourist boats out from Oban before the season ends. And fishing trawlers until the weather gets too bad.'

'There's not so much time left to get your work here done.'

'You know, it's yourself you want to watch out for, Fred. You shouldn't let yourself get too attached. Just make sure you leave this place before it's too late.'

'Too late?'

'Before the winter sets in. You don't want to be on this godforsaken rock all winter.'

CHAPTER 23

Chrissie

ST KILDA, 1927

If anyone in the village felt blame towards my brother Callum over the death of Lachie, then no one showed it.

'It was the will of God,' Mary said to me as we milked the cows at the back of the bothies, 'that Lachie should go to him now that his time on earth was done.'

After the three days of mourning, we went back to the fulmar cliffs. Almost a thousand birds were now lying in feathered piles of death on the rocks by the water or had been salted away in barrels. The weather was heartlessly beautiful, a blue sky, summer heat. The two whales moored in the bay had quietly swollen and split open to release their poisonous gases, polluting the cool breeze that came in from the sea.

The whaler came back that night, another dead beast in tow. They fastened the two swollen carcasses to the back of the boat and by the morning had left for the Bunavoneader whaling station on Harris.

Archie left with them to find a boat that would take him on to Skye or the mainland. With all that had happened in the village, I could understand his wish to leave quietly and respectfully. But I still could not quell a feeling that there was something amiss in Archie Macleod's soul, for he fled us like a fugitive, and it was only I and the slipping of the grey dawn into day that saw him rowed out to the stinking whaler. Going back on that stench-filled boat and with a rising swell to turn any sailor's stomach, I could not think that it would be a very grand voyage for our laird's son.

And there was something else I had seen as I passed him on the path before he left. His narrow face, furtive and pinched. I'd never seen him so clearly and so bereft of all the glamour I had covered him in, a tired and ordinary man who needed a shave and a good night's sleep. An unhappy man, it seemed to me, always seeking for a centre to himself. My poor Archie.

I stood in front of our sleep-sunk house looking out across the sea, the whaler rapidly fading away into a plume of smoke. The morning was fresh as fresh, curlews or oystercatchers piping clear and lamentingly hopeful on the shore. I drew the shawl tighter round my shoulders with a shiver and I told myself what my heart already knew. A pair of smiling brown eyes set deep under a steady brow, a smile teasing and honest, and a man who was little taller than me but with a strength and a grace that I found so pleasing. Come what may, whether he knew it or not, I was in love with Fred Lawson.

Love may be an imagined thing, looked for, hoped for. So I had fastened my hopes on to the form of Archie Macleod. But I understood now that I had never known anything about love, for as true and as real as the rock of our island that I stood on, I loved Fred down to his every imperfection. It was a surprise to me, to recognize the truth of it, and not altogether good news. For truly, why should he love me in return, a girl from such a backward place in the eyes of the world, a girl with little education?

When we spoke it ended in arguing together for he wanted me to think like him. 'How can you talk of the love of God when you are barely clinging on to life here on your rock? When the winter storms your God sends are so damaging and vengeful. Is this the same pally sort of God you catch sight of as you roam across the hills in summer? Which one is he? Now come on, Chrissie. Where's the logic?'

Then my heart broke for him, since I understood well that he was talking about himself and the storms that left him alone in the world. All I could do then was quietly take his hand in mine, if we were alone together, to let him know all I wanted to say. That he might know the comfort of His nearness as it breaks through into the day, borne on the sun and the wind. You are loved and you are not alone, I wanted to say, through storms and through hard times, you are very greatly loved.

CHAPTER 24

Fred
FRANCE, 1940

Just seventeen, handsome and smooth-cheeked, our guide Richard had the unshakeable confidence of youth. And with it, perhaps, a readiness to take needless risks. Madame Curtil listened to my concerns, tamped the tobacco down in her pipe, lit it and drew the air through the tobacco until it began to glow red, her white hair and beret shrouded in smoke. 'We have found that the younger a guide looks, the less suspicion from the Germans. And Richard is wiser than he seems. He cared for his brothers and sisters after his mother was mown down while the family were fleeing the invasion. He's determined to make it to England and join the Free French but for now he's part of the network returning soldiers and downed airmen home to fight once again. And, of course, I will come with you to the station to make sure that you get on the train to Paris, just in case there are any little problems.'

'Paris? But surely that's walking straight into the worst possible place for two servicemen on the run,' I protested.

Madame Curtil shrugged amiably. 'In Paris you can be anonymous. You will be hidden in plain sight. For the journey, I will do the talking, occupy myself with the tickets. Your only task is to not be noticed.'

Madame Curtil sat up front with the truck driver and Richard, Angus and I in the back, the boxes of wine bottles jangling along with my nerves. At the station, Richard went in to buy the tickets. He came back with bad news. 'The place is crawling with German guards checking everyone's papers at the barrier.'

Madame Curtil took a wine bottle from the back, smeared her cheek with some dirt from the side of the truck and dishevelled her hair. We were to follow a few steps behind, Richard walking apart from us. She managed to make enough of a tipsy scene at the ticket gate to prevent the guards studying our passes too fully.

Once on the train, Richard gave us each a newspaper to hide behind, told us not to speak to anyone, blend in. I only hoped Angus's typical Scots freckles and pale auburn hair, now half-hidden under his beret, would pass for some type of Breton genes. I feigned sleep, alert to every sound and smell.

Arriving at the Gare du Nord in Paris, we left the train and followed Richard towards the barrier. He spoke with the guard who let us through with no problems.

'How did you convince him to let us pass so easily?' I asked, impressed.

'*Cent francs.*' He shrugged, scanning the crowds. He moved towards a girl in a school uniform and a red beret, and began to walk behind her. We too followed at a distance. She looked even younger than Richard. Children with nothing but their courage fighting Germans with tanks and guns; Angus only a year or two older and already seen too much. At the station entrance, the girl paused. Richard disappeared into the crowd. She glanced behind at us for a brief moment, then carried on walking.

I had no idea what part of Paris we were headed to, or who she was as we trailed her through the streets. In a quieter part of town, she stopped in front of tall double doors, pushed them open onto a quiet hallway leading to a stone staircase with a curving iron bannister. At the top, on the third floor, she looked behind, smiled for the first time and turned her key in the door.

Inside was a gracious flat with windows overlooking the trees of the avenue, gilt chairs and a grand piano. A woman in an expensive wool suit, her hair swept up in well-tamed curls, came forward to greet us as if we had responded to her invitation to cocktails. Her daughter kissed her on the cheek to her mother's '*Bien fait, chérie.*' Madame Mercier introduced us to the other guests in her flat, two airmen, a Canadian and an RAF pilot, who had had to bail out over Picardy.

'And now, if you would like to have a bath or a nap, please, Honorine will show you to your room.'

I understood from that as we followed the maid in her cap and white apron that we were in need of a good sprucing up. It hadn't been the first thing on our minds of late.

We took it in turns to wash and have a hot shave. Rubbing my skin and feeling no stubble, hair slicked back and a clean shirt brought through by Honorine, I realized I hadn't felt so human for a long time. She'd taken away our trousers and jackets and returned them brushed and pressed. Cleaned our shoes.

We ate in the dining room, Mr Mercier pouring small drinks of vermouth before we sat down. He was a thin man, with a high forehead and tortoiseshell spectacles and the same careful cultured French as his wife. No, I hadn't been to Paris before, I answered him, to my regret.

'Ah, but she's so sad now. *C'est triste.* Red banners everywhere and German soldiers on every corner. Impossible to go to a restaurant or a cafe now without seeing them. Better to stay at home, don't you think?'

The Merciers' flat overlooked a courtyard garden at the back and in the quiet days that followed I spent a lot of time looking out of those long windows while the frost turned the bushes and the espalier trees shades of blue in the early shadows of afternoon. The two pilots had stories to tell of dogfights over the Channel, and news of terrible damage from the Blitz. 'But we've shown them we're no pushover,' Tony said, a big man who must have had some difficulty fitting inside a small Spitfire cockpit. 'Wiped the smile off Goering's face if he thinks his Luftwaffe are going to beat us.'

Christmas came and went. Madame Tissier made a special effort with the menu, a meat stew – horsemeat, she admitted ruefully, but what can one do? New Year had Angus demonstrating the Highland Fling and Monsieur bringing out his precious Scotch whisky.

In the dog days of winter when everything seemed so dead, I spent endless days looking out over the frozen garden, all my thoughts of the island, of you. And bitter thoughts too, for Archie and his betrayal.

In that last year at Cambridge, after our summer on St Kilda, I hardly saw Archie again. I moved out of college and got rooms in a student boarding house at the back of town. I was careful to avoid the corridors and quads around where he lived. I avoided the library and pubs and streets where he might walk. I never wanted to see his face again.

I didn't attend my graduation ceremony, sick at the thought of meeting him there, took the first job I was offered on the basis that it was overseas, and so began my itinerant life as a geological consultant to various oil firms trying to expand into new territories, South America, the Middle East, then Malaysia for several years where I never managed to rise up and break away from the heat and torpor of warm rain and thick jungle. Until the sounds of war reached even there.

I wondered where Archie was now. Had he joined up? I doubted it.

And if I found you, Chrissie, what was it that I was really hoping for? A new beginning? To restore the years the locust had eaten?

If there was a way to go back and start again, make it right, Chrissie, oh I'd run at it, seize it with both hands.

But for now, all I could do was wait, cooped up in the Paris flat with Angus and the two airmen, endangering the lives of Monsieur and Madame Mercier and their daughter while all around us Paris was held by a cheerful and victorious German army.

We were champing at the bit to start the next stage of our journey towards the Spanish border with the help of another brave *passeur*, but who this would be or any details of our route, Monsieur Mercier could not discuss with us. 'It is best to know only what you need to and at the last moment. Once the guide arrives, then you will be told your next destination. Until then, all you need to do is trust us.'

CHAPTER 25

Chrissie
ST KILDA, 1927

When I had checked on the calf in the byre that evening, I went home to the bothy and found my mother weeping. She was folding a newly sewn jacket, stroking the tweed cloth and holding the bundle tight against her chest with great gulping sobs. It was a garment she had been making with great care for a long time. For we knew what was to come. The boat that brought the minister home would take my brother away.

My brother Callum never recovered from the shame and grief of being the man to lose Lachie over the cliffs, he who had always been nimble as a Soay sheep on the rock face since he left school.

Callum was rising sixteen when he'd written to our great-uncle, Alex Ferguson, the year before, to see if he might find some work for him in the Glasgow shipyards. Mr Alex Ferguson had friends among the shipyard managers and he wrote back to say that they were always willing to take in a St Kilda boy since they were known as being hard-working and conscientious.

Mother said he could go when he was seventeen and not before. It was the best she could do to put off his going, but she'd always known the time would come. She'd only hoped he might be a good few years older before he left us.

She'd woven a length of special tweed, though she did not say what it was for. The warp was made from the rare black wool that you sometimes get from our Soay sheep. The weft she wove from the colours of home. The pale ginger of brown sheep's wool mixed with white, and of the pale gold colour of the dye made from the white rock lichen, and a thread running through it of blue indigo, the colour of the woollen dresses that the mothers wore, as did our mother.

I helped, since the work is long and arduous for every piece of cloth we make. I had climbed the hill to scrape the crotal lichen from the grey rocks with the flat-sided spoon and collected the egg-yellow curls to make the dye. I had sat with the neighbours around the growing pile of carded wool rolls, long into the night, our chairs in a crowded circle as we brushed the wool back and forth till it was fine as baby's hair while the old ones told their tales, the stories mixing with the fibres of the wool. I took my turn at the spinning wheel, changing the cloud of wool into a thread that grew and disappeared under my fingers. I stood by the three-legged witches' pot on the grass, feeding the hanks of wool into the water, sometimes yellow sometimes blue.

The weaving itself my mother did not let me help with, for this was a cloth only she was to do, working into the night by the light of a cruachan lamp, its fulmar's oil filling the cottage with its oily smoke – gone out by the time we awoke, my mother already risen from her small sleep.

I took my turn peeing into the big pot we keep out in the byre and in feeding the newly woven cloth into the boiling ammonia to set the dye, and helped rinse the cloth clean in the stream. Then I sat with the other women around a board and we pounded the wet tweed, grasping and dragging it over to our neighbour, again and again, the length travelling back and forth between us to the rhythm of a song that became stuck to the fibres as we sang. When the loose weave had knitted into a fabric so thick and felted it could endure any rain and shrug off any breeze then it was ready. Our tweed was thick and good, prized by gamekeepers and deer stalkers, though not always by ladies, who claim it is too rough for the skin.

'This will not wear out, not before it is long out of fashion and you are long tired of it,' said Mr MacKinnon who helped Mother cut it out and sew it.

I took a piece of the off-cuts to keep. You could spend a long time looking into the different colours of the island woven into that cloth.

You had never seen a more handsome boy than Callum as he stood in the kitchen in his new jacket. The *Dunara* was in the bay that evening, and in the morning it would leave along with the tweeds for Alex Ferguson to sell in Glasgow and two tons of salted ling – and with Callum.

We had one last evening together, mutton and cheese, and after supper Father took the Bible and made worship. He read from Exodus and we sang a psalm together. Number 23, the one that mothers teach their children to keep them safe from the Devil and his works. Father led us in prayer as we listened to the wind get up in the bay. All day the weather had been getting worse and we knew what the message would be before Ewen Ian arrived at ten o'clock and knocked on our door. It was no longer safe for the *Dunara* to ride at anchor in the swell and so the rowing boats were going out to load the last of the provisions now and not in the morning. Callum was to get down to the jetty where Finlay Gillies was already waiting, since he too was to travel to the hospital in Glasgow on account of his bad lungs.

His face set, Father went down to help the men.

All in a bother, her last evening with Callum slipping out of her grasp, my mother flitted about the kitchen, wondering what he might have forgotten to pack. Had he the new socks she had knitted? Should he take a cheese? And she fetched three sovereigns that she had saved in a tin on the press and put them on the table for him.

Then it was time to go. Callum stoked up the peats, looked around the room, saying, I will be back soon enough. But we knew it was a long way home from Glasgow. And there might be months before a letter could find its way here.

I walked down with Callum and Mother, though she thought of one more thing she wanted Callum to take. She ran back while we waited, the sea silver and the ring of jagged outcrops along the arm of the Dùn black against a sky empty of all but a pale light.

I felt I had one last chance to stop him going, to turn aside the thing that had made him go.

'Oh, Callum, won't you stay? Is it because of Lachie? You know it wasn't your fault that Lachie died. You can't blame yourself. You know that no one here blames you.'

'We were all to blame, taking drink from Archie's flask. But, Chrissie. . .' He turned to face me, took my hands. 'There's something I want you to know. I can't bear it if you think badly of me.'

'What are you telling me?'

'But first, will you promise to keep this to yourself?'

'Yes, if you want me to. But whatever is it? Tell me.'

'It wasn't me who let Lachie go.'

I knew then before he said it.

'It was Archie who was supposed to be holding the rope down to Lachie. Archie who let it go. He hadn't got the rope enough round his shoulders and then it happened so quickly.'

'Archie? Then why do you let everyone think it was you? Callum, you must say. Don't you see, there's no need for you to go?'

'No. Archie is my friend. I promised him. And I am to blame too. I shouldn't have let him have the rope like that.'

An anger rose up in me.

'Archie Macleod is no friend if he will let you take the blame on yourself, let you tell a lie for him. You must say.'

'Promise now you won't tell anyone, only I couldn't bear for you to keep thinking that I could let a man fall.'

'Oh, Callum, please don't go. It's here you're needed.'

'I'm sorry, Chrissie. It's done.'

He ducked his head, picked up his bag, moving away from me already in his silence. Our mother was coming back down the slope with Father, not too quickly, trying to draw out the time. She had a small black book, our grandfather's Bible. She put the book in Callum's hands.

'You will keep up the family prayers, carry on when you have your own bairns. Tell them of us.' The idea of those children she would not see was too much and she hid her eyes with the edge of her shawl.

Ten o'clock, the last of the gloaming turning to dark. All the village gathered on the jetty. I had so much I wanted to say to Callum still, but he was lost to me as he embraced every last person. Such a wailing and keening from the women as the little village boat began to pull away. I heard a strange voice, my own voice among them, wailing for him to come back. We watched him diminish across the bay and climb aboard the *Dunara* by the light of a lamp.

'But what is he doing?' asked my mother as he remained on the deck and facing out at us, began to make arm movements.

'It's semaphore.'

'Semaphore. You know semaphore, Chrissie. What is it? What's he telling us?'

'I – have – left,'

'Oh no, the sovereigns. They'll be on the table.'

'No. Wait. He says, I have left. . . I have left with you my heart.'

Callum stayed in deck holding up the lamp as the boat sailed, and we waved and watched him until we could see the light no more.

I held on to my mother's hand so that she could know that I at least would never leave her. She winced for I was holding her hand so tightly. It was the anger in me, a cold rage against Archie that he could let Callum take his shame – and so take my Callum.

And yet I had promised Callum not to tell. No one I could speak to, to let the anger out of my chest.

One day, the next time I saw Archie, I was certainly going to tell him what I knew, and how greatly I despised him. I could not go back in the house for I feared my anger would burst the walls.

I climbed up to The Gap where I could sit in the space hung between the two hills, the great cliffs at my feet. And there I saw what I had hoped for: the dark shape of the boat crossing the sea under a night-blue sky, moving towards where the water was polished with a silver glow. I watched until the boat was all gone to light, and then I was left with only my anger.

Archie Macleod, so tall and so handsome with his fair hair like a prince from a fairy tale, the creature I had known since my childhood, how could I not have fallen in love with him? But the real Archie was as flitting as sand in the wind, no substance to him other than what suited Archie Macleod.

I sat a long time looking out over the sea, thinking of the long island and the mainland beyond where Callum was going, and all that wide world where I would never follow.

Which was a problem for me. For as I sat there, I saw one I truly loved. He was not so tall, those deep-set eyes and cheeks that flamed if he was teased, but with a kindness and a solidness and a steady way of seeing you with that bright gaze. And whose lips I would wish to feel against my cheek. And I thought of how Fred would leave here too one day soon, no other way about it. So what would be the use of me ever telling him how I felt, even though the words burned on my tongue?

Fred would leave, and the passing fancy he'd had that he might feel some affection for me would fade away like a shore seen from a departing ship

And it was so great a problem to resolve that for the first time I wondered if perhaps Fred was right, that perhaps God did not arrange all things for the good of those who trust him. For it was clear to me in that moment, perched high on the cliff, that I would rather go to hell with my Fred than go to heaven without him. The damp had crept up on me, the wind turned chill over the dark sea and the darker sky. I felt for the first time how cold it must feel to live in this world without hope of the great being who watches over us. Then I walked back to my mother's house as cold as if I had lain down in the sea.

CHAPTER 26

Chrissie
ST KILDA, 1927

I told Fred that I would no longer come in each morning, afraid of myself to be alone with him so much. But he swore he needed some aid in the food preparation and seemed so earnest that, in the end, I agreed to help with cooking his food just twice a week and he showed me the courtesy of not appearing in the kitchen until I was about to leave.

Oh, but I loved those mornings, moving around the kitchen doing the small tasks to prepare breakfast, singing quietly to myself for I couldn't help it. I put wildflowers on the little table, set down the patterned bowl and plate, and stood by the fire stirring the oatmeal. All the while, he was there on the other side of the wooden partition, sleeping or getting up from his bed. This was how it must feel to belong to someone every day, I thought, to share a home and do small things to help each other. I knew I was playing at homemaking, imagining a life that could not be, but those mornings were precious to me.

I think he must have listened out each morning, for the moment I fetched my shawl from the peg he would appear, saying thank you and standing aside so I could pass by. We spoke a little in the doorway, always more to say than the time we had. I loaned him a novel or two from the school library shelf since he had finished all he had brought with him, and sometimes he explained his research and showed me books from his studies that he thought I might understand.

Often he came to our house of an evening to ceilidh by the fire, writing down notes of our customs, asking for old stories, curious to find hints of the ancient ones who had once lived here.

Archie's excavation inside the old dwelling in the glen that we call the warrior queen's house was almost finished. He said it might have been the home of a Norse warrior, a very ancient place. And he'd talked of a dark feeling inside there – the whisky, Fred said. He wanted to know if we knew any stories about the house, but all we knew were the times the cows were giving so much milk that we girls slept there and set the cheese, keeping the milk cool inside the old stone bothy that stands on the grass like an upturned stone basket. I found him one morning setting out to examine the place as I was going over the hill to milk the cows and so we walked together.

We walked in silence, the day being one so absorbing in its beauty. Around the slopes of the hill, the sea was finely rippled silk with the glassy blue paths of currents twisting and setting out who knows where. The turf was filled with flowers no higher than a thumb. Pale bee orchids, trumpet orchids in darker pink, yellow lady's slipper and daisy-eyed tormentil. A flock of bog cotton tufts like bird down caught on the reeds, shivering, shining with light as if lit with lamps. Up on the hills of the glen the sea sounds were quieter, the waves breaking small at the foot of the cliffs. There was little breeze, the smell of warmed peat breathed out from the earth, sometimes the leathery smell of cow dung. The birds peeped and chucked with their distant worries. All was blue and green and dazzle. He walked ahead, carrying the bucket for the milk and my scythe to cut hay from the upper slopes. I had nothing but a handful of dock leaves to carry in consequence, feeling oddly light as I stepped from mossy tuft to rock.

There was no one else there, all far away on the other side of the island with their own concerns. I saw how he walked as if his burdens were nothing. I watched the movement of the muscles in his back, in the back of his calves, sure and steady as he stepped from rock to tuft, how the sun had browned his strong arms, a golden down of fine hairs like no animal I could name. He turned back and smiled, waited for me to catch up and fall in step with him, but the slope was too steep as we descended, and against all my pride in never being the last to climb up or climb down, I found I fell in behind him once again, following his footsteps along the barely visible path through the reeds and grass and moss. And as we descended, the smell of the damper earth came up to greet us in the warmth of the sun, stronger, wrapping us round in its moistly warm blanket, sleepy and enveloping. My forehead and the back of my neck prickling with the sweat.

Fred was the first to sit down. He pulled the yellow cloth from round his neck, wiped his face, and surveyed the scene before us, the great bowl of the glen with no one for company but the cattle and the bay that is bitten out by the sea. Four miles away across the water there was Boreray, wandering across the blue with its two smaller calves, misty blue and insubstantial in the haze. I put down the bundle of dock leaves plucked for the cows, for how else should I get them to stop while I take their milk?

I was aware how still he was as he sat beside me, his smell of canvas and soap, the warmth emanating from his body, every detail of his physical presence vivid and near. Even with my eyes shut I saw him. And it seemed to me that the world had faded far away and the knowledge of him near was like the scent of a rare plant on the hillside that cracks its carapace and spills its odour on the wind, saying, it is time, it is time to consider only this one thing. I felt how he moved his hand nearer mine, how the hairs on my arm rose like a fear. I did not move. I felt the warmth of his skin, a little damp, against the sunburned skin of my arm. Then on my neck, so I flinched and shivered, and I turned towards him in one contraction of my body, a kiss that I realized I had wanted for so long.

It was only a kiss. A kiss that split the rocks of the island in two and turned north to south, transmuted the land to sea. I pulled away breathless and we stared at each other, two fighters about to wrestle for their lives as he held on hard to my upper arms.

And I moved again towards him, but there was a resistance, and I realized that his hands held me away, and he said, 'I mustn't, Chrissie. For all I want to, it would be to take advantage of you.'

But he kissed me again, worse, and wonderful. Then he was up in one swoop and clamber, so fast and pacing, and he was gone, striding out back over the hill like a man whose house is on fire, and I was left with the scythe and the bucket and the bundle of dock leaves – and the knowledge that he cannot love me after all if he would leave me like this. The burn of his fleeting kiss tattooed on my lips, I saw how my kiss was unwanted and already falling away from him as he grew smaller and left me standing foolish and bereft among the blond summer grasses.

I hoped not to see him all through the next day, though I saw him there before me every waking minute, the heat of his arm next to mine in the moment before he moved towards me, the kiss of him breaking over me like the sea, drowning me deeper into a world where only the sea people swam, twining round and round in a dance of the sea.

For I had become a new creature now, born of a longing only for him, every minute of every hour, and as the brightness of the day began to turn towards the summer dusk then I found myself once again drawn to the glow of the lamp in his bothy, as a moth is drawn inescapably to the flame.

He was, I could see, sitting by the window, reading a book, catching the last of the light and supplementing it with the lamp.

I stood for a long while a little way along from his cottage, pressed against the flank of the old byre's rougher stones and hidden away from the village. I could hear the sea breathing in and out, the sad calling of the birds on the shore for all the things they will never have. The dusk was erasing the steep rise of Mullach Mòr with the blue stones bleeding out from its slope, while I stood on the flagstone path, a pilgrim on the edge of all I hoped for.

There was a flutter in the light in his window and I saw that he was leaning down with his hands on the sill to look out over the sea, too restless to read. He looked out over the sweep of the bay that leaves and then returns to us at the village, and the broken part of the circle where all the Atlantic lies open and unbounded. I took a step away, but he had seen me, or felt me there perhaps, because he came to the door that stood open to the evening air, a pale figure framed in the darkness of his home. I came closer, and on his face the look of someone who has held a thing in the mind, and wonders and disbelieves to see it there.

My steps walked me towards him, solemnly, unstoppable. I stood before him on the threshold, shy of a sudden, ashamed of my boldness, my shawl pulled tight around my shoulders. Then he reached out and took my wrist so very lightly and led me inside.

I had never been alone with him at evening before, unsure what I should do or where I should go. He led the way into the kitchen, which was set out as like our own, but with a sense of makeshiftness in the things around the room, scoured as they were from abandoned things or loaned from the manse and the factor's house. He'd taped pieces of newspaper across the top of the hearth to draw the smoke as the chimney was not ventilating away as it should that evening. There were notebooks and drying socks and baccy tins and tins of cocoa and all the untidiness of a bachelor at evening time. There was the kettle hanging from a chain as there always was, and he played the host and filled it with water from the pail and set it to boil. He took the books off one of the chairs and I sat down to watch him spoon tea from a tin and set the pot to warm in a way that was touching to see in a man. I could not settle, but walked around the room, picking up cups from the dresser as if I had never before seen them, each single thing rare and wonderful because they were his, even the line of pebbles and shells in the windowsill.

The water boiled, he tipped it in the pot and poured it into two thick mugs patterned round with blue flowers and pink lacy patterns. I sat back down in the chair, the mug, too hot to hold, set down on the kist by me, and I picked up a book, turning the pages as if this were the very thing I had come to see. Wondering in my head just what might happen if he came near, and already knowing the answer.

I stayed too long and what was done can never be undone now. He held me tight after, and said we would be married one day.

When I left and went outside I was surprised to see the bay still there and the village unchanged. Oh, but it was changed for me. I went up behind the village a way, came back along the path before the bothies so that it was not clear where I had come from, which was a deception I was ashamed of, but it was not time yet to tell the world of what Fred and I would become one day soon – what we already were. Though I knew all the happiness of it was writ clear in my face, for Fred and I had made our solemn vow to never be parted for the rest of our lives. The joy of it was so great in my chest that I longed to shout it out to the bay, but I knew I must not yet. Instead, it came out in songs and tunes that I pealed out across the hillside as I walked alone over to the glen.

CHAPTER 27

Fred
PARIS, 1941

In the hard cold of February and a thick, city fog, our next *passeur* appeared, or rather, our *passeuse*, a dark-haired woman of around thirty who wore an elegant hat and tailored suit that must have cost a small fortune. She was medium height, a generous curvy figure inside a well-cut suit, her hat tilted over dark curly hair. It seemed as though the whole of France, from poor farmers to wealthy wives, were in a secret conspiracy to thwart the great battalions of tanks that had sliced across their cornfields in early June like a plague of mechanized locusts.

We shook hands, a firm grip, warm and confident, someone used to ordering around her cook and driver, I thought. Nancy Fiocca looked more like a woman from the pages of the *Tatler* than someone who could cope with the strain of shepherding four English-looking men through France, especially since we were going to have to cross the tightly guarded border from occupied France into Vichy territory on foot, dodging any guards.

'*Enchanté*,' I began.

'Oh, do speak English,' she said, her dark eyes twinkling, a solid Aussie accent. 'And I know what you're all thinking, but don't be deceived by all this beauty,' she gave a half twirl. 'I'm tough as old boots. All this is my secret weapon.'

Nancy, we learned, was married to a wealthy French businessman, part of the cream of Marseille society, and ready to risk her life for the four strangers before her. Along with her accent she had retained the no-nonsense capability of a girl who had grown up on a farm in the outback, caring for her brothers and sisters from a young age. She'd escaped at sixteen to travel the world, a journalist and an independent woman, determined never to marry, and ended up falling in love in Marseille.

She looked at us dubiously as we came over one by one to shake her hand.

'I see I'm going to have to teach you lot how to walk.'

She made us slouch across the sitting room, shoulders rounded, eyes on the floor, any lessons about stand up straight or hands out of pockets banished as a dead giveaway. She examined our shoes, donated by our hostess since our army boots were another red flag. The airmen had polished their shoes, but Nancy told us to scuff them up a bit, the French didn't have a thing about shiny shoes.

Early morning, biting cold and the smell of chicory and ersatz coffee from the cafes at the entrance of the Gare Montparnasse, the concourse echoing with the hiss of trains and loud German voices. Judging by the number of German soldiers milling around in relaxed mood, occupied Paris was considered a holiday spot for the conquerors. The guards at the ticket gate were less sanguine, scowling at each *ausweis* as they checked tickets. I began to feel a prickle of sweat in spite of the cold as we moved with the crowd towards them. Nancy, a few steps in front, a charming smile, held out her arms prettily saying, 'So, who wants to search me, boys?' Smiles all round from the German guards, laughter, a bow. We slipped through with hardly any attention paid to our papers. But there would be more guards on the train. She forbade us to open our mouths and stationed us two to a carriage to dilute the Anglo-Saxon fairness of Angus and the airmen.

Hunched in the corner, I watched the bastions of Paris tenement buildings begin to disappear as the train jerked taut and the carriages pulled away, wisps of smoke coming in a gap at the top of the window. My neighbour asked permission to close it. My eyes shut, I pretended not to have heard him. He wrapped his coat around him, shut it and sat down. It was cold in the carriage. I would have given a lot for a cup of tea. More people got on at the next stop, the train so crowded that a woman came into our carriage and stood between the seats. We were half an hour from Tours, no hitches, when Bill Bowers woke up and saw the woman standing in front of him. He automatically leapt to his feet, all six foot of him, saying in English, 'Please, have my seat.'

The woman thanked him in English and took his place.

I froze, a long moment waiting for the ensuing commotion. No sound but the clacking of the train. All eyes averted as if the last few moments had never taken place. Bill stood swaying in the carriage, looking sick.

At Tours, we changed to a local train, got off at a small town near the River Cher – the line of demarcation between occupied France and supposedly free Vichy France. All bridges were heavily guarded, passes examined in detail, but Nancy had other plans. A fine drizzle was sifting down, cold in the wintery afternoon. We walked a mile along the river. Nancy was looking anxious for the first time, scanning the feathery rushes and willow brush along the banks.

'Oh, for pity's sake.' Then her face lit up. 'There it is. Who wants to row?'

Angus was used to manning fishing boats out to the islands along Uist. He volunteered to be the oarsman. We were to go over in two lots, Nancy and one of the airmen going first, the two of them waiting discreetly in the wooded thicket nearby while Angus came back and the rest of us rowed over.

I was helping Angus to pull the boat up the bank ready to stow it in bushes when I was horrified to see two Germans running across the field waving their arms, guns over their shoulders.

No point in running now. We were in plain sight and it would be an open admission of our guilt to try and escape. But they didn't swing their guns round, reached us out of breath and laughing. They wanted us to row them over. I realized they thought Angus was a ferryman.

'*Combien?*' one of them asked.

Angus did his version of a Gallic shrug.

'*Dix francs,*' the German tried.

'*Vingt,*' I said.

They got in the boat. I gathered they were talking about girls they were going to meet in Tours, an evening at a pleasant *estaminet.*

Nancy thought our story of charging the Reich to let us escape hilarious. 'But remember, it's no laughing matter if the police or the Germans pick you up. You won't make it as far as Marseille. You'll be interned at one of the little prison camps around here.'

Ten miles to Louches where we would pick up the train for Marseille. We walked along the edges of bare fields of stubble or faded grass, sometimes passing hamlets of low, white houses with tall shutters and slate roofs. A mist was falling, chill with fading light, the thickets of bare woodland scribbled black at the margins. I caught up with Nancy, her heart-shaped face and thick black hair beaded with fine wet, dark eyes that were direct and kind.

'You know we can't thank you enough. And your husband, to let you risk doing this.'

'I am my own woman, Mr Lawson.' She smiled to herself. 'The truth is, he backs me up one hundred per cent. Just one of the many reasons I love him. And I expect there's someone special you're longing to get home to.'

'There was someone, once. We lost touch.'

'Well, you've got to find her. Whatever went wrong?'

I walked on for a while, turning her question over. 'I suppose I was young and too proud to ever try and really understand what happened. I let the years pass by.'

'As soon as you get back. D'you hear me, Mr Lawson? If she's the one, rip down every wall and find her.'

Ahead of us the pointed towers of a small town pricked the mist. Thankfully, the station halt was a little set apart. It was worrying to see two of the French police in their black uniforms going through each carriage as we boarded, but they were simply checking that the windows were sufficiently blacked out.

Nancy's words, spelled out in her firm Australian accent, stayed with me as the train rocked its way towards the coast. Why had I given up? Too ready to believe the world had no happy endings, no good hearts. And yet here, in the middle of a war, I was finding people of such courage and kindness, people who would endanger their lives for a stranger.

And where was my courage? Oh, Chrissie, my dear, I had been a coward.

CHAPTER 28

Fred
ST KILDA, 1927

The end of August and Archie was back at last. I could see him standing up and waving on the dinghy from the tourist boat, the sightseers in their gabardines and woollen coats looking up in alarm.

Back in the cottage, he unpacked new books and provisions. Clearly, he meant to work.

And I could tell that he was in a strange mood.

He'd been down to London and joined in with what they call the season. 'A host of girls in white looking for a man to trap,' he muttered into a glass of whisky as the peat smoke soaked into his jersey that evening, evicting the lye and lavender of the Dunvegan laundries.

'And were any of them successful?'

He bent to place another crumbling brick on the flames, young peat with the white turf roots curling in the heat and then dissolving.

'Tedious, the whole business. Honestly, what do they want from us? They lead you on with a merry dance. You put one foot wrong and it's all hell to pay.'

'You mean there's been an understanding?'

He laughed. 'What? Am I engaged? Oh, I think not. They won't let their precious daughters near me at the moment. There was a certain girl I liked – that much I'll admit – but you know how girls like to make a fuss. All I wanted was to get back here where at least people are honest about what they want. I tell you, a girl from here would blow ten of those snooty types out of the water any day.' He put down his glass, closing down the topic. 'And so how have you been here?' He gave me all his attention, sitting forward, firmly instigating a more cheerful tone.

'One would always like more time, but I can see my paper being finished soon. Perhaps, even, by the beginning of term.'

'Now I'm jealous. I should follow your example. There's the reward of not wasting one's time on the fair sex.'

I was quiet, dropping my head, deciding not to bring up Chrissie since he'd been so down on the whole topic of sweethearts, but he knew me too well.

'Something else you have to tell me?'

'I have to confess. Something did occur. That is, a realization.'

'Spit it out, man.' He took a large sip from the glass.

'Chrissie. I've spent some time with her of late. And it seems to me... in fact, I know it. I really am very much in love with Chrissie.'

'Chrissie, from here, from St Kilda? We are talking about the same village girl?'

'Why, yes.'

'Look, she's a fine girl. We all love her, but it's not really something one takes seriously.'

'No, you are not listening to me. I've never been more serious in my life. I love her. I want to spend the rest of my life with her.'

'And what does she have to say?'

'She feels the same way.'

'And so how far has this gone?'

'I'm going to marry her.'

'Now, hang on a moment. You think you are going to take Chrissie back to Cambridge with you? Your wife? Can you see that?'

'Well, not easily, but there's always a way when—'

'Or are you thinking of staying here for ever? Climb down the rocks and wring birds' necks for your supper. Fine to live the bucolic dream for a few months, Fred, dear boy, but for a lifetime? You've let this place rot your brains. You've let her sink her claws into you, like a cat with its prey, and you'll not come out of it well if you keep up with this idea, I promise you.'

I laughed. 'These are dark predictions. Chrissie Gillies is a wonderful girl, intelligent, strong, clear-headed.'

'You have to break it off now.'

'I can't. I won't.'

He put down his glass. His face was hard. 'What promises has she got out of you? You don't have to throw your life away in recompense for one heated moment.'

I felt the blood in my face, to have what we shared reduced to such a base transaction. 'It isn't like that.'

He stared at me, eyes wide, and whistled. 'So it has gone that far. And now you think you have to marry the little trollop.'

'You can't speak like that about Chrissie. And please. We'll tell everyone soon enough, but for now, please, this is in confidence. You are the only one who knows about us.'

'Listen to me, Fred, you really aren't thinking. Drop this whole sorry business and come back with me to civilization. We'll finish up here as fast as possible and then we'll leave, before you go completely native and lose all you have achieved.'

'I won't change my mind.'

'We'll see.' He poured another measure, drained it and banged down the glass. 'That's me turning in then.' Standing up, he lingered a moment, looking at the blue flames across the peat. 'You do know what this is really about, don't you?'

'What this is about?'

'Chrissie and I, we go back years, to when we were children. And I admit I've always had a soft spot for the girl. The mistake I made was some childish promise we'd marry some day. I'd forgotten all about it, but I realize now how much she was hoping. It's entirely ridiculous, and I've tried to let her down gently, tried not to hurt her feelings. But once Chrissie has an idea, she doesn't give up, especially where pride is involved. Don't you see that all this is just an attempt on her part to make me jealous?'

I studied his face, so sharp and taut. 'So let me see if I have this correctly. This is all about Chrissie trying to get your attention?'

'Well, yes. I'm sorry.'

'Archie, go to bed. I think the world will keep on turning if you shut your eyes and fall asleep a while. It may even be a better place for it.'

'I tried to warn you.'

All night I lay and worried that I'd told Archie too much. And I was angry with him for the cheap doubts he had cast on Chrissie's love. I had always understood that Archie carried a wound, growing up as he did; his brother in the full sun of his father's affections, Archie left in the cold shade. I'd always made allowances for my oldest and truest friend, forgiven his occasional spiteful outburst.

But this present bitter mood was something new and disturbing, a stream that had burst its banks and no one knew where it might go.

Tormod came with a message the next morning. Chrissie was wanted over the glen to help with the milking and setting the cheeses for the next few days, but he himself could come in and do the fire for us. I told him we would manage, and sent him off with a bag of peppermints from the supplies. I was sure Chrissie was needed, but part of me suspected that she had wisely volunteered to be busy elsewhere.

It helped that Archie and I were now in a season that required concentrated work if we were to get our papers completed before term began, the last days of summer ticking down now. It was not hard to work long into the small hours since the light stayed with us so late. Midnight seemed nothing more than a passing shadow before the landscape lay bleached and still as an eclipse once again, gradually regaining its colour. That was how I was still working at my desk when I saw Chrissie out on the grass in front of the bothies one morning.

I hadn't spoken to her much other than to say hello or good evening all week. I unbent myself from the desk, stiff and stale, and hurried outside into the chill wind and the wistful calls of oystercatchers from the shore. We sat on the low wall that ran between the crofts and the bothies, facing the sea. It was the first time that I'd been alone with Chrissie since Archie's return. I could see that she too was hesitant in how we should be after so many days apart, aware of all that had passed between us, sitting together, unshielded from the eyes of the village along the glen. I wanted to take her in my arms, rest my lips against her head and breathe her in, but we sat a little apart. She seemed shy, troubled.

'I am glad you are up about early,' I said, 'before the village is awake.'

'But it's not so early,' she said. 'It's a Sunday, people having their lie-in on the Lord's day of rest, though the cows still need milking. They will be coming out for the chapel service soon. Perhaps I will see you in there, sit across from you and think of you all the while.'

'Damn. I forgot it was Sunday.' I was in no mood to break off my work and sit in the chilly building for an interminably long morning of piety. 'I think today I will contemplate the Lord's creation from the window here.'

I saw Chrissie look over at the house, a blush on her cheeks. Archie was at the door, dressed and shining with his hair combed and a clean shirt. He called out that he'd be ready to go soon, then disappeared back inside.

'You won't come too?' she said. I read disappointment in her eyes.

'Why would you think I would? I never do.'

'I just thought, from all the things you said when we talked so much, it was as if we understood each other so well. . .'

'But, Chrissie, I've never said I was a church man.'

'Yes but, you know, you know full well that I cannot think of a world without the love of our God, not any more than you might drain the sea away from the island. I thought, being so close, we were surely to understand each other.'

I heard the worry and confusion in her voice.

'Chrissie, dear, why does it bother you so much, such a little thing?'

'It's no little thing. If a man does not have a faith in the Lord, I wonder how people might have faith in him and his promises? How can a man know who he is?'

'I don't see a connection.'

'Don't you?'

Along the village row people were appearing in their Sunday best, the older women with a white pleat under their scarf, the men in tweed jackets. Archie came striding down, wearing the jacket that Mr MacKinnon had tailored for him, the pale rust of the tweed so like the pale gold of his hair.

'And we're ready?' he said.

I held up my hands. 'You go on.'

'Quite sure you won't come, you old heathen?' he said affably.

And they were gone, Archie leading Chrissie away along the bothies.

I had the impression that Chrissie purposefully avoided me for the rest of the day. I finally found her in the byre. She had an arm over the back of her little brown calf, her head against its flank. She was singing softly in Gaelic. A prayer. The St Kildans pray at every event, the old biddies and fellows even kneeling down and praying in the byre for their cows each evening as they tend them, their beasts being both pets and friends, givers of vital milk and income. I stood and watched her in the smoky light of the cruachan lamp. She must have sensed me there for she looked round.

There were tears in her eyes.

'Chrissie, what's the matter?'

She wouldn't answer for a moment. 'So now you will think me foolish for praying with my cows?' she said. But her look was defiant.

'You must do as you think fit.'

'But all the same, you think that my thinking is lacking. So sure that your way is so superior, with your cities and universities and all the glory of the world out there.'

'Chrissie, why are you saying this? You know I love you. I respect you, all that you are. You have a fine mind, and if you were ever at university with me then I doubt I'd ever keep up.'

'But I'm not, Fred dear, and I never will be. And your world thinks so very poorly of my world, I understand that much.'

'Please don't be sad like this, Chrissie. Look, if it makes you happy, I will stay here. I've never been as happy as I have these past weeks, with you.'

'Perhaps. Perhaps you will, Fred. And it is true that I love you with all my heart, but I cannot see our way ahead.'

I took her hands in mine, pulled her up close to me, and after a moment she raised her face to kiss me. For a long time I held her in the smoky air of the cow byre, warm against me, the red-haired cow every so often stamping its hoof like the thud of a sudden heartbeat. She pushed me away.

'It's no good now, for when a girl has done what I have done, it's shameful. Oh, a man can do so, and be still a man, but a girl becomes something different. Something bad in the eyes of the world. And that is how it is. That is me now.'

'Chrissie, don't say such things. You are my own dearest girl, my wife.'

She shook her head, angry and unconsoled. Then she was gone.

Archie hurried to scrape together enough notes to pass as an essay and two weeks later was ready to leave with the last tourist boat of the season. I knew joining him was the right decision if I was to be sure of making it back to Cambridge in time for the new term, but I had decided to chance a few more weeks, leave the island on some passing trawler. After all, the start of term was still a good month away.

'What if the storms set in early and you're stuck here for another two months, or even more? It won't go down well with the dean. Come on, Fred. You know it's time to go.'

But my mind was made up. I could not bear to leave, and certainly not with Chrissie still so distant and dark in her moods.

'Very well, then. If you're so set on staying, then I'll stay too.' An arm around my shoulder, pulling me tight to him. 'And if no boat turns up before winter sets in, then so be it. We'll stay here till next spring.'

'Archie, now you're making me feel so guilty I'll have to leave with you. But it won't work, I won't change my mind.'

'Fine, fine. But neither will I. When the *Dunara* comes in for the last time, we will stand on the jetty together and wave her goodbye. We stay together or we go together. And believe me, Fred, we will go.'

CHAPTER 29

Chrissie
ST KILDA, 1927

I had seen little of Fred over the past couple of weeks while he and Archie bent their heads to their work. There was so much I longed to talk with Fred about and I did look forward greatly to the peace that would return when Archie left, Archie always bringing a storm with him.

Above all, I worried that Fred had decided that he'd not be leaving with Archie, feeling it in my bones that he was running a risk by lingering on here and not returning to the life that claimed him beyond these shores.

But I preferred to not think of such worries, reluctant to dwell on a time when my dear Fred might be gone.

I tried to avoid Archie as he came and went in the Great Glen seeking his bits of pottery inside the dwelling we call the warrior queen's house. It was hard for me not to blurt out the truth to Fred, but I had made a promise to Callum to never say who had really let Lachie fall. I knew why Archie's eyes looked sunk back in their sockets as if he slept badly each night. Why he was never still and comfortable, always jiggling a knee or tapping a hand.

I settled on the bank to milk my russet cow, after milking my grandmother's beasts, the bucket with their milk already in the warrior queen's house. It had been dug up inside as a result of Archie's seekings, but we could still keep the milk on the ledge at the side, cool and away from the sun. Not that there was any sun that day as I worked. A bank of cloud had rolled across the sea, stretching from east to west, eating up Boreray and advancing stealthily up the hill. I watched it come near, felt it creeping with wispy breath into my mouth and hair, wet and cold. Soon I was lost in a thick gloom, breathing in more damp than air. I finished milking the last cow, found her by the sound of her tearing at the grass. The bucket heavy, I walked up to the ancient dwelling, thinking of the people who had lived there in that strange beehive of stones that keeps out the rain well even now, but which always gives me a shiver of fear, expecting the stones above to fall heavy on my head so long as I am inside.

The Great Glen is where we keep our fairy tales, of meetings with enchanted folk, with ghosts who carry away the unsuspecting, so it made me jump to see a figure detach itself from the shape of the beehive and move towards me in the mist.

I stopped dead, but hearing a voice calling my name, I took courage, laughing at my own foolishness. It was only Archie, come to work on his uncovering of the past.

'Here,' he said, taking the handle of the pail. 'Give me that.' He carried it inside and placed it on the stone bench where ancient ones must have slept or sat. The cold in there made me reluctant to linger but Archie called for me to stay and admire two broken beakers and some burned antlers from a time when deer and men must have lived together on the island, the one eating the other.

'You know, I'm glad to find you, Chrissie. I'll be gone with the ship by the end of the day, and who knows when I will see you again. My dear own Chrissie.' His laugh was rueful and sad. 'Remember when we were children? How we promised to marry one day?'

'The talk of children indeed. I thought you were from a story book back then, Archie.'

'And I took your devotion for granted. Chrissie, you can't know how much it kept me going, to think that you, at least, thought well of me. Loved me even. Not that I expect you to feel the same way now. I understand. I can see how far things have gone between you and Fred.'

I felt a jolt of warning. Unsure what Archie meant. What did he know about the private moments between Fred and me? None of his business. And I didn't like it because wherever Archie goes, whatever Archie touches, then something will be broken.

'You know what the decent thing to do is, don't you, Chrissie?'

'The decent thing?'

'Yes. You know how damaging it could be to Fred's chances of a good degree if he's not back in Cambridge when term begins. Really, you should tell Fred that he must get on the *Dunara* when she comes in today. You know perfectly well that he shouldn't risk being stranded here for the winter.'

'Fred will do as he thinks fit. It's not for you or for me to tell him.'

'Come on, Chrissie. He'll do as you tell him. And if you do tell him to stay, he'll be ruined. There'll be no second chance for him if he wastes this last year of his degree. My father's estate won't pay for his studies twice. He might as well learn to catch birds on the cliff.'

I turned away, angry that Archie had needled his way into my soul so quickly.

'You know I'm right, don't you?'

And what could I say to contradict him when I too was worried about Fred's hasty willingness to risk his future?

Archie was close behind me, his hands suddenly on my shoulders, rubbing with consoling strokes of his thumbs on my shoulder blades.

'Oh, Chrissie, all this with Fred, it's a passing fancy. You loved me before. Why did you stop loving me, Chrissie? You were the only one who believed in me, all those lonely years. You don't know how much I want to see that in your eyes again.'

I turned round to answer him but all in a rush he was pressing his lips on mine, his arms circling my back and pulling me tight, his mouth stopping my breath, too hard and too rough. I could smell the sourness of whisky. I pushed back at his chest with all my might, catching a glimpse of him as he hit his head against the sloping wall as I ran outside. In the space of a moment he followed, hurling himself at me so that we fell to the earth, the damp and the water soaking dirt into my shawl and skirt as he scrabbled at my clothes.

But so much hard toil had made me the match of any man. I pushed him away again, pummelling him hard each time he grasped at me, still not believing that such things could be happening. Finally, I staggered up. So did he, and we stood like two dogs halfway through a fight.

'What's the matter with you?' I shouted. 'It's me, Chrissie. Are you mad?'

Then I ran. I could hear him crying out, 'Chrissie, I'm sorry.'

I could not see where I went, the cold air scratching at my lungs. All I could do in the thick mist was follow the slope up the hill towards home, listening for the screeches of the birds on the cliff to know how close I was to the drop. Slithering and slipping down the slopes on the other side. The mist thinned as I came down the slopes of Mullach Mòr and with great relief I saw the familiar line of bothies, their lamps already lit in the windows.

I got inside, no one else there, never more grateful to find myself alone. I took off my muddied clothes and steeped them in a bucket. I wrapped myself up in a blanket and took to my bed, shaking and cold, not wanting anyone to see me like this with the shame of Archie's disrespect still on me. Had I done something wrong to draw this down? And how could I ever tell Fred what had happened? No wisdom to follow in this other than my own wits and nerves all stormed up and jangled.

All I knew was that Archie Macleod was wrong. My love for Fred was constant and real and would stay true until the day I died.

And yet. And yet. Could I really ask my Fred to stay here and throw his life's prospects away on me?

If I loved Fred, if I truly loved him, shouldn't I let him go before the summer was out?

A ship's whistle sounded out in the bay.

Not yet. Not on this boat.

My mother came in, wanting to know what was ailing me. I told her I'd tumbled in the mist on the wet slopes. She felt my forehead and told me to sleep, took the clothes away to wash and gave me brandy for the chills. I felt so weary. I would talk to Fred in time, soon, of what had passed, and I would try and persuade him that he should go home for now, perhaps.

But now I wanted only sleep.

Mother said she would be walking up to the nurse's house for a while to help her wind some white wool she wanted to knit into gloves, but she'd stay if I wanted. I said to her to go and then I let sleep take me. All problems put aside for another day. Somewhere in my dreams, I heard a door close, and in the distance, the whistle of the boat.

And then my mother was by me, shaking me to say Fred was outside. That he wanted to speak to me or else he would be away on the boat. Would I not come out and speak with him? He was in an awful pother.

I blinked at her words. Fred was thinking of leaving? Now? Tears sprang to my eyes. I sat up as fast as I could, scrabbling for a shawl to wrap around my nightshirt. And then I stopped. Sat very still. For I knew now what I should do.

CHAPTER 30

Fred
ST KILDA, 1927

I had worked at the desk in the bothy window all morning, watching a dreich fog come down as if autumn were already here. On St Kilda, the summer is a brief season and the bright days that meet hand to hand at midnight were already drawing apart, ceding to the long dark that would soon return.

I heard the plaintive whistle of a boat out in the mist. The *Dunara* was in – the last tourist steamer of the summer, and the boat on which Archie would be leaving. I'd known all along that his protestations he was going stay on with me were not serious.

He'd already made some attempt at packing, but had left a lot still to do. He'd hurried over to the Great Glen for the morning to glean what he could at the last minute and would no doubt be back soon.

Down on the jetty the village was gathering to meet the tourists, the *Dunara's* dinghy slowly coming into focus through the gloom. I walked listlessly down to join them. Even the dogs were quiet and subdued in the mist, padding in circles on the jetty, whining and fretting.

All morning the fog stayed with us while the men took the last of their bolts of pale ginger and reddish tweed down to the jetty to be shipped back to Alex Ferguson in Glasgow who now acted as middle man for the sale of most of their goods. The cleits were being emptied of barrels of dried fish. Knitted goods, cheese, and several of the cinnamon and black Soay lambs were also rowed out through the wet mist to go to Dunvegan for rent.

The handful of tourists had walked up to the village, the village women fluttering around them, knitted socks and gloves hanging over their arms in hopes of a sale. Finlay, for the occasion, had brought out a stuffed puffin.

Archie was still nowhere to be seen. No sign of Chrissie either, but I knew she'd also left early to go over to the glen and milk the cows. No point wandering over trying to find her in this opaque and grey atmosphere. You could walk past someone a couple of yards away and not know it.

I went back and stayed working at my table by the window, the light so gloomy that I had to light the lamp by early afternoon. Still no sign of Archie. And I'd still not seen Chrissie go past or heard her voice along the path. For no good reason, I felt uneasy. Surely she'd be back by now?

I went out to find her.

No one answered when I knocked on the door of her bothy, the windows dark. No sign of her down in the schoolroom where she liked to play her tunes on the piano when it was quiet there. She wasn't working with the animals in the byre. Back down on the jetty to ask Tormod and the other small boys who roam the island. They'd not seen her, all busy doing their best to get in the way of the men who were readying the final loads to row out to the boat.

The captain came over, not looking happy. 'Tell Mr Macleod that we'll be wanting to go soon. There's a wind getting up. If he's coming with us, then he'll need to get a move on.' He checked his pocket watch. 'We'll leave tonight, by ten at the latest.'

'So Archie's definitely going back with you?' I was relieved to hear it.

'Aye. He came running down in a hurry a short while back and that's what he said. He's up in the village getting his things but needs to look sharp.'

I ran back to the bothy. Sure enough, Archie was there, his trunk open, books and clothes being tumbled into it.

'So you're going?'

'The captain says he's quite sure this might be the last boat for a while with the weather turning bad. Look, Fred, you ought to get away now too. Grab your notes and we can have the rest of your things sent on as soon as possible. Come on, man, think. Do you really want to be stuck here till next spring, eating nothing but sea birds and sending little rafts with a message home? Risk flunking out of a whole term – your entire degree, perhaps?'

I knew Archie was trying to stampede me into going. I didn't mind. He was doing what he thought best for me.

'You won't change my mind, Archie,' I told him cheerfully. 'Now, the least I can do is give you a hand getting on that boat. It leaves at ten.'

His affairs finally packed, I strung one of his bags over my shoulder. He looked around the room as if searching for a new line of persuasion, picked up a case and his jacket and stormed out.

Down at the jetty, I put his bag down and embraced him, thumped his back. He shrugged me off. Eyed me in a strange way. I sighed. I knew he was going to have one more try.

'Chrissie's not the girl you think she is,' his voice hard and bitter. He came closer, eyes two blue shards of glass. 'She's a very willing sort of girl, isn't she, your little Chrissie?'

I stepped back. 'I'd rather you didn't talk about Chrissie like that. If you think that, just because I confided in you—'

'Oh, Fred. If that was all. If you only knew. I didn't want to have to tell you this, but you should know you're not the only one your little Chrissie's been so generous with. She came over to me in the glen today. I suppose she's always carried a candle for me. You know how wild she can be. I shouldn't have let her, I suppose, but how's a boy not to get swept away?'

'Nonsense. It's not true.' I felt sick to my stomach at Archie's lie that he'd lain with Chrissie. And as if it were a comparable thing. What Chrissie and I had shared had been precious, for life.

'No? Ask her then. See if she can deny it. I'm telling you, Fred, get out of here while you can. There will be a boat waiting by the pier for a while. Change your mind and come.'

'I shall go straight to Chrissie. If she ever heard what you said. . .'

He shrugged, picked up his bag and climbed down into the dinghy. Left me on the jetty, the land buckling beneath my feet.

'Remember, the boat will be here a while longer,' he called out. I watched as his dinghy gradually faded in the mist until there was only the sound of the dipping oars across the water.

I could never tell Chrissie the lies he had told about her. And yet, it was there. He'd sown a doubt. And only Chrissie could answer it.

I ran back up to the village. Still no sign of her. I knocked on her door again but there was no reply, the cottage remained in darkness. At last I saw her mother returning along the path.

'Mrs Gillies, have you seen Chrissie?'

'She is here inside.'

'Could she come out and speak with me a moment?'

'I'll ask her but she came back from milking all dirtied and in such a strange mood. I left her to sleep.'

'But what's wrong?'

'I can't say. But she's not herself.'

'Please. I must speak to her. They are saying I should leave on this boat if I'm to get back to Cambridge in time. But I wanted to speak to Chrissie first. Please. Tell her. I need to speak to her.'

I waited on the path, much longer than I liked. Why wasn't she coming?

Finally, her mother came back, her kind face worried. 'She says she won't come.'

'But you told her that I might leave on the boat.'

'I did, Mr Lawson. But she still says she won't come.'

I went back to my bothy and sat down on the chair in a stupor. Why wouldn't she speak to me? One word from her was all I needed. I waited for her to run in at the door, out of breath. But the minutes went by, each seared with pain. She'd never been so cold and careless before. Could it really be that something had happened between her and Archie?

Her silence was all the proof I needed.

That Chrissie should give herself to Archie, as if the love and the words she and I exchanged had meant nothing.

The door stood open and I could hear the faint sound of evening prayers across the glen from the village bothies, the wailing of their psalms in that wild, unknowable language. Oh, what a fool I'd been to be taken in by all that. As if the world could be a good place, as if it were in the heart of man to follow ideals and faithfulness. I thought of my two uncles and all the broken men sent back from the trenches, the moments of despair that made them and so many others choose to end it rather than endure the pain of living.

My love for Chrissie broken in two, for the first time, I could see the logic in their self-destruction.

I began hurriedly packing up my things. Cambridge would be empty with everyone down for summer, but I couldn't stay on the island any more. I'd keep out of Archie's way.

And already I felt the pain leaving this place.

I was just in time to find the boatmen down at the jetty. They rowed out in a hurry, although once I was on board the ship, the weather kept us in the bay all night.

A long, blank night without sleep. I lay, hoping that a boat might still come from the village. A message from Chrissie. At dawn, the swell eased enough for us to get away. Sunday again, the devout men in the crew assembling on deck for the morning service, sober and humble, and all of them deluded in their superstition, deluded in themselves.

CHAPTER 31

Fred

The Seaman's Mission in Marseille was a run-down two-storey building near the docks, badly in need of a coat of paint. The Reverend Donald Caskie had resurrected the derelict place with the express purpose of smuggling soldiers and airmen out of France, supplying all they needed to pose as merchant seamen while he made plans to get them over the border into neutral Spain. His code name, the Tartan Pimpernel, was even passed around among prisoners of war interned in France and Germany. His Seaman's Mission was the place to try and reach if you wanted to get across the Pyrenees.

At all costs we needed to avoid ending up in the internment prison at Saint-Hippolyte where all active servicemen picked up in the town by the police were banged up in dire conditions.

Inside the mission, a converted set of garages from the look of it, we found a boy wiping down tables. He called us over, asked our business then sent us hastily up a flight of stairs to knock on the door at the top.

Caskie greeted us, a short Scotsman of a certain age, alert and convivial and sharp as a tack, reserving his opinions while he quizzed us on our story. The Vichy police had not been able to pin anything on Caskie so far, but that, we soon came to realize, was only down to the meticulous operation he ran. Every time the police raided the mission searching for illegal servicemen, they found nothing out of order.

Once Caskie had satisfied himself that we were who we claimed to be, men from the 51st escaped from German captivity and trying to get home, he became warmer towards us and put us in his own room at the top of the house along with another man from the 51st, Alan Bowrie, a bank clerk from Tarbert in Harris. He'd walked down from St Valery, eating raw vegetables from the fields and sleeping rough. When Caskie brought up bowls of soup he wolfed his portion down like the starving man he was. Caskie took his tattered uniform to dispose of it and found him clean clothes.

Caskie laid out mattresses on the floor and showed us a secret panel with a crawl space if there was a raid. I slept fitfully, listening for steps on the staircase. Outside, the noises of a busy port city.

The bliss of hot coffee and fresh bread in the morning when it's laced with the hope that we might make it home one day soon.

But Caskie had sobering news.

'I have to tell you that over the past couple of days there have been arrests in the safe-house line in the north, including the Abbé in Lille who fixed your passes. Looks like we might have someone on the inside passing information to the Gestapo.'

I shook my head sadly. We both knew that the Abbé would be tortured and shot, but he would never betray his fellow countrymen.

'And you've no idea who it could be?'

'Everyone's under a cloud until this gets sorted out. In the meantime, I'm sorry to say we'll need to change our route across the Pyrenees, check the *passeurs* and that, as you may well imagine, will take a while. The men on the last trip were stopped and arrested. On their way to the rendezvous with the guide, a boy came up with a letter purportedly from me. It told them to go to a different meeting point, but sent them straight into the arms of the police. I suspect it's the same source passing on information, and it must be someone well trusted.' He sighed. 'We'll need to be extra vigilant, and when you combine that with how the German police have been tightening up lately, very anxious to stop downed airmen getting back home, then I'm afraid you will have to endure waiting a while longer before we can move you on.'

The following days were long. Caskie came up and sat with us with a bottle of whisky in the evening after curfew. Alan got out his harmonica and played a few tunes, old Scots melodies.

I turned to Caskie. 'While you were in Glasgow, you didn't come across any of the folk from St Kilda after they were evacuated, Reverend?'

'We've always had one or two passing through Glasgow, at the Gaelic church, St Columba's. Was there someone in particular you were thinking of?'

'Chrissie. Chrissie Gillies. Her mother was Mary Gillies.'

He shook his head. 'I don't know that family. But the St Kilda folk were very spread about after they left the island, and sadly too many of them were taken by the tuberculosis. The pastor there in Morvern was a friend of mine. I don't know if the ones who went there were given bad cottages or they were particularly vulnerable to the mainland viruses, but he said it took almost all of the MacKinnon family, several children.'

'The MacKinnons? But I knew them. That is a blow. But you've heard nothing about a Christina Gillies?'

He gave me a wry look. 'Am I right in thinking we are talking about a past sweetheart of yours?'

'A long time ago. I can't tell you how much I regret that I never went back to see her.'

Caskie sighed and looked into his glass, swirling the whisky around. 'The war does that, shows you what really matters.'

It was getting late. I had a feeling that Caskie had his own memories but he wasn't forthcoming.

Perhaps it was talking about the island but I dreamed of you again that night. You were singing the song that I'd held in my head for months, ever since I heard it again in the prison barracks. You were sitting by the fire in the bothy, drying your hair after the rain had caught you on the hill.

When I woke on the thin mattress on the floor of the Seaman's Mission, I was bereft. And yet there was a comfort there too, a feeling, a message almost, that you were waiting for me somewhere. But there was bitterness too, for Archie and what he did. That day had changed the course of our future. And now, were you married, perhaps, our love forgotten? If I could only stand near you again, drink in the Chrissie you have become. Just to know that you are well, a smile. It would be enough.

CHAPTER 32

Chrissie
ST KILDA, 1927

It had taken every fibre of my body to stop me running out to call Fred back, but I knew I must let him go. And when he had finished all that he must do at his university, then his love would bring him back to me. I did not doubt it, though the pain of him going would be great.

As to Archie, I cast him from my mind, only glad that Fred had known nothing of his friend's readiness to betray him.

It was hard seeing the bothy at the end of the village abandoned again, the windows dark each night. I went and sat inside there sometimes, picking up the things that Fred had left behind, holding them. A jumper that needed mending, a chipped cup he used to drink from. He would be back soon, I felt it, for our love was a living thing still, growing and breathing as surely as all the birds in the air. I saw him stepping from a rowing boat and running up to the village where we would meet each other again.

'She's met a fairy on the hill,' was what Allie said when mother remarked on how I always had my thoughts far away of late.

We could feel the chill in the air each evening as the days shortened and autumn approached. A huge and bitter storm swept across the island and tore away the green tops of the potato crop, poisoned what lay in the ground with salt. At least the grass still had time enough for one last growth so we might cut it for winter hay for the beasts. The village was out as one, working to scythe and twist stooks, or storing the hay in the cleits, slotting handfuls between the gaps in the stones to let the wind do its drying work faster.

I was up on the slopes of the glen, working with the scythe, when I first felt a strange weariness that I had never known before, a weakness that carried on day after day. I began to wonder if I was ill or simply heartbroken. The fog came back, cold and wet, and left us in a small space where you could see no further than the next bothy, the tops of the hills now only a memory. How I longed to be away from our island then, standing wherever Fred might be. When I helped Mrs Munro in the schoolroom, I looked at pictures of forests or fields, of city streets, and wondered, is this what it is like where Fred is?

By the time October ended, I knew the problem. Come May, there would be a child. Perhaps I should leave the island well before that date to spare the shame on my family? And yet, even as I sat in the chapel and listened to the minister's sermon on sin, I could not feel sad on behalf of the child growing in me, for this child had done nothing wrong any more than the lambs or the flowers or the winds that are God's creation. The text for the day was, 'Behold, I am making all things new.' Angus MacDonald expounded on the text for a long time, but all I heard was this assurance, a message for me: the child would not have the sins of the past but only its future in the Lord's creation.

The men were out on the hills now to catch the sheep. Sometimes they rowed across to Soay where the little brown sheep were as wild as goats and needed all the dogs and men to get them dipped. As I helped my father at the fank with the dipping of the black-faced sheep up at the gap, I realized that my time of weakness had passed. The child pressed inside me, making me more solid in my stomach, so I was gaining in strength and energy. At night I pondered on the child, the sky perfect in its own darkness, stars sharp as glass, a moon like a polished lamp watching over us.

The winter season was ever a time of much work for us. Supper done, we went along to each other's bothies turn by turn to ceilidh and card the rough wool into tufts like smooth waves ready for spinning long into each night. In the day there were other tasks: my father and the men slaughtered sheep and I helped my mother make tripe and puddings. There was cheese-making, the cow's milk still rich from the summer grass. We mixed it together with the sheep's milk to give our cheese the sweetness it was famous for, though we did not let the tourists ever watch us milk the sheep lest they laugh at us. I helped lift what remained of the potatoes on the day when the village went out to bring them in. We had precious little growing in the soil after the storm. As I worked, even though I was hot, I never once took off the shawl wrapped across my front for I feared that my secret was beginning to show.

And all the while, my thoughts were on Fred. I felt it in my bones, strong as any belief in God, that he would come back for me one day. I could have put my hand out in the dark and found the solidness of him, I believed so strong. For how could he not feel the same and so come back to me?

The hurricanes came in with no relent, the village boat put up for winter under a layer of turf and boulders. So he could not have come back to me even if he wanted to, with the waves marching on us in droves and making the cliffs shudder beneath their fists. In the day, the little children were not allowed to go to school alone, their fathers and older brothers holding tight to them with one hand and to the walls of the bothies with the other, trusting to God in the gaps between. No, there would be no boats coming near in such weather, and so how could I be disappointed?

One morning, almost four months after Fred left, I made my way with difficulty and care through the gale to aid Mrs Munro as usual in the schoolroom, grateful for the lessening of the wind's din inside the school's thick walls. The window on the seaward side had been boarded up with a plank where the wind had smashed a pane. It was gloomier than usual in the room and Mrs Munro had lit a lamp as well as banking up the fire. I sat and heard the small children read and then I helped them with their sums, all the while the heat from the fire making me wish I might remove my shawl.

At the end of the day, Mrs Munro asked me to wait after the children were gone. Her long face was kind and sadly serious. A wisp from her grey hair pleat was bothering her and she pushed it back twice.

'Chrissie, does your mother know?'

I said nothing, but my hands went to cover my stomach. I shook my head.

'This is a sad day. I did not expect this of you, Chrissie. You know you cannot come and teach the children any more. It would not be the right example.'

I hung my head. 'Yes.'

'And can you tell me who the father is?'

To this I made no reply.

'Well, I can make a guess. But only you can know the truth of it, and if you will not say. . . Oh, here's a sorry story, Chrissie. Will you tell your mother to come and see us at the manse this evening?'

I nodded, tears running down my face. 'Have you anything else to tell me, Chrissie?' She waited a long while, my tears falling onto the wooden floor, making dark drops on the dusty planks, but I had no voice.

'Well, you had better get home then.' Then she came and put her arms around me. I realized she too was crying. 'You've chosen a hard path for yourself. It will not be easy, not any of it.'

★

Early in December, snow fell, the whole island transformed by a pristine white scrim. I stared out at the bleached land, blue shadows marking the contours, and it seemed that we were on an island newly formed. I held my hands across the pressure of my rounded middle and thought of the little white bones forming smooth inside, bone of my bone, a child of this place. Against the dazzling white, the sea and the sky were delicate blues, pale and lovely. I kept going out just to look at it, almost intoxicated on the wonder of it all as though I'd been at the brandy in the cupboard. I thought, well, it is the time of Mary, who had no earthly father to show for her child, a time when every mother is glad of her miracle even though it is so difficult. And then I was sad, because didn't Mary have her hard-working, steadfast Joseph?

By noonday, the sky had begun to take on a pink stain in the clouds, a lilac line dusky at the horizon reminding us that the day was already leaving. And it was around that time of snow that Ewen Ian came to call most nights, cluttering up our kitchen with his big long legs, taking a hank of sheep's wool from the basket to card it to and fro in that slow deliberate way he had until I felt my very nerves worn down and ragged, waiting for what I knew he would say sooner or later.

Ewen Ian helped my father put up the loom, the sound of hammering along the village street as every home did the same. My father and my mother worked late each night, taking it in turns to lengthen the tweed bolts. I tried to help, but soon fell asleep over the threads, and they walked me through to my room where I slept with the thud of the shuttle weaving back and fro, the clack of the foot boards being pulled and pushed in a rhythm that went with the beating of my heart and the pumping of blood as the child inside me knit together and grew.

I thought of a letter from him, what he might say if he wrote, how I might write back and let him know what had happened to me, the happiness he would surely feel then.

At last, Tormod brought word that he'd seen a trawler sheltering from the storm over in Glen Bay. It took two more days before the winds would let the trawler into Village Bay, the sea rising and sinking like our hopes. Perhaps it was a boat that had picked up our mail. The old ones especially were sorely longing for letters from their children, and for the supplies and money that they sent home. Finlay was out there with the old lifeboat that is our only boat now, anxious to see if he could persuade the captain to let him have some tobacco, but he came back with the news that the boat had not brought our letters. The captain would, however, take our letters and post them in Fleetwood. A great flurry in the village to get letters off with the boat.

I wrote my letter in my thoughts.

Christmas came, though we did not make much of Christmas in the way that the nurse and the minister's wife did, since we keep the old dates. But the children went to the manse for a party with paper hats and cake and sweets. On New Year's Day, with the snow deep across the village, every wall and stone buried or added to, and the sky above the white hills a heavy blue grey, Ewen Ian came to our house again. He asked my father if he and I might be married.

I could see the hope in my parents' faces as my father passed on the message with Ewen Ian still standing there. 'But it is up to Chrissie,' Father said.

You could discern the shape of the child beneath my clothes now, no disguising it any more. It was a generous offer he made. It seemed I had no other options. It was clear to the village by then that I had been more than friends to one of the boys who had stayed that summer past, though I would not say a word on the matter. So what hope was there for me now? And I knew that Ewen Ian did truly love me. All three faces, so hopeful and wanting one answer. They had to shake their ears when I told Ewen that I could not marry him.

My mother swallowed her disappointment, and my father was grave. Poor Ewen Ian stood his ground and said, 'If you change your mind, Chrissie, I will be here. I will wait and you will see, we will make a good home. And the child I will raise as my own.'

'I am sorry, Ewen Ian. For all I admire you as a brave and honest man, I can't do it.'

My parents said no more about Ewen Ian after he had gone. They never did press me though it was all they wanted. There never was a home more silent than ours that night. But I had heard my mother speak to Ewen Ian as he left. 'Give her time. It's aye hard to raise a bairn on your own.'

CHAPTER 33

Chrissie
ST KILDA, JANUARY 1928

The rest of the winter was harsh. No more boats came. I wrote a letter and folded it inside a tobacco box, tied it to a piece of wood that might float. I struggled down to the rocks where they had launched mail buoys before in the worst of the winter famines in years gone by in the hope that they might reach the mainland. I threw my letter into the waves, hoping it might make land – though I did not write his name upon it.

I went to sit with Allie MacCrimmon in her sooty cottage and took her a twist of black tea. I knew she had run out since she drinks it so strong.

'Oh, if only the trawler was in from Aberdeen, I could ask the captain for tea and sugar for they always help us,' she sighed.

'Oh, Allie, are you out of the sugar too?'

She reached across and gripped my wrist. 'It's not me I worry for. You must take care of yourself, Chrissie, for no one else can care for the precious child inside you.'

I nodded. Old Allie had birthed children in the years before they had the knowledge that antiseptic and boiled water could fight the tetanus fever. It had carried off all eight of her babies.

'I will, Allie. I'll take good care.'

'And I'll give you a bottle of my fulmar oil, to put on the cord when they cut it. The best medicine.'

'I don't think the nurse will let us do that any more. But I like the wool you have spun very much.'

She had got some of the rarest wool from the white Soays, and spun the thread very fine. I held the skein in my hands, the wool soft enough for the most delicate skin – and with a little washing, the smokiness from Allie's home would come out in time. I took the needles from the pocket in my apron and began to cast on enough stitches for a little jacket.

'And I won't have Callum to help me dig the crofts this year,' she said. 'But I'm sure Tormod will help now he's too big for school.'

'Poor Tormod. Aren't they saying he will do everything now there's so few men on the island?'

'It's a heavy burden for you young ones that are left with too many among us old.'

I distracted Allie from her gloomy mood by asking her to sing. But halfway through the song of the seal maid, she fell asleep. I put my knitting away, banked up the peats to keep the fire going and crept out.

Not until February did we see another trawler call by in the bay. The village men rowed out to ask if the crew could let us have flour and tea and paraffin, and take an order for food supplies to the mainland. Starved of news and tobacco they went on deck to talk a while with men from the outside world. And we were left with a boat cold once again, with all the village sick and old Allie dying of it, though you and I did not get it, Rachel Anne. I was determined to keep you safe, you see.

March brought everyone out to dig the crofts, carrying seaweed up to add to the new potato beds in front of the homes, freshly dug into new rigs.

The days were lightening and our hearts lifted as some secret message told thousands upon thousands of birds that it was time to return once more; fulmars gliding and floating level with the land along the cliff tops; the black-tipped, chiselled wings of the gannets flying into the rocky bastions of Boreray.

'Listen,' I said to you while the birds filled the air with messages and songs and crackles and chatter. The first time you had heard our music here. The song of your home.

The weaving was finished and the looms were coming down when at last the puffins came back, more and more each day until the sky above us each evening was that dizzying, dipping wheel of black feathers again, birds spilling from the cliffs like a giant plucking of feathers into the wind.

By now we had the first fulmars taken from the cliffs, the winter-lean adults. And it was cruel to take them before they could lay their chicks, but we had not eaten fresh meat for so many weeks and my body was craving good sustenance more than it ever had. There were moments when you moved and I could feel the shape of a foot, an elbow, the rounded hardness of a head pressing under my skin, before you turned again and became a smooth world all to yourself.

The first week in May, and after long discussions in front of the post office that morning, the men had gone down to paint the boat. My mother and the women were setting up the barrels of water to begin waulking the tweeds, felting them down into cloth that would be tight enough to keep out the weather. They were sitting around a board placed across two chairs and passing the cloth back from one bowl to the other, thumping the wool onto the plank in time to a song so old that most of the words had become a nonsense, when I knew you were coming.

I stayed in the house as long as I could, pacing up and down, singing to myself, for I did not want to disturb anyone on such a busy morning for work – though I wished there was someone who knew my news and would rush in and say how glad they were that you would soon be here, someone who would hold my hand and smile at me with shining eyes for the joy of you. I kept my pains and my quiet joy to myself. Around noon, when the village ate their cheese and oatcakes, my mother came to fetch my father's food to take over to him, and she saw me kneeling by the bed with my arms out, groaning.

The nurse was not pleased that I had left it so long before calling her down. Nurse Williamina Barclay was a thin little lady with a clipped Edinburgh voice and a hooked nose like a bird, as sharp as antiseptic. She had a man's indefatigability but was the kindest of souls. She fetched her tins of Keating's powder and clean sheets and had my mother and the neighbours putting water to boil. I'd seen my cow birth her calf, so there were few surprises for me as to how things went from there on, except that I was lost in a world of dizziness and pains with the sound of the women along the village street beating the board with the wet cloth and singing a song, 'Feathers and eggs, feathers and eggs, oh the birds the birds and feathers.' The pain came in waves until I expected I would die, but sooner than anyone thought, the nurse cried, Chrissie, you have a girl. They gave you to my mother while the nurse tied the cord and doused me in antiseptic, then washed and wrapped you in a square of fresh sheet.

And all this time, you had not cried. I raised myself up on my elbow for I knew the quiet of a lamb that needs to have breath blown in its nostrils. By the time they gave you to me, the minister had already arrived in the room to pray, and I feared they had given you to me to say goodbye. It was a long time before we saw you breathing well and even then you were such a quiet child. I named you Rachel Anne, for my mother's mother. I sat and held you in the darkening as the sound of evening prayer came from along the village and my father stood in silent prayer by the hearth. You fed a little through the night, and each time I held you close in a goodbye, for you seemed so frail and quiet. I had remembered you before I opened my eyes in the morning in the half-light, and oh, it was a joy to me when I saw your blue eyes, open and watching me so calmly and so new.

Everyone in the village came to see you with such solemn, fierce happiness over the next days, for we had kept you safe and kept you with us. There is no child on St Kilda that is not held precious. All you needed came with them, old garments stored in trunks or newly made by the women's hands. You did not have a named father, my Rachel Anne, but you had a whole village to care for you. For there are no people more glad on earth than the people of St Kilda to see a baby, and you had so many grandfathers and grannies to rock your crib or bring you fresh milk as you grew or eggs or lamb when they were brought over from Soay or Dùn.

I had no father to give to you, not yet, but I had this people to give you. And I believed in my heart that there was no better place or family that a child might have than this island, this jewel that had fallen from the pocket of God and where all men feel Him near and find the blessed solace of being welcome at every hearth along the strand of lighted bothies, be it even in the greatest and the darkest of storms. And soon, I whispered over your downy head, soon he will come home to us. For what is faith but the sure hope of things that will come but are not yet seen.

It was not a hard thing to endure the months and months and all through the winter. The summer would be here again, and then he would return. I would give you to your father, the joy of you in his eyes, your small hand in his own.

CHAPTER 34

Fred

MARSEILLE, 1941

A loud banging on the door downstairs. If the French police were going to carry out a raid, it was always in the morning. We swung into action, quietly moving floorboards and bookcases with hidden alcoves to slide inside the stuffy spaces. I heard Caskie straightening the room then going downstairs with a calm, steady step.

The police were there for at least an hour, turning over beds and emptying drawers in their frustration. I could hear them barking for men to show their papers, all clean. They spent a long time in Caskie's room but failed to find the logbook where he recorded every man that came or went. Not that it would have helped them since all Caskie's notes were in shorthand Gaelic.

Later that afternoon, our forged papers arrived courtesy of a boy with a basket of fish.

'No more hiding under the floorboards you'll be pleased to hear,' said Caskie. 'You can take yourself off to the rest of the building, boys, there's billiards, a reading room, but no going out into Marseille alone for now.' He took me to one side. 'And I want you to meet the man who will be organizing the next stage over the Pyrenees. A great friend of mine, one of the founders of the escape route, and no better man.'

We walked down into the same room where we'd first presented ourselves as dusty escapees, now officially merchant seamen. So long as we were civilians with documents it was perfectly legal for Brits to be in Marseille under Vichy law.

Our contact was already at the bar, his back to us, short cropped fair hair, a grey suit. He stood and turned towards us, the flash of a gold tiepin, neatly polished shoes. I all but stumbled on a rough floorboard. There was Archie Macleod, his arm outstretched in greeting. I stopped dead, unable to move for a moment.

'Fred Lawson. After all these years.' A look of shock on his face.

'You know each other?' said Caskie.

'Went to university together,' Archie said.

'We were both on St Kilda,' I added.

'Then you'll know what safe hands you are in.' Caskie called to the boy laying tables. 'Tony, could you get us some tea if you've a moment?' The boy came back with three thick seaman's mugs.

'I think this calls for a little something,' said Archie, taking a silver flask from his coat pocket. He tipped a measure into his tea and offered the flask round. I shook my head, as did Caskie. Archie raised his mug to us and drank.

I tried to take in Archie's words as he spoke, essential information about crossing over into Spain, but I'd been swept back to that last day, raw and bereft. Even more distracting was the lump of rage I felt in my chest. I wanted to thrash Archie Macleod. The last man I would trust. I searched his face for a trace of the boy I had known. So this was Colonel Macleod now, working out of the British Embassy in Madrid, so he claimed. His face was heavier, cheeks pulled down by the extra flesh, the puffy eyes of a drinker, though the same boyish blue. His hand seemed to have become blurred and larger, straying towards the flask in his coat, tipping out a little more. The years had treated Archie badly. He looked middle-aged. Every so often, his eyes went to mine, unsure, as if checking my reaction, but I swiftly disengaged. I wasn't going to let him believe his charm could work on me. I had forgotten nothing.

'Main point is,' he was saying, 'we'll need to scout out a new route. I don't think we need to change the *passeur*, I'm pretty sure he's solid. But we'll see. And in the meantime, if your papers are in order then it's a case of lying low here in Marseille until we're ready.'

'Papers yes, but still no ration cards,' said Caskie. 'If these boys are staying a while they'll need them.'

Archie nodded at me. 'I can do something about that, if one of you can go to the American Embassy with me to sign.'

'Thank you, Archie,' said Caskie. 'And now I have errands to run if we are to have supper tonight. You've no doubt much to talk about after so long.'

We sat in silence, Archie swirling his cold tea. I rubbed the side of my jaw, realizing that I'd been clenching my teeth.

'So, how did you come to be in Marseille?' I asked.

'Probably like you,' Archie replied. 'Fought with my unit, always in retreat, across northern France as the Boches pressed in. We were on the outskirts of St Valery when we saw it go up in flames, heard we'd surrendered. So a group of us set out to walk south. Never want to eat a raw potato again or sleep in a field. Made it this far and ended up as part of Caskie's little band of hope. Along with a few others in the town. And you?'

'Captured a couple of times, made it down to Marseille. Hoping to get home.'

'And you will. You must.' He stared into the dregs in his mug. 'I am glad to see you again. I can't tell you how much.' He looked up from under a wrinkled brow.

I gave a smile, or something like it.

'I've missed you no end, Fred. Do you think about when we were younger, the island?'

'I think about it.'

He sniffed, shifted on his stool, pulling at his jacket so he wasn't sitting on the hem. 'You know, I tried to look you up.'

'I was away a lot. Overseas.'

Another silence. Perhaps he had tried to contact Lachlan before he passed away. I'd never know.

'Why don't I come by and pick you up first thing tomorrow? There may be some queuing to do at the embassy.' He stood up to go. Paused. 'Look, Fred,' he began, 'about Chrissie—'

I held up my hands. 'Stop right there, if you don't mind. That's all in the past and we're going to have to work together now, so let's just leave it at that.'

'Right. All right. We'll leave it there.'

He was gone. I held tightly to the bar, rigid with the shock of seeing him again.

It wasn't all right, it would never be right – and this was the man I was going to have to trust with my life. An unthinkable idea had begun to form as I stared into the stains stuck to the sides of my cold mug of tea. No one knew the identity of the traitor in the chain of safe houses and *passeurs* from Lille to Spain.

Anyone, Caskie had said. It could be anyone.

All day, I thought of talking to Caskie, telling him my misgivings about Archie, but what did I have to go on, really? A past quarrel and a gut feeling. Not enough to hang a man. But I would be watching Archie Macleod like a hawk.

Later, lying in the stuffy back room in the dark, I thought, but it wasn't just Archie to blame, was it? I let my mind go to a thought I didn't like to dwell on. Dark and painful. Because in the end, hadn't Chrissie chosen Archie that day?

I'd never been able to understood how it could be so. I'd felt married to her heart and soul for all the differences there were between us. And thought she had felt the same.

And my part, my fault in the matter? Leaving in anger, refusing to hear what you might have had to tell me, Chrissie.

And regrets? And forgiveness? I left, blaming you. But what terrible times did you go through as the island was cleared? When I was never there to help you, never by your side?

And now the years had gone by. Probably, you'd married, someone on the mainland, children perhaps.

But what if you hadn't? What if there was a chance, just a chance, that if I saw you again then we could start anew, find in the ashes something of what we shared so long ago?

CHAPTER 35

Chrissie
ST KILDA, JUNE 1928

I met every boat at the jetty that summer, could feel a boat coming from miles away. I was there in front of Neil's tin hut each time the mails were handed out, waiting to hear my name called, and each time disappointed.

In June, we welcomed home two distant relatives on a visit from Australia, a Reverend MacQueen and his wife. Their grandparents had left the island some seventy years ago, after the Great Disruption, when the Spirit fell on the islands in the days when a gospel ship was seen blazing on dry land and holy fire and languages came down on the people in a great revival. The laird here would not let people choose their own minister of inspiration as they wished. He locked the church to make the people see sense and accept the minister he chose. So thirty people from the village had left for Australia where they could worship as they saw fit.

The Reverend MacQueen and his wife had heard about our island paradise from their grandparents, a place that had lived not by money but by kindness and community, by faith and hard work, where all that the people wore and ate was taken from the land God had given them, grinding the corn by hand with a stone quern, sewing their own jackets while seated outside on the grass. A jewel of an island.

You could see in their faces how shocked they were by the island, by the little we had and how simply we lived – living in squalor, as I heard him tell his wife.

They were all for asking the entire village to come away with them to Australia where life would be so much easier and better.

'And didn't half the St Kildans who left us in fifty-two die on the ship from the measles?' said old Finlay. No one was of a mind to go.

'If you want me to leave here then you will have to send the policeman to drag me out of my house,' Neil told them.

In the end, the only change our cousins caused was to leave an Australian flag, which we flew from the school chimney in their honour till the wind whipped it away.

Which was the morning that saw me stop going down to meet every boat? What happened to make me no longer want to go? The realization that summer was almost over and yet he had not written. I could no longer bear the pain of being disappointed. All the same, whenever a boat was in the bay, so long as there was a faint chance that someone might come running to the bothy with a message – 'A letter for you, Chrissie, found in the bottom of the sack' – then my skin prickled with a hopeless anticipation until the boat was gone.

Perhaps I was the only one to feel our isolation as a blessing through that next winter. There was a peacefulness in not expecting any news as the months went by.

And you were such a bonny child, sitting up and looking around. The dog, your dearest friend who let you grab his hair, and I spent long hours watching the fleeting expressions dawning new on your face as you tried to fathom the life around you, tiny frowns and startles and smiles. I carded the wool and rocked your crib with my foot each evening, Mother's spinning wheel creaking its own rhythm as we sang the old songs and new ones that came to me while you slept and rocked like a little boat in the bay. The loom's clacking and the soft shush of the shuttle going until two or three in the morning, waking after a few hours' sleep to begin the work of the day, caring for the beasts in the byre and putting on the meal to cook. Soaking out the salt in the fulmar flesh so that you did not turn your head from the spoon.

At last, a lull in the winter storms. We could hardly believe our ears, but there truly was a steam whistle sounding in the bay. It was Captain Tonner's ship, the only one of the Fleetwood trawler captains who would still take the mails for us while the dispute with the boat owners and the post office carried on, the boat owners saying they will not allow the captains to bring the winter mail unless the post office pays the cost. I waited in the bothy doorway with you bundled up in your blanket, watching everyone run down to the jetty to see the rowing boat launched, how it bounced up and down on the unsettled sea, how you held out your arms, laughing at the sparkle of it in the winter sun.

After so long, there were eight sacks of letters, greetings from the young ones far away, gifts and money for their parents, two red bags of post just for the manse. I took you down to join the people clustered around the steps of Neil's post office hut as he called out the names. My heart going faster and faster until there it was, Christina Gillies. A parcel passed over heads. By the time it was in my hand I'd a whole story in my mind of how Fred must have somehow heard, how he'd wrapped up a gift for the baby, how he was planning to come and get us.

It was Callum's careful school script on the brown paper. He'd posted a doll for you, a pink plastic creature hard as a nail with wispy yellow hair. You have it still, and we were grateful for it, though my heart broke a little more each time I saw it, recalling the disappointment that came with it.

★

Soon the land in front of the bothies was a small patchwork of brown rigs and new barley once again, not the wide sweeps of barley and potatoes that the old ones remembered but as much as we could plant. The sheep and the great shaggy cattle had been fenced out above the dyke wall so that they could not eat the new shoots. You sat outside on the grass as the irises pushed up and flowered yellow, and the children played with you and brought you the new puppies to hold like dolls. You were a year old now, and Fred had never once seen our beautiful child, never heard your name.

I thought of writing a letter to Archie, but I did not trust him not to make trouble from it, so I listened when the factor came in case he might speak of the boys who had once lived in the cottage at the end. But he never mentioned Fred's name. I heard from Mrs Munro that Archie had taken work far away in France, in Paris, but of Fred there was not one bit of news.

I turned my mind to work, of which there was plenty. It was a relentless life and the fatigue never left your bones with so many too old to do the heavy labour but who still needed turf to keep the fire burning and food to put on the table. And always so many tasks still to be done.

I stood outside with you, holding you by your hands as you tried out your first steps along our village row, the walls of the houses not whitewashed any more but streaked with grey and damp, the street sprouting grass where once it was kept so neat, the roof falling in at the end of an empty house. I saw with a pinched heart that our village had the look of a place already abandoned.

The laird did not press us too hard for our rents since we had not the means to pay him, but he took what he could from the island in recompense. Tweed and salted ling. Old Mr MacDonald was too embarrassed to tell the steward that when he took away the only bolt of tweed he'd made that year, he took all that the old man had left to sell. So how was Mr MacDonald to fill his cupboard for the winter? And more than ever, after so many cold autumns and bad harvests, we had need of money to buy in stores for the time of the long dark.

Nurse Barclay had gone along the village taking it upon herself to remind the reverend's wife and everyone else to put in their order for winter supplies in good time. She chided us because our lists were all too short. I marvelled that she did not understand how truly poor we were in the village. But she was a good soul, kept busy all summer with so many ailments from the old ones.

That summer brought more tourists than we had ever seen. I was sitting outside the bothy with Mother's spinning wheel while you played on the path – the tourists love to watch the thread grow and disappear as if it were some secret incantation unknown to the modern race – when a man came and sat on the bench nearby. I could feel from his attention that this was not an average tourist. He took out a small notebook and pencil. He introduced himself as one of the newspaper men, a Mr Alpin MacGregor from *The Times* of London. He wore the clothes of the gentry, but everything so flamboyant as if he were play-acting a Scottish gent of the highlands, the plus fours wide and baggy and a great bonnet cap. The smallest and shiniest brogues, long padded cheeks and a sharp nose.

'Call me Alasdair,' he said, and he spent some time admiring the child for her cleverness. I kept my face half hid by the hood of my shawl, a demure St Kildan. I had no wish to talk to one of the paper men.

Then he asked me if I thought St Kilda would last another winter.

I snapped my thread I was so annoyed, my foot too hard on the pedal.

'I don't mean to offend you, and if I lived here I can see that I would never want to leave, not on a day like this, but you must admit that the St Kildans are in a daily struggle against nature and I ask myself if you are not beginning to lose the battle. Next winter, perhaps?'

'We have managed before and why should we not again,' I told him. Just a babe, but you looked up, alarmed by the sharpness in my voice.

'But with such a decline in able-bodied men to man the boats and fish and cut turf and do the tasks necessary to your survival here? I hear that you can't get out to Boreray any more and the sheep there are being left to go wild. Can your fragile economy really survive the depredations of another winter, cut off for months? And what of the fishing boats with their mail strike? What if someone should become acutely ill?'

I gathered up my Rachel Anne.

'I do not think it is any business of yours, Mr Alpin. And I would ask that you leave us be.'

'Come now. You must know how closely the public have followed St Kilda's fortunes for years. The relief ships sent out in time of need, weren't they arranged by newspapermen?'

My father appeared then. He had heard the man's insistent questioning. You were beginning to cry.

'We will bid you good day, sir,' he said.

We went in and closed the door. The newspaper man stayed out on the path with his notebook, but the worries he had spelled out, they came right inside with us, sat down by the fireplace.

The last tourist boat left. A quiet fell on the village. The feathery stacks of puffins and fulmars in flight around the cliffs gone. All was stone and wind again. I took you to the empty schoolroom where there was still the piano. It had been tuned by a visitor from the summer boats and I showed you some of the tunes I knew, your little hand on mine to feel the notes. One of the high keys would not play any more, but we could still make do. And, oh, you were clever, humming the melody and standing with your chin up so you could better see the notes as you reached to test the songs with your little hands, looking for the note you wanted. You were puzzled when we went back a month later and the damp had warped the strings out of tune again.

As we headed back across the grass, I heard a great whooshing of wind coming down Conachair. A storm rushing in like a banshee. We got back to the bothy before the gale hit. It pummelled the houses like a vengeance, the walls shuddering with the blows. The rains ruined the crops and the hay. We had to go down on the cliffs to pull grass so that the cattle might have something to eat through the long dark. I felt a clenching in my stomach, knowing that we would be asking for charity again before the winter was out.

But worse was to come. I saw Captain Tonner in front of Neil's post office, the gloomy looks on the men's faces as the men listened to him.

'I am very sorry about it,' Captain Tonner was saying. 'Fifty pounds in coal it took me to get in last winter with the letters, and I'm only paid ten by the post office, you see. I can't do it any more.'

Old Finlay spent the winter writing letters of complaint to the government. But his letters stayed on his dresser, waiting for a boat to take them. 'It is the mainland that makes itself far away from us,' Finlay said as he sat in our kitchen. 'If they would send us mail on the lighthouse ship as they did in the war, then we might live well here.'

'When I was a child,' said my grandmother Rachel, 'the boats never came in winter, but we lived on our own stores with no help from outside.'

'And didn't we have fifty men then to grow those crops so we could store enough to last the winter? And even back then, the winter was often hungry,' Finlay reminded her.

She sighed, pulled her knitting closer to her eyes in the lamplight. 'We must trust in God,' she said.

My father and the men took the boat over to Dùn to fetch off a sheep. But in the narrow gap between the island and Hirta, the wind came in so hard that it swept the boat over and the men had to swim for shore. My father when we found him on the beach was barely alive. He lingered a few more days but the pneumonia was in his lungs. And no one will ever know if he might have lived if we had a doctor or a hospital near, or a passing ship to take him off the island. Nurse Barclay saw it as her failure. Mother told her it was the will of God that he should go.

We laid him in our small cemetery, covered him with earth so that the irises and daisies would mark where he lay and set a boulder there taken from the sea. For three days we mourned him, and then the island claimed us again to wrest our living from what it gave us.

And my father's death meant we no longer had enough men to row a boat as far as Soay. The sheep there, the gannet harvest on Boreray, all lost to us now.

Our supplies and our sprits low, cut off from the world, we dreaded the winter to come.

CHAPTER 36

Chrissie
ST KILDA, 1929

If you could eat the majesty of the wild splendour of the seas in winter, then we would never have gone hungry, black waves with towers of spray coming up over the top of Dùn, or rampaging a hundred feet high against Oiseval's cliffs. There were days when the howling of the gales left us deaf, ears ringing. To go out at night and feel yourself in the mighty hand of the Atlantic wind was to be humbled indeed. No human strength could ever match it.

The MacKinnons with their eight children were soon low on their stores and surviving on thin porridge. Their bairns had no boots that winter, went barefoot across the frozen grass, rubbing their cold feet together to try and make some warmth as they sat in the schoolroom.

Even the minister and his family had run out of lard and tea and flour. The nurse chided them for not listening to her warnings to put in a large enough order. But no one told her that our situation in the village was far worse, for to let her know would be the same as asking for gifts from her cupboard. But how we looked forward to her invitation to go to tea.

Every week she would ask the women and the children to come to tea with her and give them advice on any little troubles they had. She gave the children a few sweets each time from the jar on her dresser. 'They are such good children,' she said. 'I have never met bairns who did not eat sweets at once. Yours save them for later with such restraint.'

What she did not understand was that the children took the sweets home to share with their parents and grandparents since those sweets were the only sugar seen in the St Kildan homes. We soon had nothing left to eat but potatoes and oatmeal and the birds we had from the island. We rarely took a lamb for the table since they were our rent for when the factor came. Often, we went hungry that year, though not you, Rachel Anne, for you were well over a year old and growing fast.

Christmas was hardest, not a word from our loved ones. We had our New Year service warmed only by the gas sconces in the walls, the weather outside black and howling. As soon as the minister opened the door for us to walk back to our bothies, the wind tore it out of his hand and smashed it broken against the wall.

By January, we were living on thin oat gruel, eking out the salted fulmar. Ewen Ian came by with a little wooden sheep he had carved for you, Rachel Anne. He sat solemn by the fire, and said that if it weren't for his mother and the old ones then he would go tomorrow if a boat came by.

'Don't say so, Ewen Ian,' my mother told him. 'Come the spring we will recover as we always have.'

He shook his head. 'We are too few and too alone.'

We were left more shaken by his words than by any storm. We had never had such a silent supper.

We ran low on paraffin so that we had to weave by the light of the smoky fulmar oil in a cruachan lamp, which we had mostly consigned to the byre for many years, and which gave a poor light for the eyes. Mother and I took it in turns at the loom since we were a house of women now. I pushed the shuttle to and fro, dreaming of potatoes hot with butter, of bacon and bread, of sweet biscuits and hot tea with a sugar in it.

I was in the schoolroom one afternoon, searching for a book I might read again, when I heard voices through the open door into the church. It was the nurse speaking with the minister's wife. She was fretting at how much sickness we had had in the village, wet eczema and bad chest infections. Little Kirsty with the TB.

'They have low herd immunity with their poor diet,' the nurse said. 'They need fresh food to give the children a chance. They refuse to admit it and leave but I fear St Kilda is dying.'

I replaced the book quietly and tiptoed out, but my heart was going fast, filled with anger at what she'd spoken. Angry with the truth of it.

Hungry, depressed by our isolation, we were in our beds with influenza when the *Nona* struggled through a storm to bring us our Christmas letters. We gathered around the captain, coughing, wrapped in our shawls and blankets, and such lists of provisions from all sides – not that most of us had the money to pay for it. He promised to take a message to the world of how badly the island was faring so that the government might send us some mercy aid, and return with more supplies.

But while we waited, the thing that we fear most arrived. Mary Gillies, who was expecting her third child, was taken to bed with appendicitis. Nurse Barclay did all she could but she said that it was a hospital was needed to save Mary. No radio mast, no boat to go for help, what could we do?

It was only by chance that a Norway drifter came by, wanting to shelter from the storms. We watched Mary as she was rowed out to the ship, wrapped in a shawl and waving to her children.

She died in the Glasgow hospital and the child with her. The illness had gone on too long for them to save her. And after Mary died, we were a broken people.

CHAPTER 37

Chrissie
ST KILDA, 1930

The end of a terrible winter. Nurse Barclay had finally understood why the children had saved their sweets, and how empty our meal chests were. She asked all the villagers to come down to the factor's house. In her front room she had a white cloth on the table, and she made us all tea, boiled almost black, the way the old people liked it. She had sugar for the tea. She had jam from Glasgow. All the things that came over on the boats now that the winter storms had eased up. The MacKinnon children were eating fast.

No shortage of supplies now. Tea, jam, paraffin. Shoes for the children. But all come too late, for after Mary's death we were defeated. When the nurse asked us how we had fared that winter past, and to speak our minds about what we thought, we were quiet. But then MacKinnon, who had the eight children, said that if he could leave, then he would go now, but since he was a man without money, then what could he do to pay the passage? The tears running down his face.

Nurse Barclay took the big brown teapot and poured out another cup for those that wanted it, saying, perhaps there was a way, that she could find help from the government. 'It seems to me,' she said, 'you have reached the end of the road and for the sake of the children you must give up the island, but before I ask them, you must make the decision to go.' No one spoke. We listened to the roaring of the peat fire as a turf brick took the flame.

Then Ewen Ian and Tormod said they too were ready to leave. And one by one, the people said yes, we would leave the island, Nurse Barclay's kind, antiseptic words guiding us to make the right decision. I turned you to the window so that you did not become upset by the men and women openly weeping.

And in the gloom of a cold and heavy mist, the men gathered in the village street next morning, the strips of dark rigs waiting for the seed potatoes to be planted. But the men agreed together: they would not plant them now. When the autumn came, there would be no one on the island to harvest them.

Only Neil Ferguson was seen out on his croft, digging the rigs over ready for planting. 'I leave my house only when I leave in my coffin,' he told us.

It was Reverend Munro who wrote a letter petitioning the ministry to help us evacuate the island. He read it out and we each of us signed. Old Finlay MacQueen made his mark since he had never learned to write.

The government minister came to see us, shocked, he said he was, by the poverty here. He told us we must learn to earn money each day. They would give us jobs planting trees, though we had never seen a tree. And as to how the evacuation would be paid for, then we would pay for it, by the sale of all our cattle and our sheep.

They told us there would be room on the boats to take only what was needed for our new lives. Not the barrels for salting the birds over winter, not the gins and fowling poles for snaring gannets and fulmars on the wet cliff edge, not the dresser or the table made by my father. None of the heavy bits of furniture could be given room on the boat. Not our own front door with the long history that went with it, nor the white mist pouring down over Oiseval or the wide bay with the dish of shimmering sea at the foot of the green slopes. All the looms were left behind. And we felt it deep in our stomachs, how we were leaving all the things that had been our livelihood, but we trusted to the future, a future none of us could imagine except in stories of electric lights and cars and trees.

Suddenly, there was a great deal to do if we were to leave before the winter closed in again. The beasts to fetch down ready for loading on to the ship. The washing of blankets and readying of clothes so that the people on the mainland would understand we were a decent people and not vagabonds who lived on charity.

Each evening, the old ones reminisced of times before the stone pier was built, before any steam trawlers or whaling ships called by, travelling back to days when there were a hundred or more people in the village, the mothers over on Boreray catching puffins, the fathers scaling the cliffs of the great sea stacs of Stac an Armin, bringing home thousands of gannets. A time when hardly anyone on the island spoke English and money was a foreign idea from the mainland.

The reverend invited us in to the manse to listen to the wireless and the evacuation being debated in Parliament, old Finlay asking me to translate. One man said it was a shameful thing that in all the British Empire across the world, the only place that should need to be evacuated was here in the British Isles. Another man wanted to know what would become of the old and destitute of St Kilda, if they would have to be sent to a workhouse or some other institution. But the government minister told him the St Kildans care for their own. We were shocked by the mention of a workhouse and hardly reassured. And we heard how four hundred people had written to the government to ask if they could settle on our island after we were gone. They were all to be refused.

So many tourists came that last summer, avid to photograph us, like beasts in a zoo, shrouded about in the tragedy of our almost starvation.

They wanted souvenirs, spinning wheels, old lamps, grinding querns. 'They can smell St Kilda is dying and are scavenging on the scraps,' said Finlay. But he put a cruachan lamp and the last of his stuffed birds in his window, a notice beside them I had helped him write: For Sale. Souvenirs of the simple race.

And we felt it, how we had become such a spectacle. One of the newsmen brought a camera to make a film of our last days. But we had seen enough pictures of ourselves through their eyes, looking poor and backwards. All he got was us hiding and covering our faces, running away along the village street, or old Mrs MacDonald taking her spinning wheel back inside, shaking her fist, too besieged to come back out all day even to fetch a cup of water from the pump, her pride stronger than her thirstiness.

Three shepherds came from Uist with their long crooks to work out how much our sheep and the cattle were worth to pay for the evacuation and get them down from the hills. But St Kilda sheep do not flock for the sheep dog but must be coaxed from their rocky haunts one by one. Our dogs are trained in this way, which would be bad for our dogs when the time came. The Uist shepherds watched as we went up to do the ruaging. The sheep were taken away then, loaded into rowing boats and taken across to the *Dunara*.

Our dear cows were next, the old folk in tears to see their friends go who had been with them for so long. The poor beasts were tied to the back of the rowing boats and had to swim across the bay to the *Dunara*, winched up in a hoist, and it was empty without their lowing, the birds and the wind now free to make all the music of the island.

Our last week on the island and a letter from the post office arrived. They had finally agreed to pay for a lighthouse ship to deliver our mail in the winter. But their aid had come too late.

There were a dozen newsmen came on the tourist boat that last week, wandering over the island with their notebooks, getting in the way and peering through windows. They had to sleep lined up on the school floor. The Admiralty packed them off down to the jetty and sent them away with the last load of sheep. We still found one fellow hiding in a cleit behind the factor's house with a crate of provisions. I recognized Mr Alpin MacGregor from *The Times*, hoping to stay and write a book about his life as a Robinson Crusoe. He was sent to help Neil Ferguson with the sacks and sacks of mail that had come, asking for a St Kilda stamp or a gannet wing for a duster or a length of tweed. He and Neil were up till the small hours sorting through it. We saw the newsman rowed out to the boat with the sacks first thing.

The reverend and Mrs Munro and their bairns and Nurse Barclay were the first to leave in the village. We embraced and cried and stood as one on the jetty and the shore as the *Dunara* left with them small on the deck. I held a book that Mrs Munro had given me, and with it an invitation to visit her one day in their new parish but I never did make the journey there. After that, we worked to load our possessions into the rowing boats to be taken to the *Harebell*, bundles and kist chests roped to our backs, lamps held aloft through the small hours of the dark, trying not to see the windows in the manse and the nurse's house which had no lamp inside to light them any more.

We slept little, our last night as one, in a place where you might go into any home for help, the doors never locked. Now to be cast into new lives scattered far apart in places we could not imagine.

My mother and I made worship in the morning. Along the village street, each home left the family Bible open on the table at the chapter of Exodus. Next to it, a dish of oats for any passing traveller, or for when we might return. We each banked the peats and left a fire burning, though we knew that by tomorrow the hearths would be cold. For the first time in hundreds of years, there would be no homely fires warming the hearths on St Kilda.

The first time we had locked our front doors. All the village out in the street now, silent. No sound of dogs barking; the men from the ministry had rounded up all the dogs and had them drowned in the bay since they could not learn the ways of mainland dogs.

One last time walking across the island together to say goodbye to the places that were part of us. A long time standing by the graves we were leaving, by Father's stone deep in the iris leaves.

'I still do not understand why we must go,' old Mrs Gillies said as we waited on the jetty. 'It is but the work of despairing Sassenachs.'

We were rowed out to the ship, the line of bothies growing smaller, Mother holding tight to the spinning wheel she loved.

All on deck now, looking back at the hills, when we felt the vibration of the engines thrumming under our feet. The land began to move away from us, the bothies and the manse growing smaller until we were out beyond the bay and the sheltering arm of Dùn. We tried to hold the bothies and the chapel with our eyes but they slid behind Oiseval and vanished. Slowly, gradually, the island grew smaller and faded until it was nothing but a blue shadow, dipping below the sea. Then a wail went up from the people, for we saw the island was leaving us. The sailors turned to the wind to hide their tears at the sound of the women's sobbing. For the sun still made a silver road home, dancing with sparks of light, but we would not tread that way again. We had no rights to go back, for the island was to be given over to the birds.

At Lochaline, we had not imagined there would be such crowds to greet us. We were taken away in motor cars, going in different directions, people standing on the running boards to see us better as we moved slowly through the crowds. I saw men on bicycles, stared back. We'd known about cars, but no one had told us to expect bicycles.

That first night in the cottage in Morvern, I slept not a wink, missing the sound of the sea and the birds settling at dusk.

I had stayed a moment in the bothy as Mother went out, quickly written in the front of the Bible that we left on the table, 'We are gone to Larachbeg in Morvern.' For I did not know how else to let him know. And so I waited, in hope, for him to find us one day. But I never dreamed so many years would go by, and still no news.

CHAPTER 38

Rachel Anne
MORVERN, 1940

It's taken several nights for my mother to finish her story. I sit on the rug, arms around my knees, staring into the peats. She's close by to me and reaches out to stroke my hair. I feel myself flinch away from her touch.

'And you never found out where he went, Fred, I mean?'

'I tried. I even wrote to Dunvegan in the end, a letter addressed to Archie. It was a long time before anything came back. Archie was indeed working in Paris, a lawyer for a shipping company. He hadn't heard from Fred in years. Archie wrote back to say he'd tried to trace him, but with Fred's only relative, Lachlan, passed away, there wasn't anyone left who Archie could contact for details.'

'And you've never spoken to Fred since that day he left the island?'

'No.'

'And he's not had any news from Archie?'

'Not that I know of. I'm sorry, Rachel Anne.'

'So he really has no idea that I exist, no idea that he has a daughter, a grown daughter, whose entire childhood he's missed? Why did you make him go away like that? Why did you drive him away? What have you done?'

I can't bear to be near my mother any more with all she asks of me with her secrets. I run out into the night, letting the door bang hard. More solace in the cold wind and clouds bright with moon and frost than in my mother.

She has her memories of the island and of my father. I have nothing.

I walk until I am almost falling with fatigue, stumbling on the rough places on the road when the moon goes in. I turn and head back in the darkness.

CHAPTER 39

Chrissie
MORVERN, 1940

She's gone, filled with accusations and hurt, and I've no answer for her. I sit with my hands clasped hard together, trying to feel the warmth of the fire. It's a story I never wanted to tell.

Perhaps she is right: I am to blame. If I had never loved Archie so much once, if I had not let him walk with me and get so close, then surely he would not have pressed and expected things that day. Got into such an anger with the drink in him when I pushed him away.

I hadn't known about Archie's lie about me until later, when Archie told me in a letter and asked me to forgive him. But was it my fault too that Fred went away? I'd told myself that if I truly loved him, then I must let Fred go and finish his studies – and when they were done he would come back to me.

But sometimes, in my darker moments, I wondered, was it my shame rather than my love that had made me push Fred to leave?

CHAPTER 40

Fred
MARSEILLE, 1941

A brisk day outside, the wind like a knife off the sea as I walked with Archie to the American Embassy. Archie seemed more businesslike, focused on the job in hand.

At the end of Rue de Forbin we came out onto the wide promenade of la Joliette, the masts of boats swinging in the wind like a winter forest, weak sun on the water, the spires of a cathedral on the hill across the bay. No red banners as in Paris, instead posters of Marshal Pétain, or ones declaring 'Vive La France'. The pavement cafes were open, doing good business in spite of the chill, crowds of people flowing past each other on their way to work or on morning errands.

Archie was right about the queues at the embassy, a line already curving around the hall, but he soon managed to get us to the front, sorted out the cards without problems. He asked me to wait while he popped in to see someone. I suspected that he was here to do business of one kind or another. A while later, he reappeared, walking at speed. I followed him as he strode out.

'Thought we might have a drink somewhere.'

Ambushed, irritated, I fell in. Listening as he pointed out the sights.

'Hotel du Louvre, the American Bar, that's where the Germans like to hang out. Not many in uniform, but they're here.' Flicking his head at a pink stone tower and castle wall on a rocky promontory. 'Fort Saint-Jean. British servicemen caught were interned there until last month. Quite a cushy number since they were allowed out on parole on a daily basis. Sadly, there's been a crackdown after one too many escapes and they've been moved away into the middle of nowhere at Saint-Hippolyte. Makes our job a lot trickier.'

We reached the old port, an inland basin that spread into the city's old centre, ringed around with crumbling tenements, some so derelict they were propped up with wooden buttresses like decaying cathedrals. An overpowering stench from piles of rotting fish guts on the cobbles, dried urine. A persistent wind stirring up eddies of straw and detritus. Children and dogs ran in swarms around the fishermen and the old women in black who sat mending nets or gutting tiny fish. I glimpsed side streets so narrow you could touch the tenement fronts each side, cobbled steps running with water, women gossiping. A woman helping a child pull his shorts back up after relieving himself.

'Interesting neighbourhood,' said Archie. 'Bristling with crooks, pimps and with intellectuals on the run from the Nazis. Anything's on sale here, if you don't mind the chance of being swindled.' He detoured into a cafe on the waterfront. 'Barman here's a good man, if you ever need to lie low. Just a thought.'

Two small black coffees, a draught from under the door, the air smoky with cheap tobacco. I felt uneasy and wrong-footed. Wasn't this just the district to take someone if they were about to disappear without a trace, in the narrow alleys and greasy water of the harbour?

Archie seemed tense as we sat opposite each other. Just like the old Archie, he was going to have his say.

'I know you said to drop it, but hear me out. I'll be leaving Marseille soon and you'll be crossing the mountains into Spain. I may not have another chance. There's no other way to say this. Look, I wanted you to know that I lied back then, more or less.'

I studied him, listening hard.

'You see, there was never anything between Chrissie and me that day. I was hurt and jealous, I suppose. I never was good at feeling abandoned. I'm not proud of it, but, yes, I did make it clear to Chrissie that I wanted her. I'd had a fair few drinks. I wanted to hurt you. But Chrissie was having none of it. She loved you, Fred, only you.'

I widened my eyes, trying to get the table back in focus as my heart began to race. 'And now you have to tell me this, when the damage is done, when it's too late. Don't think—'

'Wait. Wait. There's more.'

'More?'

'Fred, you have a daughter.'

I tried to take in what he had just told me. 'Chrissie had a child?'

'Your child.'

'What have you done? All this time. . . But how do you know?' And then I realized what he was saying. 'So you've kept in touch with Chrissie?'

'In a way, the odd letter, just to make sure they were all right. I told you, Fred, I tried to find you, but you were nowhere. You never came back. But the point I'm trying to make is that she loved you, Fred. You have to know that. She didn't marry anyone else.'

I held my head in my hands, spoke slowly. 'A child. She'll be thirteen, and I've never seen her.' I raised my head, tried to bear the sight of the man before me, who'd done far worse damage than I'd ever imagined. 'You've seen her?'

'From a distance. She doesn't know me. She's called Rachel Anne.'

'And you know that how?'

'A letter Chrissie wrote.'

'Are you quite sure there's nothing between you and Chrissie?'

'Only as a friend trying to right a wrong. I'm not that man any more, Fred.'

— 235 —

'But wait. So you must have her address. You know where Chrissie lives.'

'Yes.'

I scrambled in my pockets for a pencil, told him to write it down on a piece of paper.

'I'll make my own way back.'

I all but ran back to the mission, floating above the crowds and the scream of the sea birds. I had Chrissie's address. And Caskie had said he could get letters home through his contacts in the Church of Scotland.

Chrissie was alive. She had a daughter. We had a daughter.

And I knew where they were living, on the west coast of Scotland in Morvern.

CHAPTER 41

Rachel Anne
MORVERN, 1941

The months went by. A few postcards began to come through from the men of the 51st held in German prison camps. But what of the thousands still missing? I couldn't bear to listen to the news any more on the wireless, losing hope that we'd ever hear from my father.

It made Mother and me all the more grateful that my uncle was in a reserve occupation in the docks. Though we did not speak of him outside the house, not with the great silence about our men's fate hanging over the land.

'I think there's a letter from Uncle Callum,' I called, seeing the postie come up our path with his canvas sack. I opened the door and ran out to him.

I hurried into the kitchen. Mother was minding the porridge on the stove. I held out the envelope to her. She studied it as she stirred. It looked official, a typed address.

'I don't think that is from Callum. Put it there on the table, my hands are wet.'

She took her time, pouring tea, eyes on the letter.

'But who could be sending us a letter if it's not from Uncle Callum? Can I open it, Mother?'

'No, wait.' She brought the bowls to the table. Picked up the envelope and turned it over, thick paper. Miss C. Gillies. She frowned at that, took a knife to ease along the top fold.

'Why ever is the Church of Scotland sending me this? From the overseas department, it says.'

I looked over her shoulder. The letter was a printed sheet, the blanks filled in with typewritten words that were thicker and paler than the others. I started to read but she suddenly let it drop to the table.

'What is it, Mother?' I asked

She gave no reply.

I took the letter up, reading it aloud. Her eyes tight shut as I read, head shaking in denial. 'Private Frederick Lawson, posted missing believed dead, has been reported alive.'

She sobbed, a gulp and then clamped her hands over her face, as if with one word all the tears she had stored up from the years gone by would come gushing out.

'It's him isn't it? The boy with dark hair. My father. But where is he now? Is he here, Mother? Is he still in France? Why doesn't it say? And why does it have to be kept secret?'

'I don't know.'

'But why are they sending us this news? And why has it come from the church?'

'I really don't understand.' She took the letter back, reading it again. And then her face cleared, hope written across it. 'But if they've sent this here, then somehow, Fred's found our address. He's alive, Rachel Anne, and he wants me to know it.'

The tears had started to push their way out now, no stopping them. 'Oh, I had feared so much I'd hear he'd been lost in France. But he's alive, Rachel Anne. Fred is alive.'

She convulsed with sobs.

I took her shoulder, shook it. 'But we have to find out more. What if he's here, in hospital somewhere? It might be the only chance to see him. To meet him. We have to telephone the church offices this letter came from, now, and make them tell us more.'

'Rachel Anne, I don't think they can know any more than this or surely they would have said. But then, why would we have to not tell anyone. . . unless he's still in France, or in Germany, in prison perhaps like all the other soldiers we've heard about, all the thousands of men from the Scots regiments taken to Germany after Dunkirk.'

But I wasn't ready to give up.

'We could try phoning the church office. Please. Will you?'

'I will try, Rachel. I'll try and find out more.'

'And if he never comes home? What if he never knows about me, how I've waited for him?'

She put her arms around me, held on tight when I tried to pull away. She rocked my stiff and angry body until our tears were finished. Until there was no more to be done than continue with the day – and to wait and to hope.

I longed to meet my father, but sometimes, I saw myself standing in front of him, shouting, 'Where were you? Why didn't you come and find us?' I thought I'd always kept a part of my heart for my father, but had it, I wondered, become hard and scarred over with anger and too much waiting?

CHAPTER 42

Fred

Caskie came in to our room on the third morning with two overcoats, long and narrow with wide shoulders.

'Not quite the right apparel for mountain climbing but you will need protection above the snow line.'

Angus's had needed shortening, but Caskie knew an Arabic tailor in the old port who altered clothes to fit without questions. Angus smoothed down the fine tweed fabric. 'Must have been quite an aristocrat the man who wore this.'

'He was that,' Caskie said. 'But his mother will be happy to know that it is being used to help someone get home. Now for the journey. There will be just the two of you, a small inconspicuous party for now given the problems with the last trip. A far cry from the two or three trips a week we've been sending over recently, but we'll need to be cautious.'

He gave me a postcard with a picture of a basket of flowers. On the back was written, Uncle sends his love. Weather fine.

'If you can, as soon as you get to the Spanish side, post this and I'll know the route works.'

'I'll post it in Spain.'

He clapped my shoulder. 'So, you'll take the train to Toulouse with the guide, change there for Foix. Once in Foix you'll make contact with the mountain guide who will take you over the Pyrenees as far as the border where you'll carry on down to link up with a man who will move you on to Madrid. And then it's Gibraltar and home. If something goes wrong once you're across the Spanish border, main thing is to get to Madrid and make contact with the embassy, quietly, back-door sort of thing. Sadly, there'll be Spanish police, Guardia Civiles, patrolling the foothills on the Spanish side but at least if you're picked up by them there's a good chance of repatriation – eventually, Spain being neutral in theory.'

'Eventually meaning?'

'Some months at least. They have an internment camp at Miranda d'Ebro. Best avoided.'

That evening, I went and sat in the little chapel that Caskie had set up in a room off the dining room. Just a table covered in a white cloth, two candles and a cross. A smell of hot wax from the candle, a hint of engine oil from the concrete floor revealing the origins of the mission as a set of garages before Caskie had them converted into the seaman's boarding house. I hadn't sat in a church or chapel for years. The simplicity of the room, almost poverty, really, took me back to the chapel on St Kilda and the strange wailing of psalms in that unearthly way, so raw and beautiful. I never thought I'd feel homesick for that.

When I'd first arrived on the island, I'd seen the men in that chapel room as limited, their minds lacking in sophistication, but I'd come to realize that for all their material simplicity they were men of deeply considered theology, reading the Bible like a well-worn map, men who loved to debate the scriptures in their meetings like a gathering of old rabbis, and probably as learned as any college student and twice as wise. They knew who they were, their spiritual muscles, it seemed, as firm as the bodily muscles that kept them steady and safe as they navigated the soaring cliffs with the fathoms of sea a thousand feet below.

I hadn't done so for a long time, but I closed my eyes, let the quiet sink into me, and prayed, for you, and for a girl I'd never seen called Rachel Anne. I prayed for endurance, for the cold courage to keep going, no matter what, for a journey that would bring me home to you again.

Archie came and went in the days before we left, quietly, always in a hurry, brief meetings with Caskie, slipping out through a side door, suddenly there in the hallway, evidently part of the underground network of people returning airmen and soldiers back home to take up the fight once again. Wealthy Marseille residents like Nancy, teenagers, priests, soldiers stranded after St Valery with enough French to pass as natives. Together they were running a covert war.

A small thing that bothered me. Out in the old port late one afternoon on an errand to pick up some suits for some new arrivals that Caskie had ordered from his Arabic tailor, I saw Archie on a street corner, talking with a clean-shaven man in a neat trilby and a long cream mac. To me, the man had the look of an *Abwehr* agent. Something surreptitious in the way they were conferring. I held back in a doorway, watched them part. I attempted to trail Archie through the streets, lost him in the crowds on La Joliette.

I told Caskie what I'd seen. He frowned, shook his head. 'Archie is the most loyal man I know. I'd depend on him with my life. Whatever you saw, I can firmly say there will have been nothing underhand in it.'

I wondered, how well does Caskie really know Archie though?

Shortly after that, another safe house was raided, in a village outside Marseille, more arrests in the north, including Richard, the boy who had travelled with us on the train from Paris. Shaken by the news, I racked my brains to think if I'd said anything about him to Archie, or if Angus might have said something, but I couldn't remember talking about him to Archie.

Caskie was sure the problem lay closer to Lille. The plans for us to cross the Pyrenees remained the same.

Our guide on the journey to Foix, a small town in the foothills of the Pyrenees, was a French girl of no more than twenty. She stood in the corridor of the train, keeping a discreet eye on her charges. The new coats may not have been ideal gear for mountaineering, but at least we did not look out of place on the train to Toulouse.

At Toulouse we needed to change and take the local line to Foix. There were few German guards in evidence, but we knew that the station would have its share of German agents in plain clothes hanging around, along with the German-controlled French police guards. Angus and the girl walked ahead along the platform, holding hands like two sweethearts. I walked several steps behind. Then my skin began to prickle. From the corner of my eye I caught sight of a man standing a few paces ahead. He was lighting a cigarette, hands cupped around the flame – but from the tilt of his hat brim, I knew that he was watching us.

No choice but to keep walking. I was almost alongside him when the brim lifted. I stumbled. Archie Macleod. He came towards me, grasped my hand, shook it murmuring, 'Just smile, as if you expected to meet me, keep walking.' He stooped closer as we walked. 'Don't get the train to Foix,' speaking urgently now. 'Germans are waiting to pick you up. Seems someone's blown your cover. Came as soon as I heard from our contact. Go on to St Girons. I'll meet you at the station, get another *passeur* fixed up in town. You'll have to take a higher route across the mountains now, more risks of bad weather, but it can't be helped.'

'And does Caskie know about this change of plan?'

Archie shook his head. 'No time.'

I had a cold feeling in my chest when I heard that. But it was Archie I was talking to. I studied his face, looking straight into his eyes. The expression was hard, unfathomable. He slipped an envelope into my pocket. 'The tickets. Two. Tell the guide I'll be on the train. She can leave now.' Then in a louder voice, in French, 'Wonderful to see you too. We'll have dinner soon. In St Girons.'

He wheeled away, disappearing into the huddle of people around the station cafe.

I caught up with our guide, whispered the news. Her steps slowed, brow wrinkled. Given that the last trip that had been sent into the arms of the Gestapo, this was a frightening change of plan. A voice inside me whispered still, 'Can you really trust Archie?'

She sighed, pushed a strand of hair behind her ear. 'Then you should get the train for St Girons,' her eyes asking me to tell her she was right.

Angus leaned in, whispered to me before we boarded. 'I don't like it. I don't trust this Macleod. Do you?'

'We can't risk going on to Foix, if he's right.' But I had to admit, part of me agreed with Angus very much.

Late afternoon and our train pulled in to a fog-bound station. St Girons. Just one German guard with a dog meeting the head of the train. We got out of our carriage at the back, trying not to look hurried, passed through the station building without incident. Archie had reappeared up ahead, and we followed him towards the river. The foothills of the Pyrenees rose around us but were hidden behind the thick clouds that pressed down over the town. We followed Archie across a bridge to the sound of a roaring weir, a row of pollarded trees disappearing into the mist, their stunted tops like knuckles bristling with thin black shoots. The backs of houses loomed up along the bank to our left, huddled together, plain and solid against the mountain winds. Archie disappeared behind them. We trailed him through the streets to a quiet cafe in an alleyway where he seemed to know the patron.

Promising to return with news of our guide, Archie left. We drank small coffees slowly, watching the door, listening out for boots and dogs.

Dark was falling by the time Archie got back. We were in luck, he assured us, a whiff of brandy on his breath. His contact, an Andorran who knew the mountains like the back of his hand, was about to take a party over in the morning and we could join them. 'Only thing is, they're meeting up at a shepherd's hut in the foothills ready to move on at first light. It will mean walking through the night to get there.'

He led us through empty streets, windows shuttered, doors closed. This near to curfew, St Girons had become a ghost town. France might be free in the south but it was still haunted by the sound of boots. The Gestapo free to act.

At a farmhouse just outside the town, Archie knocked on a door. An old man sold us stout sticks as tall as my shoulder, a parcel of salami and hard black bread. We weren't the first escapees bound for the mountains to call there.

The foothills were part of a forbidden zone, heavily patrolled by guards looking for fugitives. We went quietly in the darkness, single file on the track. Archie walked with purpose, dogged and assured. I realized that this was a journey he had done before, many times perhaps. Was Archie the embassy contact bringing funds over from Madrid that Caskie had once alluded to?

I knew so little about this Archie.

We passed through moonlit vineyards, dark meadows in the deep shadow of a pine forest, unseen cows munching cud, then took a steeply rising path through a forest of slender birch trunks, each pale column rising straight from the sharp gradient of the hillside.

Archie stopped, hand up. In the distance, the sound of dogs barking, two of them, high-pitched and intent.

'Alsatians?' I whispered. Archie didn't reply, still listening. The sounds faded, moving away.

'We'll need to keep up the pace,' he said.

On the other side of the wood, the path opened out in rough upland moor. I came alongside Archie. Walking together in the dark.

'Like old times,' he said. 'Nights returning from escapades at college, d'you remember, drinking in various dives when we'd fail to make it back to hall before the gates were locked?'

'Scaling drainpipes to get in through a friend's windows.'

I heard that old chuckle.

'Look,' I said. 'I am glad you told me about Chrissie. Grateful that you watched out for her.'

Silence came back to me, the scrape of a boot on stone.

'I hear she's doing well. They both are. Of course, she doesn't know it was me who helped her out from time to time. I sent money for her through a general fund that helps St Kildans. A piano, the girl's musical, a scholarship for her if she wants to go to university one day. I got sent back snippets of information about them from the vicar who administers the trust.'

The slope was punishingly steep here. He paused to catch his breath, holding on to a trunk.

'No friendship ever meant more to me than yours, Fred. I threw that away, I know.'

He gripped my arm. I felt the heat and damp through the wool of my jacket. We walked on side by side for a while. 'Almost there now,' he said.

The shepherd's hut was set into a bowl in the hillside, a small, square building, a rough board door with a window each side, tightly shuttered. Here we were to wait for our mountain guide.

We found the party we were to join inside, two downed airmen and a young Jewish couple. The woman had been sleeping on a rough wooden bunk, and rose with dishevelled hair. She wore a summer dress and jacket, shoes with heels. She looked at us with suspicion and shook hands reluctantly.

'Have you heard from the guide, when he's going to get here?' the man asked.

'Anytime now, I should think,' said Archie.

It was cold in there. They hadn't dared light a fire lest the smoke give them away. We waited in the half dark, the shutters barred, too anxious to make conversation. An hour went by. Still no sign of our guide. Archie passed round his hip flask. I took a sip and closed my eyes. Felt the tiredness kick in, pulling me to lean back against the wall. How long before we'd get another chance to catch some sleep?

Archie stood up abruptly, startling me awake again, and announced he was going to go back down the path to see if something had happened to the guide.

'You think something has gone wrong?' the woman asked.

'A delay. All sorted soon, I'm sure.'

'But you have made this crossing before?' she pressed him.

'Once or twice,' Archie said evasively.

This was not in the plan. My heart sinking, I watched the door close behind him, a tired thumping of blood in my chest, my treacherous thoughts following their own path. If Archie were to betray us, then surely it would be now, corralled in this shed, himself absent.

The minutes dragged by.

The sound of an Alsatian barking. The door crashed open. A guard with a rifle pointed towards us. The dog still barking hysterically outside the door.

The guard shouted for us to raise our hands.

And where was Archie? Had Archie done this?

A sudden screech from the dog, and in the same moment a shot exploded. The woman screamed as we watched the guard tip forward.

Behind him, Archie stood in the doorway, a pistol in his hand.

'There'll be more coming soon,' Archie said. 'We leave now.'

Outside, we found a man in a dark suit and beret, wiping a knife. The Andorran guide. On the grass, the inert shapes of the Alsatian and a second guard.

We dragged the bodies into the undergrowth nearby. The first hints of pre-dawn red in the eastern sky, black before us. We set off at a quick pace along the path, Archie last out of the hut, taking the rear. I turned to let him catch up. Heard the sound of running, a glint of metal.

A guard stood below me, a rifle pointed square at my chest.

A shot exploded, a second shot, echoing against the mountain. I waited for the pain. But none came.

Archie crumpled to his knees. He had fallen directly between me and the body of the guard. His hands went to his chest as a dark hole bloomed in a stain across his coat fabric.

And then I understood. Archie had thrown himself between the guard and me, taken the shot. And in the same moment he'd fired at the guard who now lay motionless on the grass.

Archie had taken my shot. He'd stepped into the line of fire and taken the bullet meant for me.

He gave a small laugh. 'Well, that's rum,' he said. He craned his head to see his coat, the dark stain still spreading. 'That's made a bit of a mess.' He was shivering. 'Bloody cold,' he murmured.

Angus had run back down the slope. Together we picked Archie up, carefully carried him back inside and laid him on the wooden bench. I put my fingers on his neck, his pulse faint and erratic, the dark stain bleeding unstoppably across the shirt fabric. Beneath it, his heart slowing. The woman came forward. She was a nurse and tried to do what she could for Archie, but shook her head, her eyes telling me more than I wanted to know. Archie wasn't going to make it.

'Someone should go and get help,' I said, searching the faces around me. 'We need to get him to a doctor, a hospital.'

'I don't think so,' said Archie, strangely serene, his teeth chattering in little bursts. 'I rather think this is it, Fred.'

'Don't talk like that, Archie. You're going to make it.'

'Happens to all of us sooner or later. You don't mind if I beat you to it?'

'Come on, Archie,' I cried. 'Stay with us.'

'Might have a little sleep.' He flickered his eyes open again. 'But you're still here. You should be gone, you know.'

'I'm not leaving you.'

He gripped my hand, tried to rise up on his elbow. 'You have to get back to her, Fred. This is all a waste if you don't. You're not to wait about here.' He hung on to my shoulder now, his voice rasping, sweat on his forehead. 'Promise me, you'll get back. You'll stay alive.'

He became so agitated, I feared for him. 'I promise.'

He sank back.

'We can't wait,' said the Andorran.

'Go on. You should all get going. I'll follow later, try and catch up with you.'

Angus let his backpack slide from his shoulders. 'I'll wait with you.'

The Andorran shrugged. 'You have a map? A compass?'

Angus took out the small square of silk with a map of the Pyrenees printed on it. A gift from Archie through his contacts in Madrid, one of the maps made by the secret service in London in the hope that they might help men get back home. He'd given several to Caskie to hand on. Angus showed the map to the Andorran who traced the route with his finger. 'Go straight up, heading south. We will be here in the refuge within twenty-four hours. We will sleep a while, and hope you catch up.'

He took out his knife and made a little nick at the site of the refuge. Handed it back to Angus.

'Farewell, my friend,' the Andorran said to Archie, as he grasped his hand. To me, he said, 'Your friend is very courageous.' Then he took me aside near the door. 'After, we will come to take him down the mountain. And don't wait too long.'

Angus took Archie's pistol, sat watching the door. A deep quiet fell in the hut. I raised Archie on my lap, my coat around him to try and keep him warm. From time to time, he opened his eyes, gave a rueful smile.

'Always wanted to go back to the island again. Remember, Fred, one of those evenings when you sit out on the bench with a smoke in your hand, looking out over the bay. The Atlantic all gold and bronze, the horizon that faint purple. And the hills over on Boreray that shade of blue. What d'you call that blue, Fred?'

'I'm not sure.'

He sighed and went quiet for a while. 'Did I tell you I was renovating the house across the loch in Dunvegan? Don't always feel at home in the castle now my sister and her husband are installed. Turns out she's a talent for being the lady of the place and doing all those tiresome things that drove me mad. Her boy will be the new laird one day so it makes sense. It's not much to look at yet, the old dowager cottage, a ruin with some sheep in it. I've had some chaps busy fixing it up. They send me pictures. Meant to settle there one day.'

'Sounds a wonderful place.'

'It will be.' He blew out a breath, a twinge of pain. I held his hand tight against my chest, as if my heartbeat could encourage his own.

'Did you know the Macleods of Dunvegan are always buried in Kilmuir? Don't suppose I'll join them there now.'

'Don't talk like that. You'll see it yourself one day, your house, the island,' I lied.

'But you'll get back, Fred?' he whispered one last time. I nodded. Then I held his hand as he slipped away. He didn't speak again. Once or twice he gave a laboured breath, between a rattle and a snore, and then was quiet.

'I think he's gone,' Angus said.

I listened with my head on his chest. No trace of a beat.

After a while, Angus cleared his throat. 'Spanish guide said we should leave him here. He said he'd make sure he was taken to the priest's house.'

Archie still felt warm, as if he might get up soon, refreshed and himself again after a good sleep. Reluctantly, I passed my hand down over Archie's forehead to close his eyes, then covered him with his coat. One last moment with him, then we left the hut, closed the door and set out on the path, leaving Archie alone in the cold and the dark.

CHAPTER 43

Fred
PYRENEES, 1941

The pale rocks of the track ahead were clear enough to follow in the moonlight. We made good time as we climbed, moving quickly, the peaks in the distance a dark cut-out against the brilliance of the stars. I was glad to fasten my mind on my steps, keeping away the wash of grief welling up behind me, but always aware of the growing distance between our frantic movements as we climbed, and the stillness of the hut below.

A pale sky edged with gold. We walked on as the sun rose across slopes of brown grass, swathes of blue-green pines below. We went as fast as we could without twisting an ankle. The higher we walked, the more evidence of the snow's recent retreat, acres of yellowed grass, flattened as if a roller had been dragged over it.

We'd be meeting the snow line soon.

The stony hillside resolved into blocks of granite tall as a man. Scrambling up, using our hands, we were certainly missing the army boots that we'd taken so much care to replace with civvies.

Around midday, eyes burning with lack of sleep, we reached the summit, a ridge a mile long of serrated outcrops like the edge of a stone knife. Our reward? A vista of the ridges and peaks to come, scoured by icy wind. Four more ridges to cross, the highest at seven thousand feet.

I pulled up the collar of my coat and held it together as the wind battered us, reminding us to get a move on. Still a chance the border guards might track us this far. But I could see no sign of a hut or our party down in the valley. Had we swung too wide in our path, missed them altogether?

Below us, steep rock escarpments. Hard to see a way down. We began to climb down a gulley, the stones frozen iron, my jersey over my hands, holed for my thumbs. Angus did likewise.

In the valley, winter sun dazzled over the ridge ahead. We walked along a lake, a glassy sheet of ice scattered over with great blocks of ice. They'd left long, elliptical score marks on the surface, as if pushed along by some unseen force

Our water flasks were empty. In spite of the cold, we were hot and thirsty, the distances much further than they had seemed from above. Angus kicked at the edge of the lake, trying to break the ice, but I knew well what shallow water at the edge of a loch could do to a stomach and we walked on, rewarded by the sound of running water. A stream was gurgling between gnarled edges of overhanging ice, humps of yellow grass inside. The water had been frozen into rivulets but the central section was still running clear. We filled our flasks and drank deeply, filled them again.

The second summit played games with us, showing further ridges each time we thought we'd reached the top, lack of sleep fizzing in our muscles and brains. I promised Angus we'd rest on the other side. Black hummocks of grass crouched across white slopes of snow, feet crunching down into holes, a staff essential. The topmost ridge was a landscape of muddy, frozen rags, bunched up and solid. Shoulders hunched into the wind, our city-soled shoes slipped on the icy rocks as we battled forward.

To the west, dark grey clouds were rolling towards us, dense with their frozen burden, all the presages of a snow storm. We urgently needed to get down from the heights. In the distance, the first forks of lightning.

In the next valley, wraiths of cloud grey as smoke, rock ledges descending in tiers of white. I had no memory of how we scrambled down, praying not to fall. We came out onto calmer fields of snow shining with a crust of ice. Each step an arduous process of digging the staff into the snow, working our way down its shaft, trousers soaked to the knee. Then planting it below for the next step. The dusk crept up on us again. On the other side of the valley, the patches of snow were slung across the peaks like white birds in the gloom.

No feeling in my toes.

We'd been walking for almost thirty-six hours. Below the snow line, we found an overhanging rock, reasonably dry underneath, where we bedded down back to back for warmth, coats held tight. Woke with the wet soaking into our clothes and hardening to frost where it met the air. The side of my coat was stiff.

The only way to get warm was to keep walking. We shared what was left of the salami and the bread. Trudged on.

The views as we climbed higher in the dawn were breathtaking, gold on the slopes facing the new sun. Deadly if you slipped on the narrow goat track. Finally, the snow came in, thick and blinding.

There were times when I fell into a trance as we trudged on, no longer in the Pyrenees but far away on St Kilda again, following a yellow lamp between the bothies. Sometimes I walked beside you, Chrissie, the wind undoing your hair from its red scarf. And sometimes I walked alongside Archie.

I'd come to, surprised to find myself back in the dusk and the snow, Archie far away, sleeping in his own deep winter. I wanted so much to lie down and sleep in the cold too. But I knew how lethal that was and my legs kept moving forward, the pains in my toes gone to ice. Each breath a sharp stab in my side.

I looked back. Angus had stopped, slumped down in the snow, his body hunched into a curl.

'I just need to sleep now, Fred,' he said slowly. 'I can't go on any more.' He held a photo of his girl Ellie in his hand, kept looking at it. Folded it against his chest and shut his eyes. The snow had eased up, but the dark had already begun to gather again, long blue shadows around the trees. And fatal for us to be out here when night fell.

I don't know where I found the strength, but I hauled him up, slapped him to keep awake as we went on together, half-dragging him over the top, then sliding down a dark slope. Below us in the valley was the distinct shape of a small hut. I wondered if I was conjuring something from hope. But it was indeed a small shepherd's cabin. Never so glad to see a habitation, even if it was little more than a shed.

We hurried towards it, Angus hobbling on his own. The temperature falling fast as we pushed the door open. I took wood from the bundles piled up to one side and lit a small stove with one of my remaining matches. We were warming our frozen hands near the comfort of the stove's flames, the cast-iron door left open, when the door of the hut opened. I was relieved to see it was just an old woman wrapped in a black cloak, her yellowed face wizened like wood. She produced beans and root vegetables from her cloak and began to make a soup, enough for three. She was mystified to hear us talking in Gaelic as she stirred the pan.

'*Inglés?*' she asked, chin towards us.

I took a stick from the woodpile and drew in the thick ash dust around the wood stove, a map of the UK. Pointed to the west coast of Scotland.

'*Escocés?*' I nodded.

This seemed to please her. She put her hands together on her breastbone.

'*Vasco.*' She pointed to herself and then to the ground. '*Yo soy vasco.*' Then she began talking in a language I had never heard before. Basque.

She fussed around making sure we were near the stove, giving us second helpings of the bean soup. I offered the remains of the salami but she gestured for us to keep it.

We slept like the dead, woken at dawn by the pain returning to our frozen feet. I knew there would be damage from the reddened sections later, the ends of two toes already blackening.

The old lady was out early, sniffing the air and looking worried. She sprinkled her fingers, stamped her feet. I understood that she wanted us to get going before more snow came in. Wrapping herself in her cloak, her bag on her shoulders, she pointed up to the next and last ridge. Signalled for us to follow.

I sincerely doubted that she was capable of such an arduous crossing, eighty if she was a day, with the build of a wizened girl of twelve. But she gripped my arm, fingers hard as ash wood, and gave me a pull. '*Vamos ahora. Prisa.*'

I was wrong about the old girl's stamina. We were hard-pressed to keep up. She strode ahead with her quick little steps, tapping the ground through the snow with her long stick. She kept her cape wrapped tight against the wind, better protection than our fine coats. My feet felt like solid ice, but the urgency to keep moving meant that we could not stop. The cold and the weariness were terrible, but it was your voice in the wind, Chrissie, your face that kept me going.

The last ridge was the border with Spain. In the distance we could make out the faint lights of a tiny hamlet. The old woman stopped and gestured towards it, pointed to us but not to herself. She seemed to be saying that if she returned now, she should make it back to the little hut before nightfall. I hoped so anyhow. I realized that she had been on her way from Spain to France, had detoured back to help us.

The afternoon light was beginning to fade again as we began the descent on the other side. By the time we were down that mountain, the evening blue had filled the valley, lights from a village some five or maybe ten miles in front of us, difficult to say when you don't know the terrain. But they were a welcome sight, a long time since we had seen a place with lights shining freely, and we hobbled on.

No one about in the village. Was this was the place where we were supposed to meet our contact? There was no clue to the place's name. No sign of a cafe or an *estaminet* where you could go in and survey the situation in the warm. The cold was coming in hard with the dark.

Two figures appeared in the road. They wore cloaks, distinctive hats shaped like upturned boats, Guardia Civiles, Spanish police.

We had nowhere to go, no food left, half frozen. We stood still and waited as they came towards us. With Spain being neutral, there was half a chance they might help us. The only alternative left to us was to stand in the blue cold and freeze to death.

CHAPTER 44

Fred
SPAIN, 1941

There must have been over four thousand men crowded into the Spanish internment camp at Miranda d'Ebro; Spanish prisoners from the civil war, soldiers and airmen escaped from France who'd crossed the Pyrenees only to end up in this place. Many were still in the remnants of uniforms, British, Polish, French, and Canadian. The compound stood in the middle of an arid plain swept by frozen winds. In the distance a ring of stony hills and mountains with snow on their peaks. Solid walls topped with barbed wire enclosed rows of white huts. Thin soup once a day.

Inside the huts, an atmosphere of resigned depression.

'I hear there's a good chance of being repatriated through the embassy,' I said to a gaunt Gordon Highlander in the next bunk.

'Still waiting for my papers to come through after six months. More of a chance of being carried out in a box from some godforsaken disease in this place.'

The black frostbite patches on our toes did better than I thought, peeled off and left new skin underneath as the days dragged on. Cold, lice and hunger were the staples of our lives over the following weeks. With the arrival of the warmer weather, a fever went through the camp and I spent days in a sweating delirium, vivid dreams where I felt you so close, if I could only rise from my bed. You were standing with a child next to you, a girl, tall, though her face was in shadow.

Angus was next to go down. Almost didn't pull through.

Then, on a raw day in October, returning from work in the quarry, I saw a black Austin parked inside the gate, a small Union Jack flag on its bonnet. Hardly dared hope.

A few days later, Angus and I were sitting in an elegant room overlooking the British Embassy gardens in Madrid. An efficient English lady had organized new clothes, new papers. One at a time we were questioned intensively, suspect until proven otherwise. When they were finally convinced I was no German agent, they asked a lot of questions about Archie. Everything he'd done. How he'd died.

I could see relief in our interrogator's face as he closed the file. Whoever had done so much to damage the escape routes, with fifty arrested and shot by the Gestapo, it wasn't Archie who'd been the traitor. And I gathered from the intensity of the questions around small details that here was a man who had considered Archie a friend.

In the embassy basements, trestle tables were set out, camp beds, basins and shaving kits. We were given a decent meal of beef stew, beer, jam roly-poly and custard. At the end of the meal, the same man who had interrogated us came down with a bottle of brandy and three glasses. Jack Tolworth. 'Thought I'd let you see I have a more civilized side. I know it's not much of a welcome after all you've been through to get here, but there's little we can do on the ground inside France. It's a hard blow losing Archie. A good man.'

'He saved my life.'

'I don't doubt it. And you're lucky to have got away after St Valery like you did. Over ten thousand of the 51st Highland Division are in German prison camps right now, most of them deep inside occupied Poland. Very little hope of escaping from there.'

'I've had help. From a lot of people. People like Archie.'

He nodded. 'Between you and me, our friend was responsible for a lot of men making it here in one piece. A hero. Don't forget that.'

I nodded.

'Well, you've an early start tomorrow. We usually take you boys who make it over the Pyrenees down to Gibraltar on the train, but since there's an embassy car going down to the coast, you'll be travelling in style. It's the surest way, no questions asked. Spain is ostensibly neutral but crawling with *Abwehr* spies. So long as you don't mind keeping your heads down.'

In Gibraltar we had nothing to do but wait. After so many months of being close to danger, I was overcome by a deep weariness. The sea breezes coming in from the open windows, army meals; I felt my body begin to heal from months of exhaustion and hunger. I sat in the autumn sun, looking out over a blue sea, eyes half closed. Sometimes, I could almost be sitting in front of the bothy again, a faint awareness of you close by.

It was only when we were on the ship home, the wind fresh off the sea and filled with salt and hope, that I began to feel a rising excitement, a longing I had not dared to allow, the hope of seeing you again. Standing on the deck of the navy frigate, zigzagging our way through rumours and sightings of enemy ships, I willed the ship to move faster.

I thought about sending you a telegram as soon as we disembarked in the din of Portsmouth but there was too much to say. I'd intended going straight home, wherever home was, heading towards Scotland, but as soon as I disembarked I was escorted to London and a dull building in Whitehall where various men asked the same questions, over and over, and the days ticked by.

A man like me, escaped from St Valery and on the run through enemy territory for almost two years, it was only fair that they wanted to know how I'd done it. Much easier to get through if you had a German sponsor willing you to get back to Blighty to work for them as a double agent. They had a lot of questions about Archie too. Everything he'd said or done. I could see that they still had their suspicions about him.

They were wrong. I could understand the need to check things out so thoroughly, there'd been much talk of the fifty people in the underground network being shot by then. But it wasn't Archie. It was only towards the end of the war that I learned the true identity of the traitor from a fellow officer. It was a man named Harry Cole, a small-time swindler posing as a Belgian officer who ran one of the escape lines down through France and Marseille. He'd been siphoning off money sent from London to aid the escapees. As soon as he was unmasked, he turned double agent and sold fifty people from the resistance into the Gestapo's hands, including Nancy Fiocca's beloved husband, to be tortured and shot.

But for now, my London interrogators were content to wrap the matter up so far as I was concerned. I was free to go.

'But don't make any big plans, Mr Lawson,' the officer said before I left. 'You'll have your call-up papers soon. Best get straight back in the fray.'

'How long?'

'A few days, I'm sorry.'

I hurried for the station, took the night train to Glasgow, so little time to find you.

CHAPTER 45

Fred

SCOTLAND, 1941

With the address Archie had given me in my pocket, I took the bus going from Fort William to Lochaline, asked the driver to drop me just before Larachbeg. It would have been a while since Archie had been in contact with Chrissie. What if she had married since he'd last heard from her, as well she might with a daughter to care for? I hoped that she had waited for me. It hardly seemed possible. With a tight readiness for disappointment furled deep in my chest, I sat on the bus rocking its way across the winding roads of Morvern, sick, half with the movement, half with nerves and hope. Another hour or so and I might know, I'd see her and she'd tell me how it had been.

All my future was in her hands, in her forgiveness, married or not. At least then there might be some peace.

The bus stopped in the middle of nowhere, a sheep by a barred gate, a stoop of newly plated fir trees, the earth still red and raw around them. The bus driver nodded to a cart track that led away down the hill.

'It's a mile or so that way you'll be wanting to go and there's the village, though it's barely a village to speak the truth. They'll be glad to see you back home, son.'

The door slammed shut, the driver facing forward and already away. I stood in the last of the bitter engine fumes, hoisted my duffel bag on my shoulder and let my hand loosen the collar of my cheap demob shirt. Hard to breathe.

If Chrissie wasn't there?

I began to stride out through the green and brown of the autumn hills, the sky a new blue. After a while the scenery had changed and yet was still the same. I breached the brow of the hill and saw the row of white cottages below. Smoke from the chimney of the middle one.

My legs taking me too fast down the hill. Wanting and not wanting to be there and finally know my fate. I stopped and crouched down at the roadside on my haunches, lit a cigarette. A way of resting that was still a habit from the camps. As I watched the cottages, a door opened and a woman came out.

I stood up, for she had the way and the gait of my Chrissie. But Chrissie as a girl. Her hair was covered by a red beret. She fetched a bike from a shed, her movements quick, decided, all Chrissie's spark and dash. She began to cycle up the hill towards me. I couldn't move as she toiled up, steady, easy, growing in size and nearness. My Chrissie, unchanged by the years.

She passed by, saying a good morning in Gaelic. I saw it wasn't Chrissie at all, but so like her.

And then I turned to stare after her. If it wasn't Chrissie, then it was surely Chrissie's daughter.

My daughter. Nothing but the singing of birds after her passing.

I turned back towards the cottages, hurried on down the road.

The girl had come out from the middle cottage. I stood loitering a little way along, trying perhaps to catch sight of some movement in the windows. But there was no sign of life. I waited a while longer then took my courage in my hands and went up the path, past the foxgloves and the cabbages run to seed. Knocked on the door, every detail of its green paint and small glass panel with a lace curtain burned into my memory. This moment. This moment would tell.

No one answered. I stood on the step, then walked back and looked up at the house. That's when an old biddy from next door came out and asked me my business.

'A friend,' I told her. 'Back from France.'

That was enough to reassure her, along with the duffel bag and that air of a soldier that clings on to you, it seems, even in civvies. In the Highlands and Islands they all knew what so many of the men had been through by now, a trickle finally making their way back from the camps.

'She'll no be back before this afternoon when the last milking is done. But you can come in bide inside if you will. I've the kettle on the stove.'

I followed her broad back, a pinny crossed over her shoulders. I watched her red rough hands make a pot of tea. A plate of hot griddle cakes appeared, smelling of salt and butter. I still hadn't got used to ordinary food.

And Chrissie, how would time have treated her? Would I know her again? I knew I'd love her no matter the changes. And the changes in me? I'd seen in the mirror the greyness and gaunt cheeks since coming back. What right had I to ask her to consider the boy and all his failings, and hope she'd still see some good in me?

'And Mr Gillies?' I asked the neighbour. 'Is he home soon?'

'Oh my goodness, we have never known a Mr Gillies,' she said with a laugh. 'I am sure there was one, one way or another, but we have never seen hide nor hair of him. Oh, but she manages. She manages very well, our Chrissie.'

And she gave me a curious, old-fashioned look. But I wasn't minded to be worried about her curiosity. I was thinking how good it felt to hear Chrissie's name spoken with such warmth and fondness again. This, more than anything, made me know why I was here, waiting for her.

The waning afternoon had begun to send down its chill, thinning the air, when, two hours later and with all of the patient neighbour's old newspaper off by heart, the old lady beckoned me to the window. 'That's herself returning now.' And I saw a woman so like Chrissie, hair cut short, a stronger build, firm of step but the same black curls, the same energy and decision in all her movements. I felt the tears spring to my eyes and an explosion of hope in my chest. My Chrissie.

I couldn't move. I watched her go inside her house and close the door.

The old lady gave me an impatient look. 'Well, you'll no talk to her standing here.'

This time, the green door opened moments after my knock. I'd stepped back down from the step, and she stood a little above me, her eyes narrowed as if troubled in her sight.

'Yes?' she said. Impatient. Kindly. 'I'm afraid I have no work for you, but I can find you a sandwich and a glass of water if you'd like.'

I realized my one civilian suit hadn't been cared for as well as it might.

'Chrissie?' I said. 'Don't you remember me?'

She frowned and stepped closer. Took in my receding hairline and close-shaved head, the gaunt frame and the loose suit. Could she see anything of the boy I had once been? I could barely see him myself any more. 'It's Fred. Fred Lawson.'

A look of pain on her face She gripped the door jamb, and I thought she might fall she was so white and unsteady. I moved to help her but she backed away.

'It can't be,' she said. 'You left so long ago. Why are you here now?'

'Oh, Chrissie, can't we talk? Can't I come in?'

She shook her head, couldn't stop shaking it as if afflicted by a tremor. 'Is it really you?' Then she put her hand out and touched my arm, the other against her chest.

'Can't I come in, Chrissie?'

She stood searching my face as if she doubted what she saw, who I was.

'Please, Chrissie.'

Another voice, the old lady from next door, calling over the low fence. 'I took him in and gave him a cup of tea till you got back. Such a nice fellow, back from France. So is he from the old island then?' She gave me a nod and a wave.

'From the island, yes. Thank you, Mrs Baird. Very kind of you. Well, you had better come away inside then, Mr Lawson.'

It was a small cottage, bright and homely. The signs of two women everywhere. I still hadn't mentioned the girl.

She showed me to the kitchen table. Her kitchen. I watched as she made tea, keeping her distance, both of us I think glad of a chance to gather our thoughts and feelings into some order, both failing. All I knew was that I didn't want to leave this place.

When she sat down with her teacup in her hands, a mug pushed in front of me – did I want sugar? – she was still wild-eyed and white. And she was still my Chrissie, not a girl any more, a woman, but even more beautiful for it, her face filled out to a new harmony and generousness, the same full lips, the same blue eyes and dark hair. Her hands were reddened, no doubt from the farm work in the cold mornings that she'd told me about as she made the tea. Cold lye and water and scrubbing brooms scouring the concrete – my Chrissie had always known how to work. I saw with a catch in my heart how the knuckles were a little swollen, and I ached for her pain.

And what right had I to be here, when I had left her to so many pains for so many years?

Then we began to talk, halting at first, then both of us talking, telling each other all that had happened over our lost years, the evening turning to dark and the need to light a lamp before we realized how much time had passed. For time had become all in pieces for us, and I swear, Chrissie as familiar to me then as if we had parted only days before, as if there had never been a parting.

But there had been a parting, the wound between us fresh and new. I could see it in her eyes, all the hurt and questions.

'I am sorry, Chrissie. I was such a fool. You see, there was something that Archie told me, that wasn't true. . .' I began, not sure how to tell her what I had believed for so long.

'I know,' she said.

'You know?'

'Yes. I know that Archie told a lie, about me. A letter came from him, just after war broke out. He was very honest about what he'd said, trying to drive you away from the island. He wanted to tell me. I expect he knew that the war meant he might not have another chance, and he was right in the end, wasn't he?'

I nodded.

'But it wasn't just Archie. You see, I made you go that day. I knew I could have stopped you, just by running out to you and asking you to stay. But I loved you too much. I wanted you to have every opportunity, to go home and finish your degree and have all the wide world at your feet. And I knew you would come back to me one day. I just didn't think it would take so very, very long.'

'I'm sorry, Chrissie. I lost my faith in you, in your love, but I could never stop loving you. I had the world, yes, travelled it from east to west, but all I wanted in the end was to come home to you.'

'So much lost. But what else could you know but what Archie told you.'

'I could have believed in you, in what was true.'

She sighed, looked out of the window with her lips pressed together.

'I'm so sorry, Chrissie.'

She gave a tiny nod.

'And I know Archie was sorry for what he'd done. He told me that much.'

She looked at me, startled. 'Archie told you that?'

'In France. Archie saved my life, Chrissie. If it wasn't for him I would have died going over into Spain. I'd never have made it home and be sitting here now. And, Chrissie, he told me about the child. Our daughter.'

A quiet fell in the room. She sighed.

'Yes, Archie knew about Rachel Anne, and I think he tried to help, the piano, the grant for her to go to college one day. There's a charity for people who have come from St Kilda, but this was something different, specific for me and for Rachel. I suspected it was Archie who was the anonymous donor.'

I nodded. 'He wanted to make amends.'

'And now he is dead. Did he suffer?' Tears were in her eyes.

'I held him as he went. He died in peace, I think.'

The tears were flowing freely now, for both of us, and I could bear it no longer but reached out and took both her hands in mine. She did not pull away.

I heard the door open and a girl stood in the kitchen, the girl from the lane, so like Chrissie but the hair lighter, the face longer, large brown eyes. My daughter. And I could see from her eyes that she understood who I was. She waited for her mother to speak.

Chrissie had stood too, wiping at her eyes. 'Rachel Anne, do you know who this is?'

She nodded. 'I think so. The man from the photograph.'

The world seemed to have narrowed into that one moment. I heard the shake in my voice. 'I'm Fred, Fred Lawson, your father.'

She nodded, calmly. 'I see. Mr Lawson, I am pleased to meet you after so much time.'

No trace of any welcome or gladness. But then, who was I but a stranger?

'I should have come sooner. . .' I tried.

'Well, you are here,' Rachel Anne said, breezily. 'But where is it you will go now?'

'I don't know.'

'You need not worry on our account. You see, we have been well without you, Mr Lawson. After so long, it seems we have no great need of you.'

'Rachel Anne, that's not called for.'

'I will be at Aileen's. I will come back when he has left.'

And she was gone, still in her coat. 'She doesn't mean it,' said Chrissie, sinking down in her chair, deep shadows under her eyes in the lamplight. 'She will come round to the idea of you.'

'She has her mother's fiery nature, and the doggedness of her father,' I said and she smiled a little at that.

'And where were you planning to go after seeing us?' she asked.

'I hadn't any plans,' I confessed, 'beyond finding you.'

'Well, it's all but dark and there's no more buses for today, so unless you want a very long walk by torchlight I suggest you sleep on the couch here tonight, have a bite to eat together.'

'I don't want to bother you. And Rachel's waiting for me to be gone.'

'I promise, she doesn't mean that.' Chrissie went over to the shelves, busied herself with something there. 'Do you have to go?'

'No.'

'Well, then. It would be a great happiness to me if you would stay a while longer. That is all I would ask.'

She made a meal of bacon and potatoes, enough for Rachel Anne too, though it went cold on the stove as we talked and the darkness deepened, leading each other through the years that we had known. Oh, I could have wept, and I did weep, for all she had suffered without me, for all I had missed. And yet, how was it, that in being together now time seemed to have healed itself, for an ease seeped into the space between us like a silver solder, and we were as comfortable together as only old friends can be, who even after many years may take up an old conversation as if it were halted a day ago. I had not expected that, to feel so at home by her side so readily. Time had done nothing to reduce her beauty, or how much I loved her for all she was.

Did she feel the same towards me, though, or was her warmth just for an old friendship that had bloomed into too much and then faded? I couldn't tell.

She made up a bed for me on the hard little couch, the knobbles of the wool fabric rough beneath the sheet.

In the dark I heard Rachel Anne return home, eat her dinner cold from the stove and then go up.

At first light I'd shaved at the kitchen sink and folded my blankets. I sat on the back step smoking, the sky in the east bright with a red tinge. The line of dark forest at the end of a field grew from shadow to trees, gathering the light above. It was cold even with my army coat wrapped around me but I had lost the habit of houses and felt more at ease outside with my smoke in the raw air. It must have been an hour later that I conceded to the chill and went inside. The girl was sitting in the morning gloom of the kitchen, a mug of tea in her hands. She was dressed in a woollen jersey and skirt. She nodded at the pot of tea on the table, a lopsided knitted cosy that had seen better days. There were two empty mugs on the table, a jug of milk and a bowl of sugar. I poured a welcome cup of strong tea. Something I would have given a lot for in the camp and I savoured it now, standing by the window.

'You can sit down,' she said.

I pulled out a chair, an apologetic smile and sat down opposite her.

Chrissie was up too. I heard her footsteps down the stairs and she came in in a hurry.

'Why did you let me sleep?' she said. 'And now I must go directly to the farm and shan't be back a while. But you'll stay?' I could hear the wanting in her voice, an anguish almost, and I was relieved – if sorry – to hear her pain.

'Of course, if you don't mind. If you've any jobs I could help with, chopping some wood?'

This pleased her, and not because she had any such chores. I could see that too in her face.

She tucked her hair away under a knitted beret, belted her coat. 'And you'll be here, Rachel Anne. In case Mr Lawson has something he wants? Make a bit of breakfast now?'

Very quiet, a shrug, 'I'll be here.'

It was a long morning in limbo. Rachel Anne stayed in her room and I sat and read a book I had with me, taking in nothing. After a while I wandered around the room, sat down at the piano and began to pick out one of her songs from the island. A long time since I'd played. Each note a memory. I'd got the whole tune, taking it with both hands when I became aware of someone standing behind me. Rachel Anne had come downstairs and stood in the doorway. I stopped and turned. There were tears on her face.

'You took such a long time to come home,' she said.

'I'm sorry. So sorry.'

'Why did you take so long?'

'I think I stopped believing in love.'

'And now?'

'I love your mother, Rachel Anne. And I'm so sorry to have missed so much of you growing up. Now, all I can ask for is a chance to get to know you.'

She seemed undecided, a bird on the edge of flight. I played a few more notes to fill the silence. I felt a movement behind me. She crossed the room and pulled up a chair to sit beside me.

'You can ask me anything, Rachel Anne,' I said, my hands still now. And she did. All through till the late afternoon we talked, trying to fill in the years we had missed. I was in awe of this wonderful girl, my daughter, spirited and gentle, beautiful and proud. And as smart as new paint. You could see Rachel Anne could do anything she had a mind to do.

That's how Chrissie found us, out on the back step, still talking. Rachel Anne had brought down photographs of the island, an old snap of me and Archie smiling out at the sea, at the days to come, all filled with promise.

I gave the photo into Chrissie's hands as she gathered the others from Rachel. She glanced down, studying those boys from another time. So much lost and gone. But when she looked up, tears in the corners of her eyes, there it was, I caught a glimpse of the old Chrissie, those direct eyes on mine. Did she see me? And I hoped.

After supper, I walked along the lane with Chrissie in the cool evening, the scent of the dew carrying the land and the green leaves in the air, fresh and cold.

I began, 'Chrissie, I'm sorry—'

'Don't say sorry any more. I know how many boys didn't come back around here and all over the glens. So many missing, thousands of our men still in prison camps far away. I know how lucky I am to see you now. And even if you go tomorrow, I will still count myself as that.'

'Do you want me to go?'

'Of course I don't. But I don't expect anything. I know they'll call you back to fight.'

'I never want to leave. I never want to leave you again, Chrissie.'

Her hand took mine as we walked, fitted so well again inside my fingers. Then I stopped and I took her to me, or she moved to put her arms around me, and it was such a kiss, a kiss I had waited for, waited for many long years.

And two months later, on my first leave after being called up again, Chrissie and I were married in the small chapel in Larachbeg.

CHAPTER 46

Fred
FRANCE, 1950

In the summer of 1950, at the behest of the Macleod family, I made arrangements to travel out to France and bring back the remains of Archie for reburial in his family plot at Kilmuir in Skye. It was strange to be in a peacetime France, free to sit out in a pavement cafe and enjoy the sun, though the years of strain could be seen in people's faces, the bomb damage still evident through the train windows as I'd travelled down.

Of course, I had been back to France before, in 1945 as part of the British Expeditionary Force in Normandy. After months of being stationed at special operations training camps in Scotland with scant leave to go home and see Chrissie, I'd been assigned to the newly re-formed 51st Highland Division, all of us determined to bring about the liberation of Europe, and the liberation of our boys from the prisons in Germany and Poland. It was strange to be fighting our way back across the same countryside we'd seen in retreat a few years earlier, the villages and farms increasingly ravaged by war as we neared the Rhine and the Germans dug in.

At the Bremerhaven victory parade after VE day, the massed pipes and drums of the 51st led the Allies through town to take the salute, a mighty sound that vibrated deeply through my bones, reverberated in my chest along with a gratitude for the ending of those terrible times, and with pain for all the boys who had lost their lives or were still held prisoner.

It had taken a while longer before the thousands of Scots boys who'd been taken at St Valery finally started to come home. No victory parade for them. Chrissie and I had been married for almost three years when I came across the eldest of the MacKinnon boys walking along Sauchiehall Street. He'd spent four years in a German prison camp deep inside occupied Poland.

We see him often, now that we live in Glasgow for my work with an oil company. Chrissie gathers a group of St Kildans and Gaelic speakers in our kitchen most weeks. Rachel Anne comes by to listen in as the stories fly round the room, often bringing friends from university with her, though I realize lately it's one particular fellow medic she's bringing home. She tells me they want to join one of these summer work parties that go out to St Kilda, restoring the abandoned village as a historical site.

It took another five years after the war's end before the arrangements were completed to finally fetch Archie home. The burial service took place on a cool summer's morning on Skye. It might seem strange to some that a titled family choose to be buried in Kilmuir, where the small stone church on a rise of open grassland no longer has a roof, but if a cathedral with its soaring pillars is built to echo a forest, then this chapel was even more exquisite. To one side, a sycamore in full leaf had spread to provide half the roof, the open sky the rest. An ancient rowan grew within the walls like a rood screen, intricate with lichen and leaves. The walls of silver-grey granite were embellished with rosettes of fern like finely chiselled medieval carvings. Grass and chamomile filled the spaces between the flagstones of the floor.

Rachel Anne, Chrissie and I, together with the Macleod family, stood as the vicar committed Archie's remains to the earth, his name engraved on a marble plaque hewn from the rare white and greenish marble of Skye.

But the true memorial to Archie was surely the eagle soaring almost beyond sight; it was in the movement of the long blades of grass across the hillside, and the irises among them, bending with the wind. Nothing in that place was static, the sea loch and the sky moving from grey to silver to blue, the grass swaying and trembling, the speck of an eagle that hung momentarily then rose. Even the rocks, I knew, were changing under wind and frost. Imperceptibly, they rise and tilt with the pressure of the earth, and all the while, the mass of our planet hurtles on through the day, the realm of dark space and its stars beyond hidden from us by nothing more than a film of blue air.

For this much I have learned, the only things that stand are love and forgiveness, they are an island of hope glimpsed and not glimpsed among the pounding waves and the storms, but there still, always there, the lights guiding us home.

The vicar is finished, Chrissie in her dark coat and hat, a red scarf at her throat, takes my hand in hers. I know what she is thinking, of the years Archie took from us, how young we all were, how foolish, and of all that Archie did for us, giving even his life so I might find her again. Dear Archie, true friend.

ACKNOWLEDGEMENTS

I would like to thank to the many writers whose books have formed part of the research for this book, including *The Life and Death of St Kilda* by Tom Steel, *Island at the Edge of the World* by Charles MacLean and Margaret Buchanan, *The Truth about St Kilda* by Donald Gillies and *St Kilda Portraits* by David A. Quine.

I have tried to render the islands of St Kilda as faithfully as possible and hope that the reader will be able to feel they have experienced something of the unique way of life that once existed there. The characters in the story, while many are loosely based on the people who lived on St Kilda, all remain necessarily fictional since there is not enough information available to write their actual stories. I believe they would prefer it that way.

Likewise, the cast of characters for the Dunvegan Macleods is fictional. St Kilda was owned by Reginald Macleod of Macleod at the time of the evacuation but was sold to Lord Dumfries in 1931 as a bird sanctuary and is now held by the National Trust. St Kilda was the first site in Scotland to be named a World Heritage site and is home to a tenth of the British Isles' seabird population.

My thanks to Adam Nicolson whose wonderful book *The Seabird's Cry* gave such a vivid portrayal of Atlantic seabirds and their behaviour. I would also like to thank Bill Lawson of the Seallam Centre in Harris for his carefully curated exhibition of St Kilda and his books and articles on St Kilda's history. I'd like to thank artists Willie and Moira Fulton of Drinishader art gallery for their hospitality and help over the years while I have been researching books in Harris. Thanks also to Jane Knight and Christian Latham for the chance to stay in Still Waters, Grosebay, and for a peaceful time to work and explore the islands. Sea Harris took us on a wonderful boat trip to St Kilda and I'd recommend them highly, not least for the on-board cake and tea. Thank you too to Clare and Roger Gifford for the chance to stay in the Dunvegan Castle Dowager's House on Skye.

I read several journals and biographies of soldiers who escaped after St Valery and those who helped them return home, including *Return to St Valery* by Derek Lang, *A Cameron Never Can Yield* by Gregor MacDonald and *The Tartan Pimpernel* by Donald Caskie and Mike Hughes. Also Monty Halls' *Escaping Hitler: Stories of Courage and Endurance on the Freedom Trails*. Each year walkers retrace the route over the Pyrenees with the WW2 Escape Lines Memorial Society. Their website, *Le Chemin de la Liberté* was a great help. The Abbé, Nancy Fiocca and Reverend Donald Caskie are based on real characters, also Harry Cole. I hope this book pays tribute to the many people who risked their lives to return Allied servicemen home as part of the French Resistance.

As a young man of nineteen, my father-in-law, Douglas Gifford, was at the Bremerhaven Victory Parade on VE day with the British Expeditionary Force and brought back photographs of the massed drums and pipes of the reformed 51st. I now understand more of how significant and poignant that parade must have been for the 51st. His photos and his stories about Second World War escape routes helped inspire this story.

Thank you to early readers Kirsty, Hugh, George and Josh Gifford, and for the many trips to the Hebrides. I couldn't have done this book without the patient support of family both in Scotland and in England. Thank you also to readers Penny and Martin Barrowman.

Thank you to my editors at Corvus, Sara O'Keeffe, Susannah Hamilton and Poppy Mostyn-Owen. This book would not have gone forward without their enthusiasm for the project. Thank you especially to wonderful agent Jenny Hewson. Thank you to Justine Taylor for copy-editing the story with great patience. Any mistakes are mine. And thank you to Kirsty Doole and the publicity team at Corvus who tirelessly help to get books out into the world, and to the Corvus art department for the book's evocative cover.

Note on the Author

Elisabeth Gifford is the author of four novels, including *Secrets of the Sea House*, which was shortlisted for the Historical Writers' Association's Debut Crown and was a Waterstones Scotland Book of the Month. She lives in Kingston upon Thames.